# FOLLOW THE FALLEN ANGEL

Jack Hagee isn't getting any younger. And his life isn't getting any easier. A private investigator specializing in public disgrace, scraping up a living in a city as cheap and corrupt as the losers begging for his help. If they pay enough for a bed and a bottle he'd sell out to any of them. All he needs now is a buyer . . .

And Carl Miller is just the kind of guy Hagee is looking for—rich and desperate. All he has to do is locate Miller's missing fiancée, Mara—a knockout blonde with a past most dames would kill to hide. Just ask a schmuck like Miller. He's taking her secret to an early grave. Mara's friends play rough. And Mara plays rougher. If Hagee sinks any deeper into the pretty angel's private hell he can kiss tomorrow good-bye . . .

# NO FREE LUNCH

**From the acclaimed author of**
*What You Pay For*
**comes a riveting new work
of hard-core detective fiction
that cuts deep into the black heart of moral decay
and love gone bad.**

# NO FREE LUNCH

## C. J. HENDERSON

DIAMOND BOOKS, NEW YORK

NO FREE LUNCH

A Diamond Book / published by arrangement with
the author

PRINTING HISTORY
Diamond edition / August 1992

ISBN: 1-55773-756-8

Diamond Books are published by The Berkley Publishing Group,
200 Madison Avenue, New York, New York 10016.
The name "DIAMOND" and its logo are trademarks
belonging to Charter Communications, Inc.

PRINTED IN THE UNITED STATES OF AMERICA

10  9  8  7  6  5  4  3  2  1

"I give you bitter pills in sugar coating. The pills are harmless: the poison is in the sugar."

—Stanislaw Lec

"We are never deceived; we deceive ourselves."

—Goethe

# CHAPTER 1

I'D GONE DOWN to Caesar's Bay to get away from everything. It had been a foul, gray, humid day—one of disappointment—one I didn't want to remember. I'd solved another sad little case, brought another sniveling, cheating husband to ground like the big bad hero I am. I'd made the August office rent by ruining a family with pictures of Daddy grunting in the back seat of their station wagon with a woman who didn't look anything like Mommy at all. As a daily occupation, it was getting to me.

My name's Jack Hagee. I make my living, I put food on my table, buy my toothpaste and subway tokens, by rooting through people's lives and their garbage, by turning over rocks for lawyers and crying spouses and tired shopkeepers and more lawyers. I'm a private detective and that night I was hating my job as much as anyone else. The little voices had been whispering at me all day, sometimes sneering, sometimes laughing out loud. That's why, when midnight had passed and I still couldn't sleep, tossing in my bed, dying in the clogging humidity steaming off the ocean, I'd gotten dressed and driven down to Caesar's.

Caesar's is a shopping mall at the end of Bay Parkway, the main drag through Bensonhurst, the Brooklyn neighborhood in which I live. Most people stay away from it after closing. They have good reasons.

After sunset Caesar's parking lot, and the park adjacent, become one large, dark, criminal carnival land. Dopers sell their wares, Johns pick up their ladies; kids strip cars, smoke dope, shoot craps and sometimes each other. And the worst thing about it all is, Bensonhurst isn't some terribly seedy

1

neighborhood. Not a home between my apartment building and the bay would sell for under a hundred and fifty thousand. It's not a ghetto—just simply the same as the rest of New York City, bursting at the seams from too many people, all with painfully clear visions of the nowhere toward which they are headed.

For those who have never tasted the city, though, who haven't felt the cold leaden knuckle it digs into the backs of those who flock to it, let me just say that it is a hell—a black, indifferent hell, one that beckons to all types, the stupid and the arrogant, the talented, the conning, the naive the hopeful and the self-destructive, to come from around the country to lick at the festering black syrup leaking from its million-and-counting wounds, begging them to call it honey.

Some of those who had begun to catch on to what the city had in store for them, however, sat in their cars, staring, or prowled the darkness of Caesar's. I parked my Skylark at the rail meant to keep people from driving into the ocean and got out to prowl.

Lighting a cigarette, I walked down along the massive stone sea wall, looking out into the storm front crawling in toward me over the black, oily water. The Verrazano Bridge was lost in the fog, as was the parachute tower at Coney Island, both usually easily visible from my spot. Not then. That night the clouds were hanging thick—waiting.

Ignoring the clouds and whatever they were waiting for, I threw myself up and over the steel railing in front of me, settling down on the foot and a half of ledge on the sea side of the barrier. My legs dangling over the dashing waves below, I stared out at the ocean, my eyes not focusing on anything, my brain relaxing for the first time in weeks. I was tired. Tired and alone, dying of despairing old age while still in my thirties.

Leaning back against the rail, I pulled another Camel, just managing to get it lit in the wet of the surrounding mist. I sucked the smoke in deep, holding it down as long as I could, maybe hoping to choke myself. No such luck. The nicotine did start to relax me, however, which at that moment was good enough.

I'd left my apartment in a foul mood. Life had not gotten any better during the months since I'd moved to the city. My wife had left me about six months earlier. In that time, I'd quit the Pittsburgh police force to come to New York and go private. Things hadn't been one great big party since my arrival. In the half year I'd been in the city, I'd managed to go through my bankroll, climb to the point where I might be able to make a success of things, and then tumble back to zero. Loads of fun—so much I barely noticed how soaked I was getting.

I don't own an umbrella—ridiculous, effeminate props— but in my anger I'd slammed my way out leaving hat and jacket behind. The thickening mist was coating my hair and clothes, drenching me. By the time I was ready for a second smoke the sky had started drizzling to the point where I could barely keep my lighter lit long enough to fire up another Camel. I got it going, though, and downed its fumes one breath at a time, watching the lightning splash along both the far shores before me. The coasts of Brooklyn and Staten Island were illuminated over and over, the random split seconds of light revealing the increasing press of the waves below and the rain above.

The truth of the image depressed me. Even nature seemed to work for New York. The city squeezes people, crushing them, forcing them to huddle and shiver, always prepared to wash them away forever for the slightest mistake. Part of me railed at the image but a larger part spoke in calmer tones, implying that perhaps hopelessness was the only sensible feeling one could have living in New York.

I leaned back with eyes closed, the rain lashing, surf below pounding hard enough to almost reach my shoes. I thought of all the reasons people come to the city and wondered what mine had been. As a friend had once said, "People don't pull up in covered wagons to the center of Times Square and say, 'Here it is, honey—a good land, a strong land, a decent land where our children can grow pure and free.'" They didn't say it when people actually rode around in covered wagons, and they sure as hell don't say it now. New York is not a good land or a strong land, and it certainly is not a place to bring children. Not by a long shot.

New York is an aching scum hole, a never-closing maw always willing to let anyone—no matter how corrupt, or illiterate, or evil—call it home and hang up their shingle. It is a giant con, a government-owned-and-operated money drain, constantly sucking the life and joy and wealth out of its inhabitants the way a dying man sucks oxygen— greedily—as if each breath were the last. It grabs everything in sight, using guilt and laws and lies and finally thuggery, if nothing lesser will suffice, to strip those who can't fight it every single minute of every day, week in, decade out, of everything they have—their money their needs their dreams and wretched, desperate hopes—until finally it either gets the last juice left within them, piling their useless bones with the rest, or drives them away in pitiful defeat, frustrated and humiliated and wondering how anyone as tough as them could have lost—everything—so easily, to an enemy so impartial.

And, I thought, still they come. Every day by the hundreds—by the hundreds, they arrive by plane and bus, in rented trucks, old cars, on bicycles, motorcycles, or they walk and hitch if they have to—all of them desperate to follow some simple-minded plan they've mapped out for themselves that is just foolproof. One that shows how easy it will be to make it on Broadway, or in television, or as a painter, a broker, writer, dancer, restaurateur, publisher, actor, reporter, agent, or whathaveyou, willing to work hard now for their bread ahead, not realizing how many waiters and convenience-store attendants and busboys, cab drivers, keyboarders, bartenders, store clerks, menials, drug dealers, hookers, homeless starvlings, and corpses the city requires for every you-have-made-it golden meal ticket it passes out.

As the rain slacked off, I tried to get another smoke going, ruefully asking myself what my excuse for being in New York was, knowing all along that I hadn't come to the city to find anything. I'd come to lose myself, to hide a person I didn't think anyone should see. I was tired when I did it, tired of corruption, tired of hate—of jealousy, pettiness, violence, and anger. I was tired of these things in myself and others.

So naturally, I came to New York, where all the above vices and sins were long ago renamed art forms, encouraged to grow with wild abandon like kudzu, or social welfare. It was the move of a desperate man—trying to hide in a sweltering sea of desperation—hoping the heightened insanity of those around him would make his own reflection look normal. It hadn't worked.

Not knowing what to do about any of it, though, I let the big problems rest and concentrated on lighting my cigarette. The job took twice as much effort as the last one. The pack in my shirt pocket had started to soak through, leaving the cigarette damp in my hand. I had to keep my palm close over the top of the lighter, burning my hand slightly, just to get the sogging smoke to catch. I sighed, remembering my old man's favorite phrase . . . there's no such thing as a free lunch. I had just spit out my first lungful when the city gave me something new to think about.

So skillfully I almost didn't notice, a pickpocket had reached through the railing my back was against, going for the wallet in my front pants pocket. His hand out with its prize, I managed to snag his wrist a split second before it could snake back behind the railing.

"Oh, no you don't!" I growled.

The pickpocket pulled hard, pushing with his feet against the rail, tearing my fingers at the knuckles as he scraped them against the steel rails. I pulled back, determined to keep my wallet, fighting for balance on the foot and a half of slick rock that made up my side of the fence.

"Let go, dammit! Let go o'me!"

Sticking his free arm through the rails, the pickpocket slammed me in the side, knocking me over the sea wall. I held his wrist in a death grip, feeling his shoulder slam against the rails as my weight pulled him tight. He cursed nonstop, his free hand tearing at my fingers around his wrist. I punched him away as best I could, hitting him sometimes, sometimes myself, sometimes the rails. My mind raced over my options, not finding much.

I could release my grip and hope to be able to catch a rail or the sea wall's edge, but the rain made my chances slim at best. It was possible I might survive the fall to the water, but it was only a 50-50 possibility. The rocks hidden beneath the violently pounding waves slamming against my legs and the wall were jagged and slimy with sea growth. Walking along the wall back to shore was impossible. So was swimming. The tide was too low for that, but quite ample to mash a man to death. I had no choice—I hung on.

"C'mon, man—let go o'me! I mean it—I mean it!"

He shook at me, pulling back and forth, jerking my armpit painfully across the edge of the rock wall. I bit at the rain, growling in agony, but didn't let go.

"Le'go, le'go, le'go—you bastard—le'go, le'go!"

"Just pull me up—fer Christ's sake!" I told him. "Let me grab the rail. You can have the goddamned money, but I'm not dying over five bucks!"

"No—shut up! Let go o'me—le'go, le'go! Shit. I makes you le'go. I makes you!"

The pickpocket reached inside his coat. Bracing myself, I thought, okay, you want it—you got it, and then dug my heels into the wall. The pickpocket's hand emerged with a straight razor. My left foot slipped back into the water. The pickpocket's free hand came through the rails at me. My foot almost caught, but slipped again. The razor took my distance, cutting open my sleeve and flaying a fine layer of hair and skin away. My foot caught. I hovered into balance, finding my center of gravity. The razor waved above my line of sight.

"Now. Now you let go."

"Not yet."

I threw my weight back, my legs pushing me out from the wall. The extra leverage broke the pickpocket's hold, bringing him slamming into the rails facefirst. The razor flipped out of his hand, arcing past my right ear. Blood splashed from his face, catching me in the eyes and mouth. Not slowing up, I leaned forward and punched, nailing the part of his face that the steel to either side of my fist had missed. Blood arced again, running over his shoulder, down his arm to mine. The blow caused me to slip but, I managed to get half my body back up on the ledge. Releasing the now limp wrist, I caught a rail in each hand, dragging myself into a secure position as fast as I could.

Once on the ledge I turned to face the pickpocket in case he was going to be any more trouble. He wasn't. He was unconscious or dead. I didn't care which. Then I spotted it—my wallet still in his hand. Catching my breath, I reached over and pried it free. He didn't stir. I slid back over to the landward side of the railing. I sat down in relief a few feet from my playmate, exhausted from my ninety seconds of past-event reruns, glad for life and breath and safety. After a few moments of being overjoyed with having remained alive, though, I noticed it was starting to rain harder. Tired of abuse for one night, I pushed myself to my feet and walked over to the pickpocket. Patting him on the back, I told him,

"Nice try."

Then I walked back to my car and drove home. When I got there, I had no trouble sleeping.

# CHAPTER 2

THE RAIN CONTINUED on through the night, still lashing at the city when I got back into my Skylark and left for the office the next morning. I grabbed for every yard of asphalt amid all the other commuters grabbing for theirs as we all fought our way through the surrounding dark rain. It came in sheets that broke up into those big drops, the kind that sound like a large dog's nails on the sidewalk as they hit your roof. It wasn't the kind of noise I wanted to hear.

Truth to tell, I didn't know what I wanted to hear, or see, or feel. All I knew was that I wanted to be anywhere but in the front seat of my car headed for my office. I saw myself fishing as a doctor-plated coupe splayed by on my right, thought about an open fire at some ski lodge while I cut off a white panel truck filthy with graffiti scrawled in ugly, undecipherable letters. A lot of other beer commercial images flashed in my brain as the Skylark and I danced the morning clog-waltz across the Manhattan Bridge.

Incredibly beautiful two-hundred-dollar-an-hour models pretending to be waitresses and snowmobile passengers and pool players and girlfriends all smiled down at me from their billboards. They winked in that certain, flirtatious, wantonly innocent manner most women lose after their second or third steady boyfriend, letting me know my crummy life would be aces if I just chilled out and had a beer. If there'd been one in the glove compartment, I'd have toasted them all with it then and there. If I'd had one in the trunk I'd have stopped the car in the middle of the bridge to get it. And I don't even like beer. Those girls earn their money.

I continued to drive, worming my way through the gray morning surrounding me, dreading the day to come. Business had been fairly slow the past few weeks; some divorce work, one lousy, small-potatoes embezzlement case, recovering some minor stolen property—not much.

One of the problems lately had been the weather. People don't seem to commit as many crimes when it's raining—especially summer rain. Maybe it's because air conditioning is still, at the least, only a necessity to the upper middle class, leaving the majority of New Yorkers to pray for rain to cool off the concrete and their tempers. Maybe it's because rain gives everyone something to complain about together. Or maybe it's just because it washes some of the filth and debris off the sidewalks and buildings, and out of the sky, leaving the city looking a little bit more like a place where people belong.

Don't ask me why. I don't know. The only thing I did know was that not too many people had needed a detective recently. Not one with my initials, anyway. Hell, if things'd kept up at that rate it wouldn't have been long before I'd have been on the streets tracking down lost dogs for the rewards. I could see the image clearly—Milk Bones in my pocket, running down the street with a giant butterfly net after some yapping poodle, all the girls from the beer commercials laughing at me. Even the damn dog laughing. I spun out in front of a fat green Caddy at the light at the end of the bridge, jumping a lane to be able to outslick everybody else in the uptown race. That would show those bitches, laughed the back of my brain. Oh, yeah, I thought, you're in a good mood.

Actually I wasn't too worried. I pulled at my collar. Despite the gloom, I could feel the sun staging a return. You could tell it would be driving the rain off soon, beckoning the skells to drag themselves out of their caves. The city would heat up by noon to where it was certain that tempers around town would be generating some kind of work for an honest P.I.

I pulled up to the newsstand across the street from my office. Freddie, the woman who runs it, keeps a ''No

Parking—Order of the Police Department'' sign in the street next to her stand to scare away the straights so I can have a parking place. Every once in a while a cop car will take it, but not often. The nearest doughnut shop is two blocks away.

Freddie is in her late fifties, early sixties, about five and a half feet tall and a good bunch of pounds over two hundred. She is also the toughest woman in the city, from the standpoints of both grit and muscle. At least in my opinion. She also carries the best selection of papers and magazines to be found in Manhattan, and hasn't allowed the Pakistani mob to annex her stand into their city-wide chain. A real tough lady.

I eased the Skylark into the spot as Freddie pulled the police marker up onto the curb. As we stashed it behind her booth, she asked,

"How's it goin', tough guy?"

"Oh, great. Got mugged last night."

"Hehahahaee—did'ja kill 'im?"

"Maybe," I told her.

"There you go again, leavin' bodies all over da street. Didn't your mother ever teach you any better than that?"

"What can I tell you, gorgeous?" I shrugged as I pulled a *Daily News* out of the middle of the pile, throwing it on top of the counter. Freddie added a grapefruit juice, which is my usual, and then a V-8, which I decided I'd grab to help me through the morning. As I pieced together enough change to cover the total, she said,

"Oh, you tough guys."

"Yeah, it's a wonderful life. I'll drop by to break your heart later."

She laughed. No surprise. All women laugh when you start getting cocky. The tougher ones just laugh louder. Thinking about it, I laughed too, and then headed across the street for my office.

• • •

The day before had been the first of the month, making it time to straighten out all my dubious finances. By the time I finished pegging down the details of my impending bankruptcy, I found myself with a stack of paid bills, $38.54 in my checking, and ten dollars in my wallet. It was a sobering experience. So much so, I went into my bottom drawer for the bottle of Gilbey's I keep there. It might be a cliché for a private detective to keep a bottle of gin in his desk, but show me the person who doesn't have a cliché or two in their lives and I'll consider getting rid of it.

I poured a few fingers worth into the grapefruit juice container, swished it around to get the last of the juice, and then knocked it all off in a couple of gulps. Feeling a little better about having less free capital than the kid from my building who works at the local McDonald's part-time after school, I mixed half the V-8 and a fist's worth of Gilbey's in the same container. Then I put my feet up on the desk, hoping for some free time to read the paper and relax.

Normally I would have come in late, considering how little sleep I'd had, but today was bill-paying day. A lot of guys can rearrange their schedule, saying they'll take care of something tomorrow, and actually get caught up later, but I've found if I let things start sliding they just turn into an avalanche. Everything considered, however, I was fairly pleased with myself at that moment. Despite my problems of the day before, I'd been able to hoist myself out of bed and into town, take care of all my bills, and get a nice buzz on, all before noon. Now, all I wanted to do was read the paper, work on my drink, and get comfortable enough to allow the rising heat to drift me off to napland. Of course, fate wasn't about to allow that to happen.

# CHAPTER 3

JUST AS I got to the funnies, an insistent pounding started on my outer door. Great, I thought. A customer—just what I don't want. I smiled at my laziness, called out a "Come in," and then folded the *News*, setting it off to the side. Running my hands through my hair, I thought about straightening my tie, decided against it, and tried to tear it off instead. The knot jammed, refusing to budge. Sighing, I let it hang as the fat man puffed through my doorway. He stood on the other side of my desk, a look on his face I couldn't quite read.

Detectives, like anyone else who works with the public, can usually get a sense of what is going on with each client who comes through the door before they open their mouths. We're not psychics—it just comes with the job. Two or three people have a cheating spouse, you come to recognize the look. Four or five times someone wants this or that type of problem solved, you start getting the idea ahead of time. This guy didn't have a look, though. Either he wanted something new, or I was drinking too much. He got his first words out. The air pushing them let me know I wasn't the only one drinking.

"Mr. Hagee . . ." My name came out of his blubbery, bearded face riding a wave of alcohol fumes, a few octaves higher than I would have guessed from the size of him. He was big; big with a semi-tamed crop of tangled, greasy hair lashing in slick strands at the frames of his black horn-rimmed glasses. His soft, beefy biceps strained against the wet-stained sleeves of his off-white shirt. His belly sagged over a Coors belt buckle, shifting up and down while he

12

moved his weight from one foot to the other, his breaths coming in laborious, fatty gasps—pretty bad for the late twenties/early thirties I figured him to be.

"Mr. Hagee . . ." It wasn't a question. Neither was what came next. "I want you to find Mara for me, Mr. Hagee." He rested his fat palms on my blotter, continuing, "I need her. You have to find her."

I decided it was time to discover who my new best friend was, and what it was he was after. I didn't really want to, but the little voices were whispering, telling me it was my job. What did I know; they might be right. I took a chance.

"Who is Mara, pal? And who are you?"

"Mara?" He said it as if he couldn't understand how anyone hadn't heard of her. "Mara is my girl. And they took her. Those bastards . . . They were always trying to ruin her life—all of them. Chasing her all the time, forcing themselves on her, making her drink, giving her drugs, getting her high, all the time . . . so they, they could, could . . ." He stared at me straight on, letting me know he was serious. "I want to kill them all."

And then, suddenly, he stopped talking. Maybe he'd caught himself in the middle of something he'd thought better about broadcasting, or maybe he'd finished. Sometimes there's no telling. Tears were welling in his sad little baked-mud brown eyes, oozing their way over his cheeks. Just as suddenly, though, he swam back to the room from wherever he'd gone off to, half-whispering,

"Please, find my Mara for me?"

He rose away from my desk then, leaving two sweaty handprints on my blotter. I waved him toward either of the padded chairs in front of the desk. He took the one to his left and sat down. Once I was sure he was with me, I repeated,

"Now—like I asked before, who is Mara, and who are you?"

"My name is Carl Miller. Mara is my girl. We're going to be married. At least we were, until she disappeared."

"What do you mean, 'disappeared'? How? When? Where?"

"It was last week. I went to her home to pick her up. We

were going to a concert. In the park. I love concerts. She does, too. Honest. Her mother didn't know where she was. We waited all night, but she—she never came home. None of her things were missing—everything I gave her is . . . everything was still there.''

"Everything?"

''A lot of her jewelry was gone, and her good clothes, but all the important things—they were still there.''

"What kind of important things?"

''Well,'' he sucked in a big mouthful of air. ''Like Buff'em.''

"Buff'em?"

''Was a doll I gave her. Just a rag doll, but she loved it. Kept it on her bed all the time. She really cared about it. She'd have never left Buff'em behind if she'd left on her own. I know it.''

Oh, yeah, I thought. Sure, pal. In your dreams. His voice was quavering, cracking occasionally. He was too upset to control himself. Too drunk. That he'd been drinking didn't really surprise me. A lot of people need a drink before they go to see a detective. Not everyone, just the ones who need help with the truth. Telling it or facing it. The fat man went back to trying the former.

''I told her mother not to worry. I said I could handle everything. I said I could get her back. I said I would, Mr. Hagee . . .'' And then, suddenly, he was out of his chair, grabbing at me.

''Help me!!''

Instinctively, I swatted his hands away. Open-fingered—stinging, not hostile. He jerked back, sticking his fingers in his mouth, one hand, then the other, smothering his yelp of pain with a thin, gurgling wet sound. I told him,

''Listen to me, Mr. Miller. Maybe your Mara is missing, maybe she isn't. It's a big world out there. Maybe she just got bored. Maybe not. I'll tell you up front that there isn't much of a percentage in disappearance cases.

''No matter what the answer is, and believe me, it isn't usually suicide, kidnapping, or murder, the searchers are never very happy with the results. No matter whether your friend is a runaway, holed up somewhere after a long drunk, or detoxing, or just on a vacation she decided not to tell anyone about, my guess is that sooner or later she'll turn up on her own.'' As much as I hate giving a sucker an even break, I gave the fat man his chance.

''Throwing good money my way is probably not going to help you any. The truth is that even if I find your friend, things are probably not going to be the way you remember them. Now, take a minute and think about it. Do you really want to spend the kind of money it'll take to see this woman again?''

He didn't bat an eye. He didn't hesitate.

''Whatever it takes.''

He was hiding something. Whether it was from me or himself, I wasn't sure. I'd given him his chance, though. Now it was time to follow the advice of the little voices and do my job. My hands had gone into my desk while I was talking, pulling out a steno pad. I hit the fat man with my questions, jotting down his answers in my own personal shorthand. Slowly I began to unravel his problem.

Her name was Maureen Phillips. She was twenty-three years old; a college-graduated artist still living with her parents—parents who'd let the fat man pick up that education's tab. According to him, she'd been a pretty wild sort before she'd met him—correction—before they could begin going out together. He'd been married when they first met—him with his wife, her one of his friends' dates.

He'd become interested in her, found her to be something special. By the time his floundering marriage washed up into a divorce, she'd slept with almost every man, and some of the women, in the fat man's circle. But then she finally latched onto him, and suddenly, sleeping with someone wasn't all that important to her anymore.

''You have to understand, Mr. Hagee. They were all using her, trying to take advantage of her. They just wanted her for her body. I was—I, I'm hoping that I'll be better for her. I'm just hoping that I'll be able to straighten her out.''

Great. Naive and a saint. Putting my pen down, giving him a chance to do a little off-the-record, I asked,

"Why do you want to see this woman again?"

"I want to know what's happened to her. I mean, she just disappeared; there was no note, no nothing. Something has happened to her, and I, I care about her—I do, Mr. Hagee. We, we were going to be married—she and I; we were supposed to, we, she and . . ."

And then the tears started inching their way over his sad, puffy cheeks again. He crumpled against the corner of my desk making gaspy, liquid sounds, every once in a while balling his fist to crack it against the side of my desk. I didn't stop him. It wasn't the worst that'd ever happened to the furniture in my office.

By the time he'd pulled himself together, I'd finished heating the coffee left over from the day before on my hot plate. I pushed a mug of it in front of him, figuring he needed it no matter how old it was. He drank at it in greedy sips, ignoring its foulness, grateful for the warmth and the diversion.

We started again. He gave me the details on her family. It looked as if I would have to drive to Plainton, their home town in Pennsylvania, to check everything out. It worried me that I was already thinking of the case as accepted. Not wanting to take advantage, I gave him one last chance, saying,

"Okay, Mr. Miller. I'm not going to lie to you. There isn't much of a chance I can do anything for you. Trying to find one person in a city of eight, nine million, is not the easiest thing in the world. This kind of case rarely leaves the client with anything except bills. If you insist, after you really think about it for a moment, I will take your case. But I do have to ask you something first."

He waited for me—silent.

"Why did you come to me, me in particular? Why did you even come to New York?"

He wiped his streaked face on his shirt cuff.

"Because they all came here. If they took her, they brought her here."

A few more questions got him back on track. It turned out that most of the group the fat man claimed his Mara had been partying around with had moved to the city. They were his home town's elite minority, its meager crop of small-time artists, writers, and philosophers, big fish not content to rule a small pond when New York was just waiting to fall on its knees to pay them homage as soon as they got here. Yeah, right. Just the types I'd expect to attract a snobbish, spoiled dilettante, which was more and more what little Mara was sounding like. I got their names and home town addresses out of the fat man, and then asked him if he had a picture of "his Mara." He did.

He handed it to me the way a kid hands his pet dog to the vet's nurse. Just like a kid's eyes, his reflected how he felt—with all the fear showing through. It was a fear that I couldn't understand the special way he did, that I couldn't care as much as him—the fear that after all I'd seen in my time, it just wouldn't matter as much to me.

And, up until I saw the picture in his shaking hand, he'd been right. The first glance changed my attitude, though. A lot. It was just one of those black-and-white, three-for-two-dollars booth shots—the kind every sailor has a wallet full of—but everything the fat man had been saying finally made sense.

She was young and soft, all curls and lace and little-girl makeup. The perfect image of what the media keeps insisting all young women are supposed to look like. She was a dazzler, with just the right nose, the right lips, right cheekbones, all perfectly designed for pouting. Her eyes and smile both sparkled with a knowing innocence, that intelligent type of upper-class wantonness that never shows itself until a very high emotional or monetary price is first met.

I found myself wondering at a number of things, like just which price Miller had been paying, and how high he'd been willing to go, and whether or not this marriage-to-be was just all in his mind, or firmly rooted in teasing hints and lies. I also found myself wondering just what shade Mara's eyes and hair were.

That, I found very disturbing.

All of my mental rummagings had only taken a few seconds. I looked at my client, then back to the small rectangle in my hand, and suddenly for some reason it struck me. She reminded me of snow—all soft and white—beautiful, clinging snow. It's always so convenient to just take a quick look through a frosted window and think about how lovely it is, never seeing past to how swiftly it turns to an oozing black slush, or how easily it can kill—or even to just how icy and hard and dead everything is underneath.

I looked up at Miller again, telling him I'd have to keep the picture. He mumbled in agreement, shrinking a little into his chair. I felt sorry for him—his only problem was that he was snow-blind, with no way out. I asked him for his New York address and some kind of advance. He scribbled his hotel's name on a piece of paper I tore out of my pad for him. It wasn't the best address in town—it wasn't even the best address in its neighborhood—didn't matter to me. I didn't have to live there.

When he asked my rates, I told him three hundred a day off the top of my head. I've gotten that in my time, but those were exceptional times. I said it to him as a last attempt to get him to reconsider what he was doing. Instead he wrote me a check for a week. I took it.

Then, with nothing else to say, Miller heaved up out of his chair and headed for the hall. The door shut behind him, leaving me alone with four pages of shorthand notes and a bad, itchy feeling behind my eyes. I thought that maybe it was only the strain from the crummy lighting in my office, possibly the last effects of the night before. I should have known better. I'd let him leave with the assurance I would take his case. I should have told him I was getting out of the private eye business to become an assistant manager at McDonald's.

The little voices starting laughing again. I felt like joining them.

# CHAPTER 4

I SAT FOR a long time after Miller was gone, staring at the notes I had taken and the picture he had left behind. Mara stared back, waiting for me to guess what shade of blue her eyes were. They had to be blue. Something about her assured me of that.

I was just deciding what to do for lunch when I realized Miller hadn't answered one of my questions. I still had no idea how he had come to pick me. Maybe Ray Trenkel had sent him over. Trenkel is the captain at the precinct house that covers the neighborhood my office is in, among many. From time to time in the past he has sent prospective clients to my door—people the law couldn't help or with whom he couldn't be bothered.

Usually I thanked him for the memory by splitting a bottle of his favorite rye with him whenever my means could afford such luxuries. This wasn't looking like one of those times. But, knowing he should be on duty then, I called to see if I could pin the blame for Miller on him. My question was answered before it was asked.

"Hey, Jack, did that big moke we sent over to you get there yet?"

"Yeah. That your idea of a joke?"

"No; why? Did the guy change his story or something?"

"What do you mean?"

Trenkel explained. "He said he needed some help. Said he had to find this broad, and he wanted us to harass some of the local taxpayers. Naturally I told him we couldn't do that."

"Well, not for him, at least. Right, Ray?"

"You bet. Who's this guy think he is . . . the mayor? Anyway, we tell him we can't just go out and harass people. So he goes, 'Who can?' Right? Funny kinda guy, huh? Anyway, then Mooney says, 'Go see Hagee. He'll harass anybody for a bottle of gin.'"

"Yeah," I said, loving the image of Mooney, Trenkel's horse-faced second-in-command, getting a laugh at my expense. "You guys are real cutups."

Trenkel laughed into the phone. "Oh, well, we do try."

"Swell. Then you guys owe me a favor."

"Such as . . . ?" The voice coming out of my phone was suddenly very full of business. Cops are always wary of granting anyone favors. They have a right to be. People ask them for some pretty unusual stuff at times. Fortunately for both of us, this was not one of those times.

"Listen. I'm going to have to drive out to this guy's home ground. I'd like you to call ahead and tell the local Plainton boys who I am and, if you can, get them to round up whatever facts they have on a little list of names Miller left with me. Okay? Seeing as how you're the guys that got me into this mess."

"Yeah. Sure. That can't keep me from making commissioner any faster, I guess. Unlike some of your other requests."

"All in the past, Ray," I joked. "This is the new Jack Hagee. You wouldn't believe the turn for the better my character has taken; all of it from associating with you, I might add."

"Sure, Jack. Sure. And I suppose your car isn't parked in front of the newsstand across the street, either."

"You know, I think that is where I'm parked today."

"Now there's a surprise."

I smiled at the phone, asking Ray "whatever can you mean" in my most shocked voice. He told me what he meant with just a verb and a pronoun. I agreed to try and then told him I'd drop off the list of names to him before I set out for Plainton, thanking him profusely for his kind consideration. He said "fine, yeah, whatever" and hung up. "Public servant" really is a contradiction in terms.

After our connection broke, I redialed, calling Hubert, one of the best networkers in the business. Calling Hu an informant would be like calling Walt Disney a successful doodler; it not only misses the degree, it misses the point. Hubert does more than snitch out junkies for dimes—he's both a top legman and dealer. He likes to get out in the street and mix in the dirty snoopwork of a case just for the fun of it. It isn't his way of making a living, though.

Hu is a mover who packages deals for people throughout the city. All kinds of people. All kinds of deals. We met after I'd been in town a couple of months. He had a politician who needed a high-profile bodyguard. I had a high profile at that time due to a case that had plastered my name throughout the media. His idea was to call attention to me so his people could protect the politician. It worked. Maurice Smartt, one of his top boys, ended up in the hospital with a lungful of blood. I got stomped so bad I was amazed I was able to get up and walk away from it. Maurice and I split a thousand dollars. Hubert got his fee, plus a commission from the two of us. He does okay.

Hubert does good work for fair prices. On the surface it seems like a fair enough deal—the problem is, Hu is also one of the most annoying people anyone's ever met. He presents an almost comical physical picture—standing only five foot three, weighing in around one hundred and twenty, limping heavily on the right side, stuttering badly, and maintaining possibly the world's most obnoxious wardrobe. None of these things are what makes him annoying, however. Simply put, Hu has one of the world's worst senses of humor. Too vulgar, too gross, too racist, sexist, corny, punning, too everything—with no sense whatsoever of when he might want to keep his mouth shut.

He is the best at what he does, however, so with the usual amount of trepidation I listened to the bell in my phone, counting off the times I could have hung up, staying on the line instead, hoping maybe he wouldn't be there.

"Hu-Hubert, here. Who-who I got?"

"It's me, Hu."

"Hey, hey, Hagee. What's up yer flagpole, Dick Tracy?"

"Not much—nothing very interesting—looks to be a typical scram-scam. Another runaway the client could find himself if he had the nerve. I've got a list of names I'd like you to give one of your people for a quick sniffing over. Anyone got the time?"

"For m-my favorite private dick? I'll do it myself."

"That's all right, Hu. It's not . . ."

"Tut, tut, my g-good man. It's a lazy day, just right for runnin' away. I'll be right over. Hey hey hey."

I tried to assure him it wasn't a problem that demanded his personal touch, but he hung up before I could get anything out that might get the truth across to him. Sighing, I figured maybe it was all for the best and replaced the phone receiver, guessing at my next move.

Before anything else could come to me, I looked again at Mara's picture. I'd already figured out what shade of blue her eyes were. She was smiling in approval. I reached for my cigarettes with one hand, turning the photo facedown with the other. That was when I saw what Miller's little playmate had written to him on the back of his treasure. The note read:

> "Lots of hugs and kisses to my big fuzzy
> Dumptruck, Mara"

I wondered at how he took it. No "love" or "take care" or even a goddamned "sincerely." Just "Mara." As if that was supposed to be enough for anybody. I turned it back over. Looking into her eyes was better than looking at that.

I lit a Camel, holding the first lungful back for a long time. Washing it down with the last of my coffee, I sat back, planning my next steps out in my mind. I figured I would head for Plainton that afternoon. Pennsylvania's not really that far away. I wanted to talk with Mara's parents about her, and maybe some of the people on Miller's hate parade as well. I also wanted to see what the local boys-in-blue knew about the whole thing. While I dug up whatever I could out there, I'd let Hubert handle the tracking here. By the time I got back I was sure he'd have found the guys who had moved to New York, where they were living, what there jobs were, and if I was real lucky, he'd know which one of them, if any, had Mara. I wouldn't have minded getting lucky for once, either. Miller's case was not the kind I looked forward to. Who would?

The problem that comes with this kind of investigation is that there really is no case. No crime. When no one's broken any laws, things get a lot harder to trace. People don't like to talk to P.I.'s in the first place. Why should they? We're just rent-a-cops anyone can blow off if they feel like it. At least when there's a crime involved you can hobble citizens with their guilt over doing their civic duty. Without that, though, things go downhill fast. Tell someone a woman has disappeared on her boyfriend and a lot of them figure that's more her business than yours.

Give them a line a little too far from the truth, which gets back to the cops, and you risk losing your license. You can hit them with a conspiratorial glance and try to make their ounce of information too heavy for them to hold, but that ploy has its own problems. There's a lot of people out there who think any woman with a magnifying glass and a face like Eleanor Roosevelt can catch a murderer with just a little bit of gumption. Yeah, it's a lot of fun being a big bad private detective.

All that aside, however, since my ruptured bank accounts had already started me on the course, I figured if Miller was determined to spend his money just to find out whether or not his Mara was all right, I was willing to be the guy who got paid to tell him. Normally I might have turned him down, or at least tried harder to explain the situation to him. I might have hammered at him a little longer than I did that there was nothing he, or I, or the police, or anyone else could do that was going to change anything for him. I might have. But Miller'd come when I was too tapped out to care. He should have come tomorrow.

By the time Hubert arrived I'd typed up a copy of Miller's list and a few carbons. He came in making cartoon duck noises, cackling his way through my outer office. He entered laughing, ambled over to my desk, and hopped up on its corner. Hubert doesn't like chairs.

He was wearing a lime-green silk shirt with burgundy

pants and yellow socks. A light pink straw hat sat on the back of his head. Something tells me he doesn't like mirrors, either.

The barrage began immediately.

"Hey, hey, Hagee. Listen to th-this one. W-what do they do with foreskins after the circumcisions?"

Admitting I didn't know got me the answer.

"They sugarcoat them and sell them to homos for chewing gum."

I groaned quietly while he laughed. Someone is required for both parts every time Hubert tells a joke. So far we've taken the same roles every time.

I diverted his attention before he could launch into another one, though, by giving him a copy of the list. He studied the names for a second, but none of them registered. Frowning, he folded the list and stuck it in his lime-green pocket. He was disappointed. Hubert always likes to try and impress people by giving them the information they want right out of his head without having to do any research. Truth to tell, I've seen him pull the trick enough times I was a little disappointed myself when nothing clicked for him. Mooching one of my cigarettes, he leaned back a little, trying to relax. He played with my paperweight, an ashtray in the shape of the '39 World's Fair's ball and cone as he flicked his ashes into it. We talked a while longer, and then I showed him the picture of Mara.

"Ooh la la—bounce her on my knee—lap it up, b-baby. Oh, Jackie-boy—tell me she's a m-m-murderer. Please. Tell me she blows her victims away."

He started pounding on my desktop, snickering and laughing at the same time, blowing air out through his closed teeth. I'd expected it. Hu always laughs at his own jokes, making his damn, dying duck noises all the while— just another reason for his well-deserved reputation. Spotting what Mara had signed on the back of the picture got him laughing harder, this time using my ashtray to pound on my desk, spilling butts and ashes across my blotter and the floor. He apologized.

"Hoo-hoo. Sorry, Jack. H-here, I'll get it."

I told him not to worry about it. After he'd started howling over the absurdity of it all, I'd started chuckling myself. I figured I owed him something for that.

"I have to get over to Trenkel's, then out to Plainton," I told him. "I'll call you tomorrow to see what you have for me."

His head was still hanging sheepishly. I repeated,

"Don't worry about the mess. It's all right."

The second "don't worry about it" had a better effect. He brightened like a puppy who, knowing it had done something wrong, also knew it had been forgiven. To prove he was a good dog, he pulled the list from his pocket again, studying it for a moment. Once he was sure he had the scent, he crammed it back into its ill-colored hiding place, saying, "Okay—sure, Hagee. T-tomorrow. Maybe we can do a bite down at Mott?"

I told him "sure" and then watched as he pushed himself off the desk and dragged himself to the door. I stuffed my cigarettes, Mara's picture, and my two remaining copies of Miller's list into my jacket. The heat filtering into my office through the windows and the walls made me think twice about wearing it, but I figured I'd better look at least semi-presentable for the small-town cops ahead of me.

Pulling at my tie, I found the knot still as impossible as it had been earlier. I fumbled with it for a second but then gave up, simply letting it hang rather than struggling to get it apart so I could just retie it. I grabbed my raincoat and hat, slinging the one over my arm and propping the other on the back of my head, just in case the rain decided to re-engage the heat for leadership in their Make-The-City-A-Hell contest, and then headed for the door. Locking it behind me, I headed down the stairs. I would drop a copy of the list with Trenkel and then head for Miller's little home town.

I left my .38 in its special hiding place in its drawer. My carry permit is good in Pennsylvania, even in Philadelphia where sometimes even the mob has trouble getting licenses, but I knew I wouldn't be needing it. At least, that was what I told myself. I don't like to carry a gun any more than I have to. What sane person does?

I came out into the street, blinking for a long moment, trying to see through the haze lifting off the sidewalks. The sun had beaten back most of the clouds, filling Union Square with heat and light, helping the overwhelming noise of the street to punish everyone on it for the crime of being in the vicinity. I worked at shrugging it off, trying to get started.

It was already past noon. Heading for his precinct house, I hoped I could mooch a few gas and toll dollars from Trenkel. I had Miller's check in my pocket, but I was in no great hurry to debate my right to my own money with some snotty eighteen-year-old bank clerk.

Lighting another cigarette, I took one last look at Mara's smile and then slid the photo back into my pocket, refusing to look at it again. At least for a while. I needed to think, and that was something I couldn't do with her orchid blues laughing at me.

I was willing to bet Miller couldn't, either.

# CHAPTER 5

SOMEHOW I MANAGED to cajole Trenkel into giving me both a clean slate with the Plainton boys and the loan I needed. He said that by doing so he no longer owed me any favors. I smiled and reminded him about a certain December night last winter.

I'd been hired by a West Side warehouse's security operation to look into a rash of thefts. In New York, everyone gets robbed sooner or later, but the owners felt they were being hit for more than their fair share. Like most security agencies, the majority of their personnel were college kids, drifters, and retirees from numerous other unrelated portions of the service economy, with hardly any real investigators on staff. In the long run it's cheaper for them to hire short-termers like myself from the outside when there's trouble than to keep any really experienced help around full-time.

What my legwork turned up on that case was a ring working the lower West Side using information supplied out of Trenkel's precinct by one of his own men. Rather than touch off another public scandal, giving the police a darker black eye, and the media another pointless nothing to scream over, I held back that part, allowing Trenkel to deal with the guilty officer in his own fashion. I never did ask what happened. Some things outsiders are best not having a good handle on.

Staring back at me sourly, Trenkel agreed that he might still owe me one more. I shrugged and let it go. There was a time that, like a lot of other people, I used to wonder what it was that made so many cops go bad. I'd heard all the stories and seen all the results of business handouts, hustler shakedowns, whores' freebies, and all the million other types of bribes and payolas the city offers. After a while, though, I also started to notice the uniform lack of respect the city reserves for her boys in blue. After watching the payroll cutbacks, the sniper increases, and the total number of cops killed in the line of duty mount higher by leaps and bounds, my attitude began to change.

Considering the low pay, the danger, the denigration, and the just plain foulness tied up in being a cop, nowadays I don't wonder so much about why cops go bad, but rather why anyone becomes one in the first place. Every time I do think about it, however, I always return to the simple out that the reasons differ from person to person.

For some guys it's the macho trip, the head-busting glory boys out to show the dealers, the muggers and the baby rapers, the big bosses and every other street skell and grabber who the real boss is; out to make the world safe—all by themselves. The guys who just know they're the one who's going to make a difference.

The aren't the only ones, of course. There are the insecure ones, tying their lives so tightly to their badge and the blue shirt it's pinned to that in the end the number stamped on their shield becomes more real to them than their own names.

Guys with no other future become cops. Failures at everything else, a grubbing, rotting destiny takes their wrist and drags them in, both the well-intentioned and those who were creeps from the beginning. It rolls them through the city, coating them with its foul reek, every day another smear or two grinding itself into their sharply creased pants.

It isn't a beginner's disease, or an occupational hazard, but a continuous, never-ending deterioration that affects them a tiny bit every day, until after a few years they find themselves as dirty as the things they set out to stop. It's like taking a handful of plant cuttings and placing them in a clear glass. The longer you leave them in without changing the water, the grayer and scummier the sides of the glass become. Leave them in long enough and eventually everything will be sucked empty, water gone, cuttings decayed, the only thing left a damp, blackened pulpy slime that blots out even the memory of what the glass used to look like.

And the real shame of it all is that none of them ever seem to see it coming.

None of them escape it. Talk to Ray Trenkel. You can smell it in his attitude. He started out to clean up the world, fighting the battle every day, digging his nails into the dirt, striking as solidly as he could at the city's ills. But as the years dragged by, the punches grew wilder—and blinder. His hair and muscles thinned and, despite the jokes and the cordial, captain's manner he's learned to display for the public, the bitterness is there. Constantly. Discouragement has caught hold of him, too, a desperation born of the realization that there's no way to win.

It may surprise those who've never thought about it, but most cops join the force thinking they really can make a difference in the way things are. It may seem like a stupid notion to some, but it should seem a lot stupider to think they joined knowing they couldn't. A lot of people don't believe me when I say that, but then how long ago I gave up caring what other people believe I couldn't tell you.

Despite what anyone thinks, the only men and women who know just how bad the streets stink are those who have to walk in them. Victims don't know what the streets smell like; they're never there long enough. The grabbers know what things are about—them and the cops. They're the only ones who know the main lesson, that there is no way to win, and that only the very strong, or the very foolish, continue to fight against something they know they can't beat. Foolishly, I continued back toward where I'd parked my Skylark.

● ● ●

It was another hour before I could fill up with regular at my favorite station, maneuver through the crosstown traffic, and finally aim toward Jersey. There wasn't much to see on the turnpike. It'd started raining again. I pulled at the tangled knot in my tie, letting the miles of highway churn past me, each looking fairly much like the one before it through the patches of windshield my wipers could keep clear. Luckily, it stopped raining around four o'clock. By five-thirty I was in Plainton, looking for the local police station.

A kid whose jeans cost more than my living room couch gave me directions which eventually took me to the cops. Once there I parked in an unpaved area designated Visitors. Heading indoors, I scraped the excess mud from my shoes and went through the screen door.

Inside I was confronted by a tired, heavyset woman in her fifties whose lapel badge read "Mrs. Bryant." She was cut off from me by a glass partition. The glass was reinforced with crisscrossing wire. What was keeping Mrs. Bryant up was not that obvious. When I told her my name, she said a Sergeant Andren was expecting me. She pointed out the office I should head for, her hooded brown eyes never really leaving the clock on the desk in front of her. I thanked her for her congeniality and then went down the hall to knock on the sergeant's door.

"Come on in. It's open."

I entered Andren's office, looking over the gray-and-green interior. It was a cop's office, with the same old desk, battered filing cabinet, and all the other worn, tired refuse that piles up in the too small rooms they give cops who hang on long enough. Of course it had some personal touches; Andren had his own coffee maker and mug. There were a few cartoons on the wall behind his desk along with a black-and-white photo of the television Superman and, as would be expected, his name was stenciled on the door.

All of which meant that if something ever happened to him, some other guy would inherit the coffee maker, most likely by stealing it out of the room before the widow could come to claim it. Then some other guy with his own mug and cartoons and photos of whatever would inherit the office through more regular channels, and after a month or so his name would get stenciled on the door when the gray paint over the words "Sergeant Andren" dried. And they say the system doesn't have its rewards.

Andren rose from behind his desk, a medium-sized man, forties just beginning to admit to the fifties around the bend, sandy-haired, raw complexion, sharp eyes. I crossed the room and took the long-fingered, outstretched hand before me. The handshake was strong, dry, and short—the type of greeting one gets from a basically direct, honest, confident type of person. For a cop, it was a nice change. In a city cop it would have been a miracle.

"You must be Jack Hagee."

When I confirmed his guess, he confirmed mine.

"Yeah. The captain said I was to help you when you got here with anything reasonable. So tell me. What do you have for me that's reasonable?"

I explained everything to him, telling it as I'd gotten it from Miller. I gave him the extra copy of the list, then asked him his opinion of the whole thing. After reading down the page he looked over at me and said,

"You certainly have gotten yourself mixed up with a bunch here, Mr. Hagee, let me tell you."

"Call me Jack. Why do you say that, Sergeant?"

"Dennis. Huumph. Guess I'll start with some of the things Carl either just plain doesn't know, or didn't feel like telling you for one reason or another. Yeah—this bunch knew Maureen, all right, but their relationships were a little bit different than the way Carl seems to have painted them.

"These guys didn't seduce her—nobody ever seduced her. Believe me"—he waved the list in his hand—"thinking like that gives these boys too much credit. And I don't suppose it's the duty of the police department to participate in character assassination, but I think I can be allowed an exception for this case." He paused for a second, fumbling for some tact. When he couldn't find any he plunged on regardless. "The only thing that keeps Maureen Phillips from being an arrestable whore is that she never gave out any set rates."

Andren's story was brief but concise, giving me a fairly good picture of the goings-on in Miller's little circle of friends. They'd all been casual drug users—small-time salesmen—some of them picked up by the cops for shoplifting in their time—all of them suspected of it.

"I mean," he said, "sometimes it's really hard to understand these kids. Byler, Cerelli, Sterling, George—all of them made college; all of them from at least reasonably good backgrounds. What a bunch.''

"What about Mara, though? What was their connection to her?''

"Now, that started with Byler. He met her at the same time he met her best friend, Jean Ward. See . . .''

Andren talked, telling me a story of small-town romance. Jean was the one Byler fell for, something Mara took as an insult. They were that standard set of girlhood friends, one good-looking, the other sort of plain. Jean had been the sort of plain one. It seemed that Jean and Mara were both somewhat younger than Byler and the rest of his crowd. When he showed his preference for plain Jean, unplain Mara got uncommonly jealous. She did her best to break up Jean and Byler. She slept with all his friends, made sure he heard about what he was missing, and in the end, she slept with him, too.

Andren seemed to think that was mostly Jean's fault. Byler'd been really hung up on her, but she wasn't interested in giving him any kind of a firm commitment. She was grateful for the attention, liked having the ego-boosting audience of an older man, let alone the use of his car and the cash in his working man's wallet. It wasn't often a girl just entering college found a college graduate nipping at her heels—not in the country, anyway.

But Jean was in no hurry to settle down with him. At least not at first. Not until he made the decision to leave town. Then, the rumor mill had it, she'd changed her tune and called him saying she'd decided they should get married after all. There was a quick marriage and then they left for New York, where there was an even quicker separation. The mill also had it that the separation had turned into a divorce. Andren smiled at me.

"I know; sounds a little Mayberryish, but that's the way it is around here. People tend to stick to their own levels in these parts. That's why I know so much about all this. Everybody knew about it. Neither girl's parents much liked what was going on. The Phillipses used to complain to us regularly, 'Keep that nasty Byler away from our little angel,' which is a lot like screaming about the vicious jar of honey attacking the innocent little grizzly.''

Apparently the Phillipses didn't really know all that much about their ''little angel.'' Andren seemed like a man who knew what the score was. I had a feeling his report on what'd happened was probably fairly close to the truth. After he wrapped up the first part of his lecture, I tried to squeeze the whole thing together.

''So, Byler, Sterling, and a truckload of others all slept with Mara, but the one she wanted wanted her best friend, and eventually married said best friend.''

''Uh-huh.'' Andren grinned.

''She was mad at Byler for going after Jean instead of her, which is what seems to be the thing that triggered her into going after everyone else in the first place. Right so far?''

Andren nodded.

''Well—then what in all of that got her together with Miller? I mean, you tell me this Byler is good-looking, athletic, clever, God's little gift—fine, okay—him I can understand. But how does a flabby moke like Miller suddenly get so lucky?''

''We aren't really sure,'' admitted Andren. ''Truth of the matter is Miller was Byler's 'plain' friend. Just like Jean never thought she'd get a chance at the kind of guys Mara could get, Miller never thought he'd get a shot at any good-looking girls. Well, for whatever reason, Mara stuck her claws into Miller when Jean and Byler moved to New York.''

''But why? What kind of assets does the guy have?''

The sergeant gave me a look to let me know I was getting a little nosier than was covered by professional courtesy. I told him,

''I don't want bank statements or anything. I just meant, the only thing I know for sure is that the guy has a checkbook. Does he have any other known assets like investments, real estate, et cetera? Anything a golddigger might consider worthwhile?''

Relaxing a little, Andren told me.

"He owns one of the hardware stores in town. He also collects antiques—traded them, sold them, the usual. Mostly just so he could pump up his gun collection, I think. Had a pretty big one—I hear. Never saw it. Anyway, he doesn't have it anymore."

"Sold it?"

"No—reported it stolen about a month ago. Lot of nice weapons up in smoke, too. Shame. No leads, yet. But," said Andren, his tone coming to a wrap-up, "that's about it, though, outside of the store."

I sighed to myself. "Any guesses, then?" I asked. "I mean, what could he do for her that she couldn't get somewhere else?"

"Who knows? Maybe she liked his temper."

I looked at Andren with more than a little puzzlement. The Dumptruck hadn't struck me as the temperamental type. I told Andren how Miller had acted at my office. He put his feet up on his desk and just shrugged, offering,

"I said he had a temper, I didn't say he was a lunatic. But, drink does tend to bring out the beast in him. Then again, Carl wasn't in his element. Maybe he played it cool with you. But, trust me, I'm not wrong on this—Carl's a big fish in a small pond here. You've probably seen the type—bar fights, gun collecting, scaring little guys with tough talk and the like. You didn't fold when he made his grab for you, so he did. He'd be petty enough to hold a grudge about it, though."

"He ever hit anybody for real?"

"Oh, yeah, sure. Other loudmouths, mostly. He was usually smart enough to wait until they were drunker than he was. Same old story; all week long he manages his store, then on the weekends it's time to tear things up in the little red-necker joints on the edges of town—him and his wimpy tag-a-long, fella named Ted Karras. Sad guys, really. Both of them.

"But—" Andren suddenly shifted back to the main topic, "as to what Maureen could have seen in Carl Miller . . . "

His eyes showed he was looking for an answer, but eventually the only thing forthcoming was an apologetic shrug.

Things were getting a bit sticky. At first I'd thought Mara was a runaway. Just another small-town girl ditching the one-chip-on-the-table back-home boyfriend for city lights he neither wanted nor understood. But suddenly, that didn't make any sense.

It was Mara who'd gone after Miller. For some reason, a blond knockout who'd proved she could turn on any man in town as easily as most women turn on their kitchen tap saddles herself with a fat, sad-looking buttonmaker like Miller. He wasn't rich, handsome, connected, or much of anything else in any way. He was probably honest, but from the sound of Mara, both what Andren had told me and what she'd told me herself in those black-and-white eyes I was still carrying in my pocket, I knew she wasn't the type to fall in love because she'd found an honest man—not if he was Carl Miller, anyway.

No, I was far from having all the pieces in place. There was something the Dumptruck could do for Mara, something she'd wanted I hadn't tumbled to yet. After she'd gotten it, or at least enough of it, she'd taken off for New York, leaving Miller behind to look into those small glossy eyes and wonder what had gone wrong—wondering what he had done wrong, and how he could erase it so he could have his Mara back.

I was feeling sorrier for him all the time.

Sensing that Andren didn't have much more for me, I asked him what I hoped would be a fruitful question. "Okay, Dennis. If you were me, where would you go next?"

"I'll tell you, Jack. I wouldn't bother with most of the places on Carl's list. Like he said, these guys have all moved to New York. I don't think their parents are going to be much help to you. But there are a few stops you could make, seeing that you already went to the trouble to drive all the way out here."

"You mean besides Mara's parents?"

"Yeah." He chuckled dryly. "Go there first. Maybe the

old man will still be sober. After that, I'd head over to Miller's pal's place, you know, Karras. See if he can tell you anything.'' It was worth a shot, I figured. There are things about you that your friends will never know—true—but on the other hand it's amazing how many things in your life they'll know about that you won't.

The sergeant stopped for a second then and shifted gears, moving from confidant back to cop. He shot me his sharp look again, sizing me up with his official Dodge City-troubleshooter's eye, then asked, ''You do know where the tracks are, and when not to cross them, don't you, Jack? I'm not going to regret this little talk, right?''

I assured him I had no interest in slapping around his citizens just to earn a fee from the Dumptruck. He relaxed back into the guy I'd first shaken hands with, pulled a pen, and then scribbled Karras' address onto the copy of my list along with the others.

''As far as I can see, the only one else who might be able to tell you anything you could use would be Cerelli's old girlfriend.'' The sergeant went on to describe the lady in question in very glowing detail. Even if she didn't talk at all, it sounded as if the trip would still be worth it.

I thanked Andren for all his help. We shook hands a last time. I filled my grip with easygoing I'm-just-doing-my-job-and-I'll-be-cool. He responded with a firm I-believe-you. That put me at ease. A lot of guys just aren't as intelligent as Andren.

The sergeant reached into his drawer and pulled out a map of Plainton the local Rotary had commissioned. He handed it to me, then poured me a Styrofoam cup of coffee to go. I thanked him for the map, and then even more for the coffee. I drained off the top sip, surprised at the taste. Good coffee always surprises me.

Starring the streets I had to find, Andren offered to lead me to the first stop on my list, but I thanked him once more, saying I could probably find it myself. I told him I'd call him if I got lost, pointing out the station number printed on the map. He smiled, looked quietly at me for a moment, giving me the chance to read his face. I could tell his only question was why would anyone get themselves involved with a crew like Miller and his pals.

It was an honest question. If I'd had an honest answer, I'd have given him a look at it. He wanted to show me out but I told him not to bother. Walking down the hall, I tipped my hat to the dozing form of Mrs. Bryant and headed for my car. I managed to get inside without either spilling the coffee Andren had given me, or getting any more mud on my shoes. Balancing the cup between the windshield and the dashboard, I backed out of the space I was in and headed for the outskirts of town.

One down, three to go.

# CHAPTER 6

I FOUND MY way to the Phillips' residence with only a minimum of wrong turns. It was a great place if you were into tree-lined, stone-walled driveways, bushes trimmed like chess pieces, stained glass, scrolled colonnades, and all the other real estate novelties of the nouveau riche. I left my car off to the corner of the hockey rink they probably considered the turnaround area of their driveway, right next to the big-lipped, white-skinned iron jockey who'd apparently undergone a race change somewhere along the line, and headed for the front door.

I tried to straighten out my tie again but the knot had claimed squatter's rights and wasn't budging. Giving up on it once more, I looked over my choice of a doorbell or a gargoyle's head that served as a knocker. Being a New Yorker I chose the buzzer, only slightly surprised at the resounding chimes.

The bells brought a woman to the door whose looks and manner made it seem likely she was Mara's mother. She asked politely what I wanted, almost making me believe she wouldn't be upset in the least if the answer brought me and the dried mud on my shoes inside across her carpeting. The rich are talented that way.

I told her who I was and why I was there. She responded to my introduction with something just approaching bored curiosity. Key words like ''Carl Miller'' and ''Mara'' set off sparks in her blue eyes, though, letting me know I had found the right house.

Finally asking me inside, she pointed me toward a chair, telling me to wait until she could find her husband. I took the designated chair-for-undesirable-visitors in the bus station she said was their living room and waited while she trooped off to track down hubby.

While she was gone I was joined by a girl of maybe eighteen who looked to be Mara's sister. Her eyes were green as well, her hair a variety of colors thanks to the sun and something out of a box. She was a wild-looking one who might have favored a different parent, but who was Mara's sister nonetheless.

It wasn't so much bone structure as attitude that gave it away. She eyed me the way a small child does a dog to whose tail she wants to tie a can. It was that sort of sideways glance of innocence, the type that automatically makes you look to see which hand they have behind their back. All she was waiting for were the final figures on how much risk was balanced against her fun.

Deciding I probably didn't bite at all, she came over, sitting down in the chair across from mine. She was dressed for poolside at the country club. Her unevenly tanned legs hung out of a suit made up of patches and thin cords—a suit stitched together as bait for whichever little boy was in favor that day—a costume that promised the chance to ply her with dinner and a gram or two of coke with the possible reward of a fast grope in a back seat in some neighborhood parking lot. She pulled a thin brown cigarette out of her leather beach bag, holding it to lips wearing their best here's-your-big-chance-to-get-lucky look.

I grinned, but not for the reason she thought. Deciding I was too shy to start our personal magic up all by myself, she asked,

"Got a light?"

"Yeah," I told her, wishing Mom and Dad would arrive. "I keep it on at night next to my bed."

"Afraid of the dark?"

"I just hate surprises."

Deciding to humor her, I pulled my lighter from my pocket and flipped it her way. She caught it out of the air neatly, clicking it open and striking the wheel against her hip with one motion. A thin red scrape blushed on her leg as she lit up. She inhaled deeply, closing her eyes. Her mouth opened after a moment, the smoke pouring out slowly, gliding upward over her heavily made-up face until suddenly she drew her lips together, pouting away the last breath of smoke into the air. One of those moves guaranteed to pop all the pimples in the back of homeroom.

She tossed my lighter back, smiling.

"Thanks."

I nodded, wishing again for Mom and Dad to hurry up so I could get the hell out of their little nightmare. Happy people's lives depressed me enough. Sis told me,

"You're here about Mara."

"Yeah," I admitted.

"She went to New York, didn't she?"

"Why would she go to New York?"

"Yes, Penny," came a voice from the hall. "Why would your sister go to New York? Why don't you tell us?"

A man with a drink in his left hand and a slur in his voice a little too thick for the first break of evening came into the living room, planting himself in an easy chair next to the front window. It was a tired move as if it and everything else, including breathing, wasn't worth the effort anymore. Penny answered him.

"She went to New York, Daddy, to get away from that stupid, sweaty fat man and his hardware store. She went there to find a type of life a bit more exciting than this early American turtle-shell of a town you crawled to to hide in, dragging us all with you, when you couldn't make it at the Exchange anymore; she left because she was tired of waiting for you to realize you'd better dry out and—"

"Penny!"

The interrupting screech came from Mrs. Phillips. She came into the room, followed by what appeared to be another of Mara's sisters. Dad was sitting quietly in his chair, sipping at his highball, serenely staring out the window, blissfully looking out across his estate, ignoring the fact that his daughter had just called him a coward and a drunk. Maybe he was just used to it. He explained it to me.

"Our Penny is a little high-strung today. If you're going

back to the club, why don't you leave now, my dear? Your mother and I would like to talk to this gentleman.''

''I'd like to do more with him than just talk,'' she smirked, darting her tongue at me. ''I'll bet Mummy would, too.''

''Penny, I think you had better be going.''

Penny shrugged, looking at her mother with the superiority of inexperience. She picked up her bag, crushing out her cigarette at the same time. ''So pleased to meet you, sir. We must do this again.''

As she left the room, the other sister fell in step behind her. She was a few years younger, not quite the age where playing goad-the-guest was as important as getting to the pool in time to stake out that evening's claim. She'd come around later, though. Penny would see to that. If she stuck around long enough, anyway.

As the pair filed out, Dad asked me, ''Now then, sir, as you may have deduced, I am Joseph Phillips. And you are . . . ?''

''My name is Hagee, Jack Hagee. I'm a detective out of New York.'' I tried to put the best face on Miller's story, knowing how ridiculous it sounded as it came out. ''A man who claims to be of your acquaintance, one Carl Miller, came to me saying that your daughter Maureen has been kidnapped by either one or several men who used to live in this town.

''Pardon me if I tell you anything you didn't know, or don't believe. He has given me a list of people who are believed to have been sexually active with your daughter. He thinks there may be some connection between them and her recent disappearance. He's hired me, and paid a retainer, to bring back your daughter, or at least to prove to him she is safe.''

''What does all of this have to do with us?'' asked Mrs. Phillips. Her motherly concern touched me, the way Medea's does. She was a tight, thinly drawn woman with a sharp bird's face. She stared at me coldly, waiting for an answer.

''I was hoping you would be able to shed some light on

this thing for me. Do you think your daughter was kidnapped?''

''Of course not. Neither do you.''

''Whatever you say, ma'am. Did you tell Carl Miller he could handle this for you?''

''I told him to do whatever he wanted to do. He was here, threatening to kill people, storming and raging, all over again, and I did not want, or need, to put up with it. Not then. Not with her finally gone. I told him to go and find her if he wanted her.''

''What did you mean when you said Miller was 'raging all over again'?'' I asked. Dad tried to answer.

''She didn't mean—'' But Mom cut him off, figuring she could talk for herself.

''You stay out of this,'' she told him. Then me, ''Carl and Mara used to argue—they fought all the time. On the phone, in stores, in restaurants, but mostly right here in this room.'' I could understand that. It was a big room; Mara'd probably loved the acoustics as much as her mother apparently did. Her voice rose again.

''Whenever she went out with someone else, and there were plenty of those occasions, he would be here sputtering at me about my faithless daughter. With her not coming back, I'd had all I was going to take from him. I told him to get out and leave us alone.

I continued to ask questions, drawing the pair of them back to the beginning. It seemed Mara was as wild as Miller and Andren had outlined. Her parents were either very modern thinkers, or just so used to everyone knowing of their daughter's exploits that trying to hide them just seemed too futile anymore. They confirmed pretty much for me what I'd already been told.

The Phillipses had tolerated the Dumptruck because they'd hoped he might be some sort of stabilizing influence on their little girl. All that had happened was that Mara had racked up a lot of presents and Miller'd reaped a bumper crop of grief, until one day the Phillipses suddenly realized their little girl's bed hadn't been slept in for too many nights in a row, and someone got the bright idea maybe this time she wasn't coming home at all. Mrs. Phillips' only hope seemed to be that Mara would continue to not come home. Mr. Phillips seemed a bit more concerned.

"Mr. Hagee, I want you to find my daughter. You don't have to bring her home kicking and screaming, nothing so dramatic. There really would be little point to that. But please do what Carl asked. Find her for us, and let us know that she's all right."

He talked as he walked to the far end of the room. There he planted himself again, this time to write a check. "Here," he said, handing it to me. "Add this to what Carl gave you. Let me know where Mara is, and you can consider it earned."

I nodded to him as he sank back into his easy chair. The air seemed to leak out of him as he did so. The effort of actually making a decision had left him a little shaken. I thanked him for the check, telling him I would do what I could. He thanked me as well, then asked his wife to show me to the door. I could hear him beginning to mix himself another highball as we left the room.

I was glad to be leaving. There was a panicky air in the Phillips house. They maintained their attitudes of disinterest fairly well, but underneath strain gripped them the way blood feuds strangle Puerto Ricans or the way a transit strike weighs on a city.

I didn't like them. They were full-fledged products of the eighties, leftover money-binge junkies, from the queen castrater at my elbow, and her apprentice razor-brigade, to the soft-fleshed sot in the corner chair. Maybe if he had been more of a man things might have turned out differently. Maybe if he had been more of a man he wouldn't have had all daughters in the first place. Then again, there was no evidence sons raised in the Phillips household would have turned out any better.

When we reached the front door, Mrs. Phillips gave a short look over her shoulder and then held out her hand. "Give it to me," she ordered.

"What? I didn't have time to find the family silver. Honest."

"You know what I mean." I did. "Hand it over."

"Any particular reason?"

"Yes. If you give it back to me now, it will save me the trouble of calling the bank to stop payment on it. Take a look at it; both our names are on the account. I can stop it. I *will* stop it. Please, don't make me go to the trouble."

I didn't care if her name was on it or not. I pulled the check from my wallet, holding it in front of me.

"You don't understand, do you?" she said, waving her arms around her in an all-encompassing gesture. "This is all a fake. This house isn't paid for. Nothing is paid for. And if he doesn't 'dry out,' as little Penny so quaintly put it, and get back to some kind of work, they're going to come and start taking things out of this barn one by one. So—just give it over, because all it can do is bring us back another mouth to feed, and with Mara's tastes, that's too expensive a mouth to have around."

I crumpled the check and dropped it into her outstretched hand. I thanked her for her help, the way you thank a wino who cleans your windshield with a gritty, dry rag, and headed for my car.

I knew it was a mistake, but it didn't matter. If I'd kept the check, it would have just made her more vindictive. Whether I returned it or not, it gave her what she wanted, more ammunition to use against Dad. Sooner or later they'd have an argument, and just when he reminded her of how he'd stood up to her and written the check to find his little girl, she'd let him know what she'd done, sending him off to mix another drink while she cried inside over his spinelessness, never for a moment realizing what had turned him into an invertebrate in the first place.

I went to my car and climbed in, feeling Mrs. Phillips' eyes the entire way. I tried not to think about her, or her husband, or any of their daughters except Mara. That one alone was trouble enough.

# CHAPTER 7

GETTING BACK OUT onto the main road, I started driving toward the center of town, wondering about the case as a way to pass time between red lights. I couldn't come up with much, but that was because there wasn't all that much of a case to wonder about yet. All I had was a lovestruck Dumptruck and a hot little number out for a good time. Mara's family hadn't been much help except in confirming what I'd figured out for myself.

Looking over Andren's map I could see I was closer to Karras' place than to Cerelli's girlfriend, so I headed there first. After fifteen more minutes of trees and frame houses, I arrived at the address. It was a four-family dwelling, of which Karras had the lower right half. I walked up to his door and rang the bell. After a short pause, a surly whine slightly resembling a male voice asked what I wanted through the door.

I called back through the woodwork, "Is there a Mr. Karras here? I'd like to talk with him." The "mister" must have been a surprise. His curiosity made him forget his defensiveness long enough to ask what I wanted.

"I'm here for a friend of his. Is he home?"

Something got through. Maybe he was only wondering who might be going around calling themselves his friend. I was told to wait a minute. His footsteps faded noisily away, as if he were kicking away newspapers, then returned. He called to me to open the door. I did.

There were no lights on inside. The curtains were also drawn, but I could see Karras' form back in the shadows. He was too thin; his long neck and awkward head tilted off his

45

spare frame like that of a sickly bird. He was tall, but weightless; the kind of guy who stumbles after sneezing. His voice came out greasily,

"I just got up. I work nights. Sorry to take so long. What's this all about?"

"My name is Hagee. I'm from New York. Your friend Carl Miller has hired me to help him find—"

"Yeah, I know," he interrupted. "That skanky slut Mara. Christ, he's never gonna learn." Suddenly he noticed I was still outside. "Oh, hey, man; sorry. Come on in, will ya?" Karras stepped back as I entered. I shut the door. He ushered me into his darkened living room.

"Sorry about the lights. I just got up right now. I can't take no lights when I just get up. Okay?"

I nodded that it was "okay" by me. I didn't know if he was trying to protect his eyes or keep mine from noticing what kind of butts were in the ashtray. Or maybe it was the puffy bruises on his face he didn't want noticed. I wasn't sure. Ignoring all of it for the moment, I waited until he got his bathrobe pulled together and then asked him,

"Have you known Carl Miller long?"

"Sure, I mean we've known each other since we were little kids, like—you know? All through school and everything. You know?"

"Yeah. This marriage to Mara. Do you think it was going to happen?"

"Aw, hell . . . who knows? I mean, she was usin' him for everything; I mean—everything. Whatever little Mara wanted, wherever she wanted to go, whatever she said, that's what would happen. 'Do this for me, Carlie; I want this or that or the other thing, Carlie.' Christ, I'll bet if she whispered, 'Cut your fuckin' throat for me, Carlie,' the dumb boob would have done that, too. You know?" I wasn't going to argue. From what I'd seen he was probably right. Karras went on. "Naw, probably not. The wedding, I mean. Hell, why should she, really. Once she had his ass cleaned out, what did she need him hanging around for?"

"Has she cleaned him out?"

"Oh. Ah, huummph. Jeez-it. I don't know. I guess.

Maybe. Sorta. She was probably close, I guess. How would I know, though?''

How would you? I thought. Aloud, I asked, ''Is that why she ran away?''

''Oh. You mean he hasn't laid his kidnapping rap on you yet?''

''Let's just say I'm open to suggestions.''

''You mean you don't believe poor Carl's little angel was stolen in the middle of the night by those 'monsters from New York'?''

''What do you think?''

''What do I think?'' He looked at me, his head bobbing back and forth at the question as if it wasn't one he'd ever heard before. ''What do I think?'' he repeated again. ''I think little Mara got sick of Fatso and decided to get something worthwhile in her pocketbook and between her legs. You know? That's what I think.''

Karras was a classy guy. There was no denying it. You could see it in the frayed tears in his robe, or just by looking around the room, what you could see of it through the gloom buried beneath the litter. The orange crate he stored his porn mags in, the paper plates still covered with smears of food and some things moving under their own power strewn underneath the lawn chair he was sitting in, or even the open two-liter bottle of Canadian Club sitting on the television—right next to the smaller ones of Night Train Express, Tiger Rose, and apricot brandy—all clear signs of his obvious higher station in life.

That wasn't important, though. How he lived his life didn't matter to me. All I wanted to do was get everything into perspective. Hoping he might be able to help me do that, I asked,

''So where did she go? Where do you think Mara is, and why?''

''Aw, Carl's right; she's in New York. She went there to get away from him. Now, now—I ain't got no facts or nuthin', you know? But my guess is that she got tired of Carl, so she gathered up what she had and went lookin' for a better offer.''

"Do you think she went after one of the guys that moved there from here?"

"Ahhhh, no." He hesitated. "She'd be after big money. She's a fuckin' whore, man. Her pussy bleeds for dollars. She don't care what she does, who she does it with . . . all she cares is what she's gettin' out of it. You know?"

I knew two things. One was that I really didn't want to hear the words "you" and "know" used together again for the rest of my life. The other thing I knew just as surely was that he was, at the least, holding something back from me, if not just plain lying.

"Are you sure?" I asked it flatly, without any accusation in my voice. "It couldn't be anything else, could it?"

"No." Sweat was creeping out from under his thinning hair. Even in the darkness I could see his eyes narrowing at me. "Not Mara. Money's all she's after. She wouldn't be bothering with no small-town losers like those guys. Honest."

Now I was sure he was lying. I stretched out my hand, touching the bruise on his face. I commented on it as he flinched away.

"Real nice patch of tar you're growing there. Anyone help you with the planting?"

"Naw. No. Nobody. It was an accident. No. I did it myself."

"You do the ones on your legs, too?"

"Yeah, yeah. Those, too."

I pretended to study the shades of yellow and purple running down his face. "About a week ago. Right?"

"Hey. This stuff is my business. You, you ain't got no fuckin' right buttin' into my stuff. You're no cop or nuthin' legal or nuthin'." He sucked in a breath. "Fuck you, man. You'd better take it out of here. You know?"

He was scared. Of what, or who, I had no idea. But something, or someone, wanted Plainton's leading derelict panicked, and had invested enough time and effort to get what they wanted. I'd hit some sort of nerve; the trick now was to find out which one.

"What's the matter, Karras? Don't you want to help your buddy Carl anymore?''

"Hey, I can't fuckin' help him. You can't help him. He can't even help his dumb-assed self. Mara is fuckin' gone, man. She ain't comin' back. You know? She ain't.'' He took a gasping smoker's breath to steady himself, then added, ''You better get goin'. I got to get ready for work.''

"Sure, Karras. I'll take off. But try to remember something.'' I shoved one of my business cards into his robe pocket as I told him, ''Just because I'll be out of sight doesn't mean I'll be out of your face. There's something going on here. We both know that. And guess what? I'm going to find out what it is.'' He began to sputter at me but I held a hand up in his face. ''Save it, weasel. You've blown enough air. You're a little cornered rat, and I don't even want to hear you say 'you know' again, let alone get rabies. Remember one thing, though. I'm on this case. I'm going to sniff out what's gone down and I'm going to hang every one of Carl Miller's problems out to dry. And if I find you're one of them—''

"Get out—get out—get out of here!!''

Smiling, I turned and walked off, leaving Karras half-hiding behind his door—trembling and screaming—the best way I could leave him. I could have pressed him for more, but I knew it wasn't worth the effort. He was the kind that clams up on answers, screaming about his rights. No matter how scared I could have made him of me, he was already more scared of someone else.

By leaving him to his own devices, I was hoping to turn his own cowardice against him, get his fear juices rumbling loud enough to tip me off to something. Cops call it ''letting the pot simmer.'' Considering Andren's warning against my rousting any of Plainton's citizens, I called it my only choice. In the meantime I figured I might as well get my last stop in Plainton over with. A guy like Karras could take a long time to simmer before he finally got scared enough to come to a boil.

Getting my car into gear, I headed for the home of a Ms. Carol Ballard as the sun started to set in the distance. One of the guys on Miller's list, Ernest Cerelli, had broken up with her before he'd left for New York. She'd stayed behind in Plainton. Andren had built her up as quite a number, as well as one of the people with whom Mara had slipped between the sheets.

Checking the map, I found the street on which she lived. Pulling off the main road, I turned left, hoping to find her place before the sun could set completely and leave me in the dark. I didn't know if she would be home but, since the majority of people in small towns don't go far from home on worknights, especially at the beginning of the work week, I figured it was worth a shot. After all, a lot of good information can be picked up from spurned lovers. Especially if they were spurned in just the right way.

I pulled up in front of her house just as the sun had finished dipping behind the trees in her backyard. It was a nice, cozy-looking place; there wasn't a picket fence around it, but I could hear an all-American dog barking somewhere. The smell of summer flowers and freshly cut grass mingled with that of dinner time meals, coming to me more readily than auto fumes or garbage lying in piles on the pavement, or the sweat of millions milling in the steaming streets, reminded me once again of what it was like not to be in New York.

I tried the knot in my tie once more—and once more gave up. Going toward the house, I walked across the still-wet grass, listening to my shoes squish against the sopping soil underneath. Heading up the walkway, I picked her evening paper out of the puddle it'd been tossed into and carried it up to the door with me. I knocked, hoping for an answer. After a few seconds I heard footsteps; then the door opened.

A red-headed figure stepped into sight. I stared into her eyes—standard move. Fix them with that open, kind, "trust me" smile they taught us in Military Intelligence. Win them over fast. They told us that it doesn't always work, of course. They were right. It didn't work on Ms. Carol Ballard. Big time.

There was an energy that crackled outward from her that gave me a jolt like being hit by twin bolts of lightning. It drew me closer to the space she reserved for herself, right to its edge. She was long and tall and very good-looking. It was hard to find a safe place to let my eyes rest because everything else demanded equal attention. So finally I just let my eyes wander back up to hers, which was the worst place of all.

"Yes?"

One word was all she gave me to work with. She said it politely, inquisitively—and yet, somehow it still seemed like a dare. She sipped from a drink in her hand, and then moved her arm up the door frame, waiting for an answer. I smiled, handing her the damp evening edition I was still holding. She took it.

"Aren't you a little bit old to be delivering newspapers?"

"My name is Jack Hagee. If you're Carol Ballard, I'd like to ask you a few questions."

"Are you with the police?" I shook my head. "Private?"

That time I nodded. She waited. I fumbled in my jacket pocket and then produced my ID a little less smoothly than on most occasions. I don't know what it is but I always feel funny around redheads, especially natural ones, and Ms. Ballard's was as natural as it comes. It jumped in long, fierce waves whenever she turned her head, crashing against her bare shoulders like the tide against white sand. It teased the blood with sparking shocks—flaming crackles, the kind of look men kill their best friends over. She handed me back my ID.

"You want to come in?"

I looked her up and down—knew it was a mistake. I nodded anyway.

"Then come on in."

She turned on her hip and strolled back into the room. She didn't walk; she strolled. There is a difference. I closed the door behind me and joined her in the living room. She pointed to a chair. I put myself into it. She coiled in one directly across from it. Then it was her turn to look me up and down.

Her eyes curled over me and, as often as I've ignored that kind of thing in the past, as sure as I knew it was all nothing more than a minute of teasing self-assurance for her, I still found myself sitting just a little bit straighter, sucking my gut just a little bit flatter. It was no surprise to me that I was as idiotic as the next guy. I just hoped it wasn't too disappointing to her.

She tossed her head, her hair flashing in the reflected sunlight coming through the window behind her like the flame of a smooth, milky candle flickering in the breeze. I was afraid if I tried to talk no words would come out of my mouth. I was hot and dry; my mouth was itchy and my palms were sweating. I didn't try to kid myself that it was due to the weather.

Deciding to try and lessen the heat in the room by attempting to do my job, I croaked out a few questions, asking her about Miller, Mara, Karras, and all the rest. Ballard was mostly in agreement with everyone else. Yes—Mara had slept with everyone, rumors said possibly even Karras, just to teach the Dumptruck some lesson or another. Yes again—like so many others, Ballard was also certain Miller was being taken for a ride.

Yes—she was sure Mara had no intention of going through with a wedding. She smiled at some private joke at that point. I almost asked what was funny, but then I figured I got it, and didn't bother.

Continuing to ask her the same questions I'd already gone over three times that day, I racked up her variations to the same answers. She was also sure Mara was in New York. To Ballard, it was obvious that no matter how much money Miller could wring out of his hardware store, Mara needed more out of life than good times and expensive gifts. Even if he did keep his hands off her. She smiled again. This time I asked.

"Oh, don't get me wrong . . . Mara likes sex," she answered. "She just likes power more. She does get a big kick out of making people do things just by spreading her legs, but she gets an even bigger kick out of getting them to do the same things without having to do anything at all. And Carl, now Carl will do anything for her. I'd be surprised if she's . . . oh, hell, if he's kissed her three times in the same night, he's twice the mover I thought he was."

I had to agree with her on most of it. Miller still had that glow about "his Mara" that high-school guys have about their first serious crush, before they finally slept on the same side of the sheets. I hadn't thought the Dumptruck'd been doing much sleeping with "his Mara."

Which brought me back around again. Why had she run? Everything had been going her way. Miller'd paid for her schooling and anything else she'd wanted, from the sound of things. Ballard felt that Mara wanted someone on the side—her parents had confirmed she went out with other people. I wasn't as sure. Mara was sizing up as the type who didn't enjoy sex—but still, to torture the Dumptruck . . . well, any woman can grit her teeth and make happy sounds for forty seconds with somebody else to drive a few spikes into some boob that loves her.

Everyone is supposed to be entitled to their opinion, however, so I figured I'd grant Ballard hers. After all, she'd known Mara a lost closer up than I had. I asked, "Do you think she went to New York after one of the guys who moved there from here?"

"Probably."

"Which one?"

"Whichever one of them has the most money."

"Any idea who that might be?"

"Not in the least."

"Feel like guessing?"

"No. Feel like dancing?"

"Depends on the dance."

"I know what you want."

Turning her back on me for a moment, she pulled a tape out of a cassette player on a stand next to her chair, replacing it with one from a pile heaped on the same stand. Hitting Play brought us into the middle of "My Funny Valentine," the Miles Davis version. Perfect music for pressing bodies together. She smiled and held out one hand. I took it without hesitation. I was probably smiling, too.

I felt a bit odd, but not enough to complain. One of the

few good things about the P.I. business is that as jading as it can get, you really just never know what's going to happen next. I had no illusions about our little dance. We were both bored people, trapped like most folks in boring lives. But it was a safe bit of fantasy that bordered on the romantic if one didn't examine it too closely. Neither of us did.

We finished the number in silence, drinking in the sad, steaming horn, behaving ourselves for the moment. We both knew the prelude wasn't over. Figuring it was my job to keep things moving, however, I decided to ask her a few questions as we started swaying to the next number.

"Do you know Miller's pal, Ted Karras?" She nodded, making a face as if the wind had just gushed past her from a squatting dog. "Do you know why anyone would want to work him over?"

"There are only a few dozen people I could name who would like to work that little eel over. If you're looking for a list, I can help you. If you want a particular name with some kind of good reason attached to it, I'm afraid I can't. Why? Did somebody beat the little creep up?" I nodded. She smiled. "Awwwwww, that's too bad."

I could tell she was real broken up over it. With nothing else up up my sleeve, I asked her, "Do you think of Carl Miller as a dangerous kind of guy?"

She hesitated for a long time before answering. "I don't really know what to say. Sometimes you think he could slap around his own mother, then . . . he'll turn around and you'll figure him for the type to be rescuing kittens out of trees.

"He's always putting on an act. The problem is you never know what's the act and what isn't."

I had to agree with her. I also had to wonder if Miller himself knew where the act started and where it stopped. The more people I talked to about the guy, the larger the circles I was going around in seemed to grow. Sensing that the inquisition had passed, Ballard asked,

"Do you want a drink?"

I thought about it for a little under a millisecond and then told her how much I'd love one. She told me she only had bourbon. I told her I didn't care. We disengaged, our fingers lingering just long enough to show the proper interest. She left the room, making enough noise with the ice trays to assure me she wasn't slipping out the back door. I felt the proper gratitude and took my same seat. When she returned, she handed me a glass of watery bourbon and disappearing ice cubes, then sat down on the arm of my chair so we could make a toast and clink tumblers.

I looked up at her, fairly sure of what came next. Thinking about it, I couldn't find any reasons to hurry back to New York. I knew it wasn't the kind of offer that entailed staying over and enjoying breakfast in the morning. I was just an adequate guy in the right place at the right time, whose presence both offered a taste of novelty and saved her the trouble of a phone call on a slow TV night. I didn't have to worry about getting any strings attached. I also couldn't expect to be able to drift into town and have it happen again, either.

I tossed back my drink, setting the glass on the table next to me. I figured, what the hell, it would be worth it if the only thing she did was manage to untangle the knot in my tie.

# CHAPTER 8

I THOUGHT ABOUT Miller and his friends throughout the drive back from Pennsylvania. Things looked as if they might begin to add up after I gathered a few more facts. I needed to know whatever Hubert had been able to find out before I'd be able to make any guesses. I also probably needed to meet Byler, Cerelli, and George. What I really needed, though, besides some sleep, was something to eat. I'd been on the move since I'd met the Dumptruck the previous day. Driving straight to Plainton and then running around gathering details on Maureen Phillips hadn't given me much time for anything else.

True, Andren'd given me a cup of coffee, but unfortunately after the first few sips I forgot about it, leaving it to grow cold, wedged in its position between the windshield and the dashboard. Ballard had even made me a sandwich to go with a second cup a little while after the National Anthem, but somehow it couldn't quite kill the appetite she'd helped me build during the rest of the evening. I'd have been disappointed if it had.

Either way, however, it was all still a lot of hours behind me. By the time I returned to Manhattan, the gnawing gurgles in my stomach convinced me to pull up at the first early-bird eatery I could find. It took a while; there isn't usually a whole lot open at 4:30 in the morning—even in New York City. Not anymore.

There'd been a time when Manhattan really had been "the city that never sleeps." But that was years ago. Before the wolfpacks and the mutants—the homeless, the muggers, the boosters, flashers, and stick-up artists—before all the grabbers and the destroyers decided to turn the entire town into their own private toilet. Of course, considering the Democrats' socialist plan to have everyone living in the streets by taking away their property, I don't blame the skells so much for leaving their prisons as much as I do the politicians who told them to go forth, be fruitful, and multiply.

I found salvation on 14th Street when I finally saw a diner with its gate already up. A large sign in the front window proclaimed their special breakfast combinations. I liked Number Four: Two eggs, any style; fried potatoes; toast, butter and/or jelly; coffee, tea, or milk; and juice—$2.25. The price was too good to be real. The fact that there were no other lights down 14th showing anything else promising was also a helpful, decision-influencing factor.

Deciding it would be safe enough to leave my car at the curb for the amount of time I would be eating, I cut the engine, locked up, and headed inside. I took a front-counter seat where I could keep an eye on the Skylark. She isn't much of a car, but she's all I have.

I looked the place over quickly. A guy a few seats to my left stared at me through his fingers while I stared at everyone else. He wasn't trouble—just one of the wormy little gray people New York is packed full of these days. His eyes slid into hiding behind his palms as he drew in on himself, physically showing me he wasn't going to be a problem. The only other customers were a quiet selection of early-morning New Yorkers, none of whom seemed ready to present any problems, either. I was glad for that; I had a lot to think about, and I didn't need any more troubles than I already had.

While I began pulling my facts together in the front of my mind, a tired, unshaven counterman came over to me, asking what I wanted in as few words as possible. I think if I had only wanted a newspaper I would have made a much bigger hit with him. Unfortunately for him I was more in the mood for a meal than a fan club. I ordered the Number Four. The counterman scratched at the darker stains on his T-shirt while he asked,

"How you want dee eggs?"

"Scrambled."

"Coffee?"

"Yeah. Dark."

My man of few words turned away for a moment and then turned back, handing me a medium-sized mug. I looked down through the rising steam as he returned to his griddle, watching the little grease blotches slide across the surface of the coffee. I couldn't tell if they were a result of the way the dishes were washed in that place or the way the brew had been made, but at the moment I didn't much care. I was tired and my stomach was calling for warmth. If it was going to let me think things through at all, I was going to have to give it something. Besides, all New York diner coffee is the same; people just don't usually look at it.

I made a slight face as I took the first sip. It wasn't the way they washed the dishes after all. Having swallowed the initial taste, though, I decided to put the mug down until the rest of the meal came. While I waited, I decided to put all my questions and answers in order. It was a fairly straightforward case, right? How hard could it be?

Fact number one: There was no doubt in my mind that Mara had left of her own accord. She hadn't been kidnapped; she wasn't a suicide, a rape victim, or any other exotic kind of missing person. She'd just split for better things. Period.

Fact number two: Mara had wanted everyone's pal, Byler. He'd wanted her friend Jean. Jean hadn't cared much one way or the other. Mara slept with all his buddies and then finally with him.

Fact number three: This all blows over and Byler still wants Jean. She still isn't crazy about him, but knows an opportunity when she sees one. Deciding she can be in love as easily as the next girl, she marries him, and they move to New York. The marriage lasts about a year and then, poof, suddenly it's over. No clues yet as to why they broke up. Or as to where Jean was now. Ballard'd heard of a nervous breakdown, and a modeling career—late bloomer, I guess— but that didn't give me the why of their break-up, or her breakdown, if that was fact in the first place.

I suddenly realized my fatigue was confusing facts with questions. Why did Mara go after the Dumptruck after losing Byler? Did she ever plan to play straight with him? What had she wanted from him? No . . .

I stopped my mind's rambling, setting it back on course.

Fact number four: There was never going to be any wedding. Mara played Miller for a sap, took him for whatever it was she wanted—cash, antiques, pistols, all of the Glidden Spred Latex he had on his shelves—whatever. Andren guessed that maybe she wanted to put his temper to work, but Miller didn't seem crazy enough for that. I was betting that underneath it all he wasn't a rough guy, just the confused, lonely one I met in my office, wondering where his Mara was.

Fact number five: Ted Karras was a lying little weasel who knew something I didn't. I was still wondering how he fit into the picture. Who beat him up? Had he slept with Mara and been told not to do it again—the hard way? By whom? Miller? Didn't add up with the way Karras talked about his old drinking buddy. But he did have something to do with the case. So who did do it? And why did they do it?

Maybe it was only because I was tired, but my fairly straightforward case was looking more confused all the time. After boiling everything down, the only thing I was sure of was that Miller deserved to know what his Mara was doing to him. I figured I owed him that much, anyway.

I stopped thinking about it all for the moment, though. I could see my early-morning pal coming back with my food. He dropped the smaller plate with my toast near the coffee, and then laid the larger platter with the rest of my breakfast in front of me.

It wasn't what I ordered, I thought. It couldn't be. I remembered what scrambled eggs were supposed to look like. I've seen them before. Scrambled eggs are fluffy, with little flecks of white breaking up the color pattern. The mess before me was a solid, pale orange, the potatoes and the eggs, both nothing more than an unbroken smear of lard-singed warmth.

I looked at it again, sighing. I tried spreading ketchup

over it. The red trail did nothing for the appearance, and even less for the taste. I shoved the platter aside after a few bites, unable to bear the thought of shoveling any more of its contents into my mostly empty stomach. True, you'll fight rats for the privilege of running your tongue over the kitchen floor for the crumbs when you're hungry enough, but I wasn't that hungry yet. I ate the toast, figuring nobody can ruin toast. Folding the slices, I dunked them one at a time in my mug, watching disks of grease slide out of the tasteless bread across the surface of the coffee, bonding with that which was already there.

It was apparently not going to be my day. A depressing thought when it crosses your mind at 5 A.M. The counterman asked me what kind of juice I wanted. I said "orange" to make it easy on both of us. He brought me a small glass a minute later, sloshing the top layer across the dull Formica when he set it down. I tossed it off in a gulp, hoping it would cut some of the various aftertastes in my mouth.

Fishing in my pocket, I found the exact change. I dropped it on the counter next to my mostly untouched platter. This was one time it didn't bother me to stiff the help. If the chef wanted a tip he could eat the eggs.

Stuffing my remaining change back into my pocket, I scooped up my hat and headed for the door. Before I could make it halfway, a sudden clatter of silverware came to life behind me. Wormy had jumped over the two seats to gulp down what I had left. It was no great loss. The chef hadn't deserved a tip, anyway.

I went through the door, pulling my hat down over my ears as I hit the wind howling up the sidewalk. The rain was back. I stood under the diner's awning until I got my keys out and ready. Waiting for a break in the downpour's heft, I chose my moment and then sprinted around the front. I got my door open and myself inside seconds before a bread truck splashed the entire length of the Skylark with a blasting arc of wheel spray. Grateful for being only mini-mally wet, I started the engine and pulled back into the meager morning traffic. Water leaked in slowly around the windshield as I drove. I had reglued it only a few weeks earlier, but it was already starting to eat through.

I gave up then, heading back to my office, tired of fighting everything around me. I was cold and weary and ready to risk getting a parking ticket in Trenkel's precinct, plus the hassle of getting it taken care of. It would be worth it just to not get any wetter than I already was.

I pulled up against the curb as close to my building's entrance as I could, infringing on a fire hydrant and a bus stop. Sliding out the passenger side, I made sure the door was locked and then ran for the shelter of the front alcove, splashing through several puddles before finally ducking inside. Two human forms lay sprawled under the building's directory, clutching wet plastic bags blindly in their sleep, one definitely male, the other undeterminable. Roaches ran down their hair, in and out of their sleeves. Normally I might have pitched them out—the building had enough bugs on its own—but it was too wet, and I was too tired.

Stepping past the Gold Dust Twins, I unlocked the front door, closed it behind me, and then trudged upstairs with all the enthusiasm of a twenty-year-old hooker the night they realize they're never even going to be rich, let alone happy. Stopping in front of my door, I watched the last of the shine ooze out of my boots as I fumbled for my office key. Once the door was open, I stepped from the dark puddle that had dripped out of me and went inside.

Clicking on the overhead light, I peeled off my soaking coat and hat, hanging them on the rack near the door. Looking down, I found my electric bill stuck to the bottom of my boot. Pulling it loose, I gathered up the several other windowed envelopes I'd trampled over and deposited them on my desk. After that, I collapsed on my waiting room couch, too tired to bother with my boots or the light. I figured things like that were better handled when a person was awake.

•  •  •

There was a constant ringing somewhere in the background. I thought for a long time, wishing hard for it to go away and bother somebody else. It had a familiar edge to it, like a voice in a dark room that you recognize but can't place. Finally I opened my eyes, wondering if the shrill clanging was only some sort of dream. It wasn't; it was the phone. Or at least it had been. The ringing stopped before I could sit up, leaving me to wonder who could be calling me at eight o'clock in the morning. Anyone who knew me at all knew I never came into the office that early. Of course, anyone who knew me at all also knew that a lot of nights I never make it home, period.

Realizing it could've been any number of people, the only sensible thing I could do was wait to see if whoever it was called back. I cursed the fact I hadn't turned on the answering machine. I thought about getting up and clicking it on, but decided not to bother. The overhead light was still burning from the night before. I should have taken care of them both but, I slumped back down into the couch instead. I decided if I couldn't see the answering machine or the light, I wouldn't have to worry about them. To make sure I couldn't, I turned my face toward the couch and shut my eyes, giving only the phone another chance to bother me later. I didn't have to wait long.

It rang again at ten, reminding me that most of the city, even that segment that didn't bother working for a living, was all up and about its daily business. With an effort that put me in the same category as Sisyphus, I pushed myself up from the cushions and clomped into the inner office to stop the ringing.

I was almost grateful to pick up the receiver. If I'd been hung over, the sound would have been painful. Only being tired made it a little less painful, but a lot more annoying. Finding Hubert on the other end of the wire didn't do much to lessen the annoyance.

"Hey, hey, Hagee. Where you b-been, Dick Tracy?"

"Did you call me earlier?"

"Why would I call you 'earlier'? Your name is Jack."

"Hubert!"

"No. N-No. I've been waiting for you to call me. You remember. You, m-me. Lunch. R-right?"

"Right."

"You sound a little out of it. I d-didn't wake you up or anything, did I?"

"No, Hu. I was just working out—thought I'd get ready for the next city marathon."

"City marathon. Ho-hoho, that's a rich one. Listen—are we still going to m-meet in Chinatown?"

"You got anything for me?"

"Everything you wanted." Hubert had found out all one man could about four others in less than a day. For some he even had pictures. I told him to meet me at Mott Street at one o'clock. He laughed his best I'm-pleased-with-myself duck laugh, told me not to take any wooden nickels, and then finally hung up.

As I cradled the receiver I tried to plan my next moves. I figured the best thing to do would be to head over to Tony's. Tony's is a small-time gym in the neighborhood where I have a standing arrangement; I don't tell Tony's wife Lisa about the girlfriends he had for a while and he doesn't charge me to use the gym.

The arrangement went back a couple of months, stemming from his wife hiring me to find out whether or not she was playing the fool. It hadn't taken long to get the proof for the answer I knew from the first moment she sat down in front of my desk. But I also knew she didn't really want proof Tony was a cheat—she wanted proof he wasn't. That isn't why a lot of people hire detectives to tail their spouses, but it does happen.

Taking matters into my own hands, I sized Tony up. He wasn't going to break her heart, take the money and run, et cetera. He was in their relationship for the long haul . . . he just wanted more attention than one woman provided. Some people are like that.

The end result was that I confronted Tony with what was coming, scaring him into being not a good boy, but at least a better one. Getting a taste of what Lisa was capable of woke him up a bit. The end result was they both got what they really wanted and I got free gymnasium privileges along with my fee. To some people this makes me a real good guy and to others it makes me a crumb. You can imagine the chills I get at night worrying about what other people think.

The short walk over to Tony's helped me wake up. The sun was making its strongest comeback yet, beating back and drying the monsoons once again. It irradiated the city, burning off the puddles, steaming the buildings and trees until the humidity was so thick it looked as if the air were hung with surgical gauze.

Tony was the only person at the gym when I got there. The heat had chased all the early birds out and it was still too early for the lunch set. I tried working through my usual weight repetitions, but I couldn't make it. I was too tired and hot and sticky. The heat boiled up out of me, soaking my hair and clothes and sneakers. Water rolled off me, making the machines I was working on too slick to use.

Giving up, I escaped the heat by heading for the back-room showers. There I took care of whatever dirt the morning rain and my sweat hadn't gotten to. I decided to shave as well, trying to keep the sweat out of my eyes so I wouldn't accidentally slit my throat and kill myself in the process. Knowing it wouldn't be that much of an accident if it ever happened, I try to keep an eye on myself.

The humidity sucked at me, reaching through the back windows, helping the empty room close in around me to the point where it started to get hard to breathe. It was almost enough to make me wish it would start raining again. Going through my locker, I found I'd left behind a change of clothes the last time I was there, which helped my situation greatly. I stuffed the things I'd been wearing on top of a pile growing halfway up the inside of the metal cabinet, taking the clean clothes from the top shelf. Putting on clean underwear and a fresh shirt made me feel even better than the shower had, which was saying a lot.

I hurried outside, promising Tony I'd stop by and have dinner with him soon, then rushed back to Union Square, where I was lucky enough to catch a downtown N train to Canal Street after only a short wait. Getting out several minutes later, I hoofed it up to Number 11 Mott Street, Hubert's and my favorite Chinese restaurant.

Hubert was already there; he always arrives early. As usual, he had a corner booth for us. He started out by telling me the difference between male and female pork chops, and between the brides and grooms in different countries' weddings, and then finally started giving me what I needed.

Miller had narrowed his New York field of vision down to four guys. Joseph Byler, Ernest Cerelli, Fred George, and William Sterling. Hubert had found all of their addresses and phone numbers. He knew where each of them worked, where all their apartments were, which ones were and weren't talking to each other, and why or why not. He even had pictures of three of them.

As always, I was impressed. Feeling good enough to throw him a bone, I asked,

"How do you do it, Hu?"

"Easy, Jack," he told me. "I pulled the old 'collectin' yearbooks' routine. That eccentric artist b-bit gets 'em every time. Caught George at home. Real ch-chatty guy. Gave me the lowdown on everybody in the school. B-Byler graduated the year before the others, so no picture there, Dick Tracy. He didn't want to give up the yearbook after we got done talkin', natural. Same old shit—once you got 'em rememberin' the ol' days o' future passed, they never want to let go.

"But, when he wasn't in the room I g-got the shots with my pocket model. Got Byler's and Sterling's addresses and phone numbers from him, too. Told him, 'I muz have a copy of zis yearbook—it's studied righteous confusion—it iz magnifizent in its earnestly innozent interpretations of za times.' Said I was hopin' they'd sell me one of theirs."

Hu dug a handful of fried noodles from the appetizer bowl and sloshed them through the hot mustard, popping the whole wad into his mouth at once. Chewing noisily, he added,

"And don't worry. I checked out everything he told me. It's all the straight goods."

"Fine."

I meant it, too. There was no questioning Hu's work. The guy just didn't make mistakes. He had even gone so far as to sketch in beards on Byler's and George's photos. I always figure he knows what he's doing. If I didn't, there was no way I'd put up with him.

I had a lot more questions, but our waiter's arrival with our meal forced them to the back burner. As usual, Hubert had ordered for the both of us before I showed up. I don't complain. He knows what I like, and besides, I'm not what you would call a fussy eater. That day, not having eaten for as long as I hadn't, made me even more complacent than usual.

Our feast started with large chunks of roast pork served on a bed of fresh snow peas and sliced red peppers. A large side of spareribs covered in black bean sauce followed, along with an order of diced chicken with peas and cashews. A specialty of the house, Buddhist Delight, ten-vegetable fried rice, topped it all off, a heaping platter that would have been meal enough for any two rational men.

I rolled the case over in my mind while we ate, whenever I could stop cramming food in my mouth long enough to pay attention to anything in the first place. Luckily table manners aren't required at Mott.

Mott's a funny place, actually. The waiters are all fairly surly guys; in all the time I've gone there I've never gotten a polite one yet—but, then again, I've never had a bad meal there in all my visits, either. And, at the prices they charge, I wasn't about to complain if the waiters didn't bow and scrape, or lick my hand just because I was good enough to come in and let them serve me. Truth to tell, that's one of the place's special attractions for me. If nothing else, it keeps out the yuppies.

While we ate, Hubert gave me his personal impressions of the four I would be calling later. "Remember I only met George and Cerelli. Th-they live together, right? Nothin' funny or nothin'. Just a couple of guys t-trying t-to scrape along together, splittin' the bills. George—he's okay— pretty good egg, but Cerelli—" He paused for a moment, looking up at the ceiling, then at me. "He's got a temper. I think they're both clean, though."

"What do you mean?"

"I d-don't think she's with either one of them."

"Why not?"

"Mainly because they're living together. And—the obvious one—because they're both poor."

Made sense to me. Hu's been around more than enough whores in his time to spot them from their pictures. You could see in her eyes that Mara wasn't the type to do charity work. And, like he said, George and Cerelli were sharing the same place. Two guys and one woman under the same roof never works for very long. Ask anyone who's tried it. Hubert knew he didn't have to explain that one any further to me.

We continued to talk and eat, more eating than talking, Hu filling in the small rough spots I needed. There wasn't a whole lot more he could tell me, but then at that point I didn't need a whole lot. He'd given me enough to gather in the guys who might be able to lead me to Mara. All I had to do was find out where she was, tell Miller, and that would be that.

Once the meal was over, Hubert started up again with the one-liners. The waiter mercifully distracted him by bringing more tea and our fortune cookies. We each cracked one open, dutifully reading the tiny print on the red slips within. Hubert cackled.

"Listen to this one. 'Love is a shining dew drop, sparkling in the m-morning sunshine.' Ain't that a hoot?" His laughter turned even the waiters' heads.

I smiled. I didn't know if the cookie was right or not. I'd found very little of either "shining dew drops" or "love" in New York. I had my doubts as to whether or not I could find them anywhere else anymore, but then I'm basically a skeptical kind of guy.

Hubert asked me what mine said. I read it to him.

"'In an ugly world, the man with the mirror is not appreciated.'"

He stopped for a second—his face scrunched as if he were thinking—then asked if he could see the fortune. I handed it to him. After a moment's study, he told me,

"Funny, this is almost a perfect haiku."

"A what?" I asked.

"Haiku. It's Japanese p-poetry. Supposed to have a certain number of syllables. This one has one syllable t-too many. T-too bad."

I wondered if the extra syllable ruined the message. I read it over again just to make sure. It seemed okay to me, but what do I know about poetry? Then again, how much can you expect from a cookie? Deciding that I didn't want to chance a poetry lecture from Hubert, I scooped up the check, and stood to get back into my jacket. The humidity from outside was still rolling down the steps and in through the front door. That changed my mind. I draped it over my arm instead as Hubert gulped down the last cup of tea. He left the tip, then followed me over to the cash register.

Once we'd both climbed back up to the street, we went through our usual Mott Street ritual. Hubert always starts it for us.

"W-What're you goin' to do now?"

"I'd better get back to the office, Hu. I want to start following up on this stuff."

"Oh, okay."

The puppy whine forced me to ask, "Anything you wanted?"

"No. No. It's okay. I just thought you m-might like, want, like to go across the street. You know, maybe to see the d-dancing chicken."

I pretended to consider waiting around for him to waste fifty cents to watch some poor dumb bird get its feet electroshocked into doing a jig, then gave him that day's variation on my standard, "I'm sorry, Hu. I really do have to get back. Maybe next time."

He nodded his head with his usual, "Sure, Hagee. I un-understand. I'll talk to you later. D-don't take no wooden nickels now, Dick Tracy."

I assured him I'd watch out and that we would talk later. Then, I turned to head back across and uptown to the train while he limped across the street to the arcade to torture the mangy hen in the glass box. I'd thought about holding up the almost-haiku's mirror for him, but decided against it. Such social niceties really have no meaning for a guy like Hu. And besides, I thought, why bother? After all, it was only a chicken.

# CHAPTER 9

I CAUGHT THE uptown N train after fifteen minutes, taking it back to Union Square. Even with Mott's swift service, it was still almost two-thirty by the time I got behind my desk again. I pulled out the list of names and numbers Hubert'd given me and started making calls.

I tried Byler first; if the big fish couldn't be reeled in for that night, it seemed useless trying to gather up the others. I caught him at his office; he'd just come back from lunch as well. After I told him that a disturbed Miller was in town, looking for "his Mara," he became very agreeable. He assured me it would be no problem for him to come to my office that night after work. We set the time for seven and then hung up on each other.

I called Cerelli at the publishing house where he'd just started. It took a while for the receptionist to find him; nobody ever gives new numbers to the switchboard. I explained things to him the same way I had to Byler, adding the fact that he probably didn't want a crazy person like Miller coming around to his new job causing trouble. I really didn't think Miller was in such bad shape yet, but anything that made getting that night's meeting together any easier was worth using.

Cerelli agreed he could make it at seven o'clock as well, and then abruptly clicked off. I didn't care. All I wanted was to see him that night in my office. I've been rude in my time on occasion. I never get too excited whenever people are rude to me.

George was a cab driver working the night shift. I caught him at home the same way Hubert had. He was as eager as everyone else to avoid a confrontation with Miller. He would be at my office along with the rest of the gang.

Unfortunately things didn't go as well with Sterling. It seemed he'd become his own boss, one who didn't like to follow any set hours. He'd bought a bar upon moving to New York, one that opened without him in the afternoons, or so they claimed anyway. The happy voice on the other end of the line wasn't sure when he'd be in—but it was quite willing to offer me an enthusiastic assurance of "later."

Not being quite as enthused, I tried his home number. The only personality in the apartment interested in answering the phone was a tape machine. If Sterling was home, he had no interest in talking with someone he didn't know, even with the magic name Carl Miller dropped in for effect. I left a message, saying I would try again later if I didn't hear from him. Then, after giving him my number clearly, I hung up, drumming my fingers on my desk, looking for another angle from which to reel him in.

Trying a dodge, I called his bar again, using another voice. I pretended to be an office manager who needed a midtown bar to rent for a company party. The happy voice came on again. At first it seemed enthusiastic at the prospect, but the longer the conversation lasted the more it seemed to feel someone from the company should come in and see the place before we actually committed ourselves to anything. When I asked if I could speak to the owner or the manager, I was told that Mr. Sterling kept his own hours and that he wasn't in at the moment, but that he would certainly be in "later in the evening." Hurray for him, I thought. At least they'd narrowed it down to the half of the day during which he might finally show up.

I thanked the voice politely, telling it I would call back later in the hopes of catching Mr. Sterling. It thanked me twice as politely with another double barrel of enthusiasm, wishing me a "real nice Big Apple day," then clicked off again. I stared at the receiver for a moment, finally hanging it back up for lack of anything better to do with it.

Sterling was beginning to look like a tough nut to crack.

On top of that, from what I'd already found out about Byler, George, and Cerelli, it also seemed he was the most likely candidate to be hiding the Dumptruck's little sweetie.

But I figured that at least by meeting with the Rover Boys I would probably be able to positively eliminate them from the running. This would help to keep Miller calmed down and make it look as if I was earning the check he'd tossed my way. Thinking about that check, I decided to toast my good fortune. Reaching into the big drawer of my desk, I took out my bottle of Gilbey's and an only slightly filmy glass. I was just preparing to pour when I heard the hall door opening. Somebody was coming into the outer office. Before I could question it, a smooth female voice asked the air,

"Is anyone here? Hello?"

I figured it was either a new client, or Goldilocks straying somewhere off the beaten track. Since I hadn't left any porridge out to cool, and couldn't afford to let any kind of client get away, I gave the voice something to home in on.

"In here."

She came through the doorway walking straight for my desk. She had poured herself into a gray tweed suit that morning—one that went well with the cream-colored blouse and gray tie beneath it. The skirt was just the right length to tease one's imagination as to whether or not the lengths of the legs behind it were as well-shaped as the lengths exposed. I was betting they were—I was giving odds. They didn't look like the kind of legs that belonged hidden behind tweed. Then again, neither did the rest of her.

Despite the crispness of her appearance, she moved across my office like silk curtains on a balmy day. Her frame was slim but firm—sturdy but delicate; it wore the starved but satisfied look of a person whose hungers were assuaged by things other than a good steak. On her it wasn't a bad look.

Her shortish black hair framed a delicate face made up almost entirely of cheekbones and eyes—mostly eyes. They were fascinating—even from a distance—there was no better word for them. Most guys would probably fall straight into them and stay there for so long it would be years before they noticed her nose was just a little bit bent, or that her smile was a trifle tilted. Those eyes made up for a lot. They could have stopped a baby's tears or a platoon of Marines. They were a deep, lacquered brown, a kind of tribute to the color, as if whoever made them had wanted to prove that the drabber shades could have their day, too. There was a reflecting brightness to them, like the underside of a well-scrubbed skillet. That kind of hardness as well.

And suddenly, for some reason or another, I realized I already knew who my guest was. A model's face is her fortune, and I had only heard of one model during the past two days. As she stopped in front of my desk, a matched set of Dresden fingers pulled away from a tweed cuff. Her hand extended over my blotter as she asked,

"Mr. Jack Hagee, correct?"

I took the hand.

"Correct, Ms. Ward. Or is it still Byler?"

"It's Ward."

"I can understand that."

Our hands stopped shaking and returned to their owners. She asked,

"Have you been checking up on me?"

"Nope. Just on some of your friends. You've known some fun people."

She turned toward one of the inner office's worn leather chairs. She sat down heavily, as heavily as a person who weighs around a hundred pounds can sit, anyway.

"You know," she told me, the world's weight squarely between her shoulder blades, "if you really can't go home again, the least you should be able to do is clean all the dirt off your shoes and leave it behind at the city limits."

I nodded. I guessed that to her it was supposed to be a really snappy line. I didn't think it was terribly clever, basically because I didn't think it was correct, but I didn't say anything. I make it a point not to argue with really beautiful women; they don't like it. They're not used to it. It gets them cranky. I just smiled and tilted the bottle of

Gilbey's her way, offering her a quick one. Not surprisingly, she declined.

"No, thank you." Not her cup of tea. She asked, "Do you have any bottled water, though?"

"Sorry." I shrugged. On a planet more than three-quarters covered with water, I never could see the sense in buying any. Of course, Exxon had been doing its best to change my mind, but old habits die hard.

"Oh well," she answered, "that's all right. Maybe I should just tell you why I'm here." When I indicated that that might be a good idea, she continued. "I'm a friend of Carl's, Carl Miller's. He told me that he had hired you to try and find out what happened to our friend Mara. He told me that you took the case. Is that right?"

"So far, so good."

"Do you think you'll be able to find her?"

"I might be able to. It's what I get paid for. Why?"

"I told you, I'm Carl's friend." She figured that was supposed to tell me everything I needed to know. It was said in that tone of voice intelligent women use when telling the truth is a bit too bothersome. After my blank expression got across the fact I wasn't smart enough to pick up on the subtleties of her style of conversational fencing, she offered me a bit more.

"I want to see him get what he wants. I used to be Mara's friend, back before . . . well, before everything that happened. I just want the two of them to be happy."

Women like Ward usually don't care if guys like Miller live from one day to the next, let alone whether or not they're happy. Buying her story didn't seem like too smart a move. And, as tired as I was, I didn't care if she knew it.

"Ms. Ward, try to understand that I've had a very bad past couple of days. I'm not making any excuses for myself, and I'm not looking for your sympathy. All I want to do is get the truth out of you.

"Why did you come here?"

My answer was a shocked look, not a blatant, bug-eyed jolt, more like the kind someone on stage gets when they're fed the wrong lines. She caught something in her throat but held it back, letting another sentence out instead. "I'm sorry if I haven't given you the right impression. I only wanted to help Carl."

"Right. Well, that's just wonderful. So—you've asked your questions, and I've answered them. And, since you don't have anything further to say, you can be leaving and I can get back to some unfinished business."

As I downed the slug of Gilbey's in my hand, Ward started to get up, but then sat back down, trying to decide something. I really had no idea what it could be. After letting the Gilbey's pour down, I wasn't sure I wanted to be bothered with anything else for a while either. The humidity was layering a thick, muggy rug in the air only certain things could cut through—gin being one of them. I'd just started pouring myself another half glass of relief when Ward suddenly remembered what it was she wanted to tell me.

"All right," she admitted. "I'm scared of Carl."

Now that was a wrinkle I hadn't been expecting. As I prodded her along, the rest of the facts began assembling themselves. Miller had maintained contact with Ward after she'd walked out on Byler. He'd called her often over the last year, looking for advice on how he should handle Mara. Ward had talked to him out of loneliness at first, the chance to speak with a man who didn't want to paw her out of her clothes, and then with the hope that Miller's relationship with Mara might succeed. If things between the two of them had any chance of working, she felt she should help all she could. At least, that was the way she was telling it. She concluded,

"But it didn't work."

"Such are the fortunes of war."

She looked at me coldly.

"You don't understand," she explained. "I'm the only person Carl knows in New York City. He's called me five times in the past three days. He talks for hours and hours, just on and on, about all the others who moved here, and Mara, and—but sometimes . . ."

She paused for a moment, as if she didn't want to

continue down the same sentence, but only for a moment. Backing up, she plowed ahead for once without worrying about what she said.

"He keeps threatening to do something on his own."

And then, before her outburst could run away from her, she collected herself, leaving me to wonder again which emotion had just been trying to bubble up to the surface. It was an eerie thing, watching an obviously emotional woman holding back tears. I'm not saying I thought it was wrong, it's just something I'm not used to. The hardness won out, however, leaving her able to continue coldly.

"I think Carl might be heading for a nervous breakdown. He keeps talking about killing people."

"Which people?" I asked, obviously curious.

"Everyone. Ernie, Fred, Bill . . . Joe." The pause before her ex's name surprised me. Maybe she still cared for him. If that was true, it certainly helped make sense out of why she'd come to my office in the first place.

"I don't want him to hurt anyone."

"Anyone in particular?"

"Me, for one. You, himself—Joey." Another pause. "I don't know what he might do. Sometimes he talks about suicide—other times . . ." She trailed off for a moment, and then suddenly she whispered, "Don't let him hurt Joey."

"What makes you think your ex is a prime target?"

"Carl hates him. Mara only slept with Fred and Ernie and all the others to get to Joe. Once she had slept with him, she tried playing all of them off against each other, but it didn't work. She was too young then; she couldn't control them like she can Carl."

Emotion had crept into her voice the way a cat enters a room when it's stalking its owner. You can be sitting reading the evening paper, and suddenly the household tabby is in your lap, and you're jumping up, wide-eyed, sputtering something stupid like "it just came out of nowhere," even though your common sense tells you that it had to have been there all the time. I looked up at her, surprised at the shift. And then it happened.

Just as startling as the unexpected cat, the tears I hadn't thought her capable of began sliding out of the corners of both the beautiful brown eyes down over and around the fabulous cheekbones. Her chin quavered as she wiped at the slightly bent nose. She started digging through her bag, scattering its contents over my desk as she cried. "Oh, please. I'm so sorry, I didn't mean to do . . . to be, not here, I wouldn't want you to think I'm, I mean . . ."

"It's okay," I told her. "Don't worry about it. Do you want some Kleenex or something?"

"No, no, please. Don't bother. I have some here." She pulled a handful of crumpled tissues from the rubble in front of her, and started dabbing at her face. It was almost a shame. It looked even better wet. Maybe not better, actually—just more human. With some of the makeup and self-assured chic coldness suddenly rubbed away, she took on a more believable tone. Once she'd managed to contain her outburst, the harder edge came back to tell me,

"I really am sorry about that. Maybe I should level with you."

"That would be nice."

"Joe and I just couldn't make it together. Our marriage was a mistake, plain and simple. I do still care about him; I really do. I don't want to see him get hurt." I watched her while she talked. Now that her concern had shaken her composure, I could see what it was that Byler had found so attractive in her. A look of desperate need mixed with a sense of longing played across her face, leaving her vulnerable, looking the way the last leaf of fall does as it clings to its branch. She continued,

"I wouldn't want Joe to know I told you all of this. I know him too well. He would think that it meant something else, and it doesn't." She looked at me directly. Her face was dry again. "Sometimes I almost wish it could, sometimes, on the lonely days, but I know better than that."

She was a strong woman; it takes a strong person to tell the truth, especially to the people who need to hear it. I had a feeling Joe Byler had heard the truth—maybe more times than he might have cared for. But then, that was conjecture.

Ward began repacking the contents of her purse. "I guess I'm really afraid that Carl might try to hurt me."

The statement intrigued me. "What makes you think he might?"

"Carl isn't well, Mr. Hagee. He's having a nervous breakdown. It's only just beginning to surface, but I can tell."

"You some kind of expert, Ms. Ward?"

She looked away. "I've been close enough to it to think that I can identify it, yes." I figured I could accept that. Most everyone has eaten an orange in their time. Most of them couldn't give you the scientific name for oranges if their lives depended on it, but how many would they have to eat to recognize the taste?

I asked her, "Do you think he's going to crack soon?"

"I don't know." She looked up again. "Not if you find Mara for him."

She said the last sentence staring straight at me, and then looked down again so she could finish restuffing her bag. As she did, she suddenly frowned. Apparently she hadn't put things back correctly; not everything fit. She stared at the leftovers, trying to decide what was worth forcing back in and what wasn't. She asked me if I'd had lunch yet. When I told her I had, she asked,

"How about dessert?"

"Only a fortune cookie."

"Then here," she said. "Have an apple." She handed me a large, crisp-feeling red one. "I'm not allowed that many calories a day, anyway," she explained.

I took it, saying "Thanks," stashing it in my top left-hand drawer. Getting rid of it seemed to help her finally set everything in order. One does what one can. She threw a few remaining odds and ends into my wastebasket and then snapped the refilled purse shut. Standing, she extended her hand once more, saying, "Thank you for your time, Mr. Hagee."

"Thank you for the apple."

"No. I'm serious." I'm not sure what made her think I wasn't. "I don't know if coming to you was the right thing to do, but I was scared. I don't need Carl showing up at one of my shooting sessions, or anywhere else for that matter.''

"Have you told him not to?"

"No," she admitted. "I just keep putting him off when he says that he wants to meet with me. The phone calls are quite enough.''

"Yeah. I can understand that.''

"I hope so." She looked at me again, softening me with the brown eyes. "Find Mara for him, please. Keep him calm. I don't know for sure if he would really do anything crazy . . . but I do know it's possible. I just don't want him, or Mara, or . . . anyone, I guess, to get hurt.''

"I'll do what I can."

"I'm sure you will, Mr. Hagee. If it helps any, I'm not as scared now as I was when I came in." I thanked her for the vote of confidence. She hung her bag over one slim shoulder and gave me her hand one last time. I held it for an eternity, sucking at the energy surrounding her—wanting her just from the touch of her fingers, the contact jolting me more than I thought possible. I let my hand move where her grip took it, pretending to be in charge of my motor functions. She told me, "Goodbye, Mr. Hagee.''

I answered her, "See you around, Ms. Ward," which I figure showed just what each of us wanted from the other. Then I sat back down as she disappeared through the office door. She shut the outer door lightly as she left. I listened to her spiked heels tap away, holding my breath so as not to lose the sound too soon. I could always get some oxygen later.

After my sadly shaken composure pulled itself back together, I thought about her visit. It had given me more subjective facts, but I wasn't sure exactly in what order I could arrange them.

I believed her when she said she was scared. It was there; I could feel it. She hadn't been nervous enough to drive a cat from her lap, but she was getting there. I didn't blame her. In her place I'd probably have been scared, too. Miller must have been upsetting her more than she was letting on—to

me or herself. I couldn't tell, though, if she was more
worried about herself or her ex-husband.

It seemed to me she might still honestly care about Byler,
but what did that prove? That was only my opinion, and I've
been wrong about women and what they cared about in the
past—plenty of times. She gave the impression she was
more concerned about Byler than herself, but that kind of
impression is usually false. After all, how many of us deep
down really care more about anyone else than we do
ourselves?

To care about someone, to really love a person, you have
to trust them first, and like my old man told me, the only
person you'll ever trust completely is yourself. When he
first said that, like most people, I didn't believe him. I spent
a lot of time over the years after he said it trying to prove
him wrong. I worked hard at it. Finally, though, as I found
myself getting older, I discovered two things. The first was
that it was becoming more and more important to disprove
my old man's adage. The second thing I found was that he
was right. No matter what I tried, it always came down to
the final wash that, just like he said, you really can't trust
anyone completely except yourself. Most people even have
trouble with that.

I wish I was wrong. I honestly would like to just once find
that someone who cares, that someone to trust. It's like
sticking your hand into a box with a trapped cat, on some
sort of dare. Praying that nothing happens, you slide your
fingers into the darkness, inching them along until your
wrist disappears into the black, and usually just when you
think you have things under control—*scratch*. Most people
try again. A lot try five or six times. Some never stop
hoping, trying just once more, knowing that this time, this
time things will be different—that the little woman will
realize, or Mom will understand, or that a guy who's been
a pal for that long would never . . . and then—*scratch*.

And the worst part about it is that the ones who keep
trying finally reach a point where they don't even feel the
claws anymore. It boils down to little more than a game in
which they keep sticking their hand back into the box more

out of desperation than with hope, praying that just this once they'll be able to get away with it. It stops being something they have any control over; no longer looking to receive love, or understanding, or even sympathy in return, their expectations are reduced to simply wanting to get in and out without getting roughed up too badly.

That was the kind of guy Miller was. It's the kind of guy a lot of us are.

At that moment, though, none of that seemed very important. I had work to do, and not a lot of time in which to do it. I still hadn't gotten through to Sterling, and I knew that was important if I was going to watch the old gang react to each other later on.

I looked at my watch; it was already four thirty. I also looked at the Gilbey's. It was still a third full. Reaching past the phone, I grabbed the bottle and pulled it back toward me. As I unscrewed the cap I figured what the hell, Sterling could wait longer than I could.

# CHAPTER 10

BYLER AND GEORGE both arrived before seven o'clock. Cerelli wandered in at ten after. Byler sat in the same chair Miller had, the same one Ward had as well. I wondered if there was something about it that drew people from Pennsylvania, or if he had just unconsciously zeroed in on some familiar scent left by Ward. Not that I was worried about it, but I do make an effort to understand why people do things. It is my job.

I don't know if I ever will, though. Trying to predetermine what most people are going to do next is about as easy as guessing what each card in a deck will be as they are turned over one by one. You can guess correctly from time to time, and of course it gets easier as you go through the deck, but I wouldn't want to do it for a living—no more than I do already.

Trying to get started, I watched Cerelli as he sat down, giving him and the others a last quick once over. Cerelli and Byler both looked bored. Maybe they weren't that worried about Miller. Maybe they'd been in New York too long. A couple of years in this city is about all it takes to give anyone a bored look, no matter what is happening. George's face was a wall of stone—hard, solid—a barrier between its owner and everything else. Byler's cracked long before his.

"Well, is this it?"

"Yeah. I tried to get your pal Sterling, but I couldn't track him down."

"Your pal, maybe," he snapped. "Theirs, maybe"—he swung a finger at the other two—"but not mine. Not that bastard." Byler seemed more than a little upset. I asked him what made Sterling such a bastard. He had no problems with telling me. A little louder and he'd have been telling all of 14th Street. "I know a lot of things came between Jean and me, but he was definitely one of the big ones."

"Aw, Christ's sake, Joe—that's all in your mind," interrupted Cerelli.

"Right—their trips to Atlantic City are just in my mind. Her singing in his club is just in my mind. Just like her first modeling jobs, pouting in the background for faggot underwear ads—he didn't arrange that, either. That's all in my mind too, right? Go on, talk some more shit for us. Tell me her gratitude stopped with a smile and a handshake and a home-cooked meal—"

"Mr. Byler—" my turn to interrupt, "this is all fascinating, but we are here to talk about Carl Miller and Mara Phillips."

"Equally interesting subjects to be sure." George's stone puss cracked a little. I asked him what prompted his comment. The fissure split open wider.

"I'll tell you. Sure—no problem. Carl Miller is the craziest fuck I know. How that sad, fat redneck ended up with a preppie tramp like Mara Phillips, I can't tell you, but I do know this—we all knew this was going to be trouble, not just trouble for Carl, but trouble for all of us—right from the start. Just like Crazy Maggie."

George certainly had a way of showing you one shoe that left you dying to see the other. Byler and Cerelli both twitched at the mention of the new name. George had obviously let some cat out of the bag. Following up, I got the story.

Crazy Maggie was the nickname my guest had given to a former girlfriend of Miller's from before his marriage. She was another one half the town had slept with, including the Rover Boys, here. I was beginning to understand my client a little better. His upset over Mara and his suspicions were starting to make a bit more sense. Ballard hadn't known, or just hadn't wanted to tell, any of this.

Maggie had been either truly crazy, or just plain vicious. No one present was sure which. She had started by leading

Miller on, both by telling him how wonderful he was and by promising to marry him. In the meantime, however, finding his buddies more interesting, she started sleeping around with them, dragging them in with pleas for help. She told the Dumptruck's friends he was mentally unbalanced, that he was threatening to kill her if she didn't marry him. As she put it, she was turning to them in the hopes they could convince Miller to leave her alone.

Meanwhile, though, she continued to string Miller along, telling him she didn't know what to do about his friends and the awful way they kept forcing themselves on her. One could hardly blame the guy for believing the woman he thought he was going to marry when she cried the blues about his horny friends. The possibility that she might be lying wouldn't have dawned on most guys, and I didn't see where I could go making any exceptions for the Dumptruck. The three told the story in a way which made it easy to believe he turned on his pals and, once they were gone, got taken to the cleaners and dumped by a bored Maggie.

After that, their view of things hooked back up with Ballard's. Basically on the rebound, he'd gotten married to a quiet girl from school, just about the only other girl he'd ever dated. When she tried to calm him down, get him to lead a more normal life, he split from her to chase after Mara, something Mara seemed to have encouraged, along with his divorce. Kimberly, his wife, couldn't stand up to him. She signed the papers without any trouble. George suspected she might have been relieved at the way things had turned out. Mara reeled Miller in then, skimmed all the cream he had left, and then took off.

It took a while to get the whole story out of the trio, but it gave me a lot more puzzle pieces to start moving around. It was a wonderful little mess, laid out with all the charm of a movie-of-the-week. All it needed was somebody dying of cancer. I felt sorry for Miller, but then, I feel sorry for any dumb animal that can't see the car for the headlights.

With all of them staring, I asked Cerelli the question that had been bothering me since my ride back from Plainton. "Okay. I thank you for all the background, gentlemen, but

I need something more. What I want to know is if you can tell me what it is that Mara got out of all this? Everyone's under the impression that Miller got his box emptied. Fine. But what is it he had that she wanted?''

"I don't know. Cash, maybe," answered Byler. "Pennsylvania's dirt-down and belly-up right now. Been getting worse for years. Lot of people out of work there. Miller had a lot of things going all the time. She could have drained him for a lot before he'd go dry."

"How? I'm not saying you're wrong. Just tell me where it was going to come from?"

Everyone turned on the "vacant" signs. They were all of the same opinion—Miller had his fingers in lots of pies—but none of them had any facts. Byler'd heard antiques; Cerelli, stocks, investment portfolios, all the current smart moves. I asked George.

"Beats me," he replied. "I ain't the detective."

"No. That's right. That's my job. I'm trying to do it now. You're supposed to be helping me. Now, why doesn't one of you try a little harder?"

No one got a chance. The window behind me suddenly erupted in time to a sharp bark echoing out in the street. Chips of flying glass slashed their way through the room, nicking everyone. Warm smears started leaking down my cheek and palm. George toppled backwards in surprise, his fingers desperate to close over the burning hole in his chest.

Yanking my .38 from its place in my side drawer, I dodged for the door around Byler and Cerelli, who'd both heaped to the floor as soon as George'd started screaming. As I ducked out of the office, Cerelli yelled,

"It's Miller!"

"Anything's possible," I agreed. "One of you—get up! Dial 911; get an ambulance. I'm going out."

I took the stairs three and four at a time, grateful no one'd decided to bed down yet for the night in the stairwell. Coming out the front door, I leaped into the densest part of the crowd and then threw myself toward the restaurant dumpster they always keep out front. The crowd I'd entered faded like week-old roses. Men waving guns isn't a common enough sight in New York City to go unnoticed just yet. They didn't go far, though; people still love a circus.

I sighted around through the fading evening light, checking the buildings across the street, the rooftops—windows. I scanned the sidewalks, too, searching for anyone who might've just blasted my office with rifle fire. Nobody looked very likely. Standing up, I eyed the same areas again without worry. I'd already relaxed my grip, finger outside the trigger guard.

Sensing nothing further was going to happen, the loose circle around me lost its structure, fading back into a crowd of passersby, a number of them giving me dirty looks for wasting their time before they walked on. I wondered where attitudes like that come from—not surprised at them—just curious.

About ten minutes later an ambulance managed to break the traffic barrier and slide over to the curb near the fireplug. Amazingly, there was nothing else parked there to block them. The attendants, a Puerto Rican teenager and a Korean woman in her twenties, jerked the back doors open to pull the stretcher free. The sheet on it was sporting at least three different blood types; the one nearest the low end was still damp. I guess I wasn't the only one having a busy night.

Wiping some of the sweat off my forehead with a rolled shirt cuff, I followed them back inside. Going up, I took the stairs one at a time. It was too hot for any more exercise.

# CHAPTER 11

RAY LOOKED AT me like a high-school principal wondering where he'd gone wrong. I wondered how long he was going to take before he started tearing into me. The fan on the filing cabinet behind him rattled the drawers with each swing to the left. If it had been two degrees hotter in the station house, the walls would have started sweating. Ray drank the top off a paper cup of water, shaking his head at me as he swallowed.

"I thought you told me something yesterday about a brand-new Jack Hagee."

"All lies—you know you can't trust the private ops in this city."

"Ain't that the truth." Ray nodded sourly. "You'd better start leading a quieter existence."

"Sure. I'll put up a 'Don't Shoot Up My Fucking Miserable Life' sign in my window tomorrow."

"You're really funny. I like it when you're funny to me, Jack. You know why?"

"It adds color to your otherwise drab, wretched days?"

"Naw. It's because it makes it so much easier for me to pull the hair off your nuts when I have to."

"This one of those times?"

"Maybe."

It was a routine we've gone through before. Ray was letting me know he was in no mood for games. As he pulled a half-empty, unlabeled bottle of something raw-colored from his bottom drawer, I thought maybe I'd better wait before pushing him any harder. The heat in the room had begun to soak into me, crawling down my shoulders into my

clothes, the chair, the floor, probably into the streets and
sewers below. I pulled another button open on my shirt,
mopping the sweat running down my chin with a blank
piece of paper from Ray's desk.

He was ignoring me for the moment, though, concentrating on his nameless fifth. Ray has what I consider a strange
habit of pouring the ends of whatever bottles he has around
into that one fifth. Over the months I've known him, the
color has ranged from almost clear to chocolate. That night
it looked green, but it might have only been the heat playing
tricks on my eyes.

As he tossed off another slug, the lights tried to shine off
whatever was inside the bottle this week but failed. He
offered one to me but I declined, asking him if we could get
the party rolling. He smiled.

"Sure, Jack, sure. Here are the house rules. You tell me
all about this Miller character—now. You tell me all about
whatever he wanted, who those dildos were that were in
your office, why you had them there, and what all of it has
to do with you keeping our great city safe. Then I'll turn you
out into the street so you can pick up some spare change
pitching quarters with the needle boys in the park."

"All of it, huh?"

He smiled again—nodding. I sucked in a deep breath.
There was no fighting it. The heat had me to the point where
the effort behind thinking up smart remarks was just behind
juggling bowling balls in effort. Also, since fighting with
Trenkel at that point would have made as much sense as
trying to juggle bowling balls, I pushed my back deeper into
the cutting slats of my chair and told Captain Ray about Carl
Miller's visit.

I gave him the story of what Miller wanted. I told him
what Miller'd told me of his reasons for suspecting Byler
and the rest, and what they'd told me of Miller and Maggie
and Kimberly. I gave him Ballard's side of things, and
Ward's, and a tour of the Phillipses ugly little home life just
for grins. We tinkered with a few ideas as to who might've
decided to start taking potshots at my office, but it was
mostly just for form.

Unless someone had given into the humidity and noise and dirt of the city and decided to let off a little steam playing Davy Crockett, there was very little to choose from in the way of suspects. Sterling, maybe—but he most likely hadn't even gotten my message by the time of the shooting. And even if he had, what reason could he have to shoot at me or the people in my office? Even implausible reasons were having a hard time surfacing.

Edging around the Dumptruck's obvious candidacy for gunman of the week, I went back to telling Ray his bedtime story. I filled him in on my visit to Karras, and everything he'd had to tell me, and then went back to giving him the details on that night.

I closed up all the loose ends, impressing him with the stupidity of my marathon dash into the street. I gave him a quick checklist of the order the ambulance, the uniforms, and his detectives had arrived in, finally admitting,

"After all the confusion died down, I tried to call Miller at his hotel. He wasn't in."

"For how long?"

"They weren't sure."

"What'd they guess?"

"They thought maybe all night."

"Doing what?"

I glared at Ray. "He didn't bring his social secretary with him this trip."

"What's that supposed to mean?"

"It means the desk clerk told me he *was out*. That he'd been out *a while*. That he couldn't tell me how *long* a while, just *a while*. Maybe *all night*. I left a message for him to call me when he got back."

"He won't have to."

"Why not?"

"Because," answered Ray, "you're going to tell me what hotel he's staying in. After you do that, I'm going to send over a plainclothes to escort your client here for a little after-dinner tea. Because, in case it's escaped that keen analytical eye of yours, your Mr. Miller is our only suspect in an attempted murder they tell me may soon balloon itself into a full-grown murder. You square?''

"Like a box," I muttered.

I gave Ray the hotel name with a growl. Unlike the detectives on television, I don't have a charismatic force field which magically stops the police from revoking my license, or from just plain slapping me around, if I don't cooperate. For some reason, people seem to believe a private detective can just smile at cops and make them forget how to do their jobs. Even the Mafia has to use money.

People who write movie and TV scenes where P.I.'s jerk cops around and then laugh in their faces are living in the *Twilight Zone*. This is not the way the world works. Cops are like everyone else—they don't like to be thwarted. Having to step aside for every minority group and political clan with a collective conscience is galling enough. Having to do it for someone like me is unthinkable. Besides, there's no way to stop a good cop when he's on the trail, especially when he might be right. There's no reason to, either.

After Ray got done explaining the situation to one of his men, and sending him over to Miller's hotel, he turned back to me.

"So, what'd you and those three talk about after the shooting?"

"Nothing. When was there any time? I waited in the street until the ambulance came. Your boys were there two minutes later."

"Your big mouth can do a lot of flappin' in two minutes."

"Lighten up, Ray. One of them was unconscious and getting slid onto a stretcher—the other two were watching. Christ—send your boys out to bring them back in—you can rubber-hose the truth out of the three of us." I stood up—sweat rolling down my face. My voice rose, pushing the situation.

"You've got it all. There just isn't any more. I've given you the full answer to each of your questions. Now move on to something else and quit dicking me around.''

Ray reached for his bottle. He took a quick nip, not bothering to offer me one this time—his way of letting me know he was not amused. I didn't care. Wiping his own sweat away with his sleeve before it could get into his eyes, Ray softened slightly, offering the sarcasm known as a cop's apology.

"That's why we're all so happy with you, Jack. You're such a pleasant person."

"And I thought it was just my even, white teeth."

"Yeah, right," drawled Ray shortly, "that, too. Now, why don't you continue keeping me happy and tell me just what the flip side to all this bullshit is."

I filled Ray in on most of what I'd been thinking. I gave him the background I'd picked up on the Rover Boys in Plainton. I told him what I suspected, and how most of the pieces seemed to fit together. I didn't give Sterling or my visit to Karras much emphasis. Those points I downplayed. I wanted some time to fish those two out for myself before I let anyone muddy the waters.

Ray was about to ask something else when one of his men rapped on the glass. The uniform got a two-finger wave, a signal I'd seen before. It translated to "make it fast." Of course, most of Ray's signals have that message in them somewhere. The rookie snapped the door open quickly, not stepping inside but only leaning around the jamb so as not to waste time.

"Got a report from Fourteenth Street, sir. Fresh shell found on top of a roof across from Mr. Hagee's building. No prints."

"Make?"

"A 9.3 x 74R, sir."

"They spring a match from Jack's wall?"

"Yes, sir. Uptown ballistics confirms a match."

Ray had word sent back to his men to rope off the roof of the building where they'd found the shell. It was too dark to order a search, especially one not very likely to turn up something else. Now that they knew the "what," "when," the "where," and the "how," Ray's trained dog act wouldn't be happy until it sniffed out something that resembled "why" and "who" as well. Especially "who." Truth to tell, having a squad of cops eager to find the trigger finger that enjoyed redecorating my office left me with mixed emotions.

On the one hand, a person should never quibble when the police take an active concern in their safety. For me, however, there was the annoying prospect of having a case concerning one of my clients solved by a grinning bunch of jokers who would like nothing better than to be able to drop the same kind of comments on me that I do on them. I had no doubt that Ray's main concern was for doing his job. I also had no doubt if he got his done before I did mine, I'd get to hear about it for a long time.

I put aside personal considerations, though, and got back to work. Ray and I kicked some ideas around about the shell. It was a European make, most likely German. I hadn't told Ray about Miller's reported fondness for gun collecting. If we were going to pretend to work together, though, it seemed like a good time.

"How about a favor?"

"Like what?" Ray growled at me, reaching back into his drawer for another slug of whatever it was he was drinking.

"Keep your boys from griefing me too much on this one."

"Why should I?"

"Because if you don't, I won't tell you that Miller is a gun collector, and that he might be a prime candidate for owning a few exotic European hunting rifles. Also that he reported the majority of his collection stolen a while back; both of those facts would leave your boys sniffing each other's asses without any trees to bark up."

Ray glared at me, letting me know the humidity and the green sludge he'd been pouring himself were not making him any the more receptive to wisecracks. I glared back at him to let him know I didn't care. Sighing, he nodded slightly, letting me know he'd keep Mooney and the others off my back. He reached for the phone, then dashed off a couple of quick calls, starting the gears rolling toward getting a list of Miller's gun registrations. I put in an order for a copy. He laughed at my chances of getting one. So much for cooperation.

We kicked around a few more points, but we both knew there wasn't much more to be said. Miller was the only real suspect we had for the shooting, the only one that made any sense, anyway. I was just about to see if Ray would let me call it a night, when we were interrupted again. We both knew what the rookie had for us by the look on his face. Ray told him,

"George didn't make it."

"No, sir. He died on the table a few minutes ago."

Ray waved the rookie away and reached back for his sludge. Hefting it without ceremony this time, he took a shot off the top, then offered me another chance at it. My client had just graduated from an assault suspect to a Murder One suspect in a case that was getting worse faster than I could count the reasons why. This time I took the bottle and kicked back a good one.

It tasted just the way it looked.

# CHAPTER 12

I WALKED UP to Sterling's club, the Blue Ostrich, at a little after eleven. If Ballard'd been right about Mara's monetary needs, he might just be the one to whom she'd flocked. On the outside the place's look indicated bucks had been spent putting it together. It was glass and chrome surrounded by pastel paints, all of it set off by something cheap that had been painted to look like marble by someone expensive.

A look through the windows showed track lighting hung everywhere, some of it installed just to highlight individual plants. None of them really very green, mind you. They were all singular, overpriced things—spindly, prickly, twisted— set out like works of art, their very existence here in the city indicating massive amounts of effort to keep them alive . . . just the kind of veneer guaranteed to generate plenty of upscale capital in New York. With a shrug, I passed through the front doors, not looking for any of the things the place had to offer.

It might seem odd to some for me to keep looking for Mara while Miller was wanted for questioning in a murder case, but only to those who don't understand exactly what it is that I do for a living. I'd been paid to do a job; if I wanted to keep the money, I had to do what the client wanted. Just because the police wanted to pin a murder rap on Miller didn't make him guilty. Hell, in New York, it was almost proof he didn't do it.

All that was beside the point, though. Pushing Miller and Trenkel and George and all the rest out of my head, I walked inside, gearing my mind to searching for Mara, saving a little extra energy to thank heaven the air conditioning was

94

working. I knew I'd be leaving soon enough—I'd told Hubert I'd meet him between midnight and half past at my place—but for now I welcomed even a brief respite from the heat and humidity that's dogged the whole town all day.

While I mopped at my now cooling neck, a stylishly chic, hard-muscled but slender figure closed in on me, eyeballing me the same way a tired father does his fourteen-year-old daughter's date who shows up with a back pocket bulged by the outline of a bottle and hands whose shake you don't like.

Clutching a menu to shield himself from me, he asked, "One . . . ?" His tone implied he didn't think I could count that high.

"I'll just try the bar, thanks."

He let his expressive eyes roll up under their lids in time to a supercilious sigh, and then deserted me to beam his attention to the again opening door. As he walked away I contemplated doing something just as childish back at him but figured, why bother? I could always pour a drink on his head or cut his tie in half or some other forties hardguy movie shenanigan on the way out if I was really feeling Curly-Joeish later.

Sitting at the bar, I began to understand why the guy I'd talked to earlier on the phone had thought I might want to see the place before booking it for an office party. The Ostrich was a gay bar/restaurant, one of those classy, quiet places with which the mid-range of Manhattan's East Side had once been covered. People called it the Bird Circuit in the fifties; all the clubs had had bird names—the Red Parrot, the Dying Sparrow, the Peacock, et cetera, a code signaling a secret oasis for those who knew.

Of course, that was in the days when such things had to be kept a secret, or at least discreet. The circuit had died in the late sixties/early seventies when the gay activists had come out and made their life style socially acceptable, at least in the big cities. For a long time, clubs like the Mine Shaft, Wally's, the Toilet, and others, kicked things up in a wild way, their patrons announcing to the world nightly what they liked and why. They all made headlines repeatedly, some amusing, some not. Finally, though, in the eighties, the spread of AIDS caused the city to close all of the bath houses and high-risk sex clubs. Too much of a good thing, I guess.

Taking the history of gay clubs into consideration, Sterling's low profile and his club's quiet demeanor made sense. The Ostrich wasn't a refuge for the lumberjack boys, the so-called Pines' clones, in their rough pants and boots and plaid shirts. This was a place for silk ties and hand-made suits—a *GQ* kind of spot for more established, upscale couples, just the spot for a sensible pair of lovers to come and discuss their needs away from home for a while, like who was using whose razor, or what color the dining room should be painted this fall, or who had brought the latest social disease into their romance after a night of tramping it up—and whether or not anyone was going to die because of it.

I dropped my hat on the bar, whistling up a quick one. The bartender, a rock-hard twenty-year-old with a soft face and a cigarette-ad moustache turned to find out what I wanted.

"Gilbey's, double rocks."

"On board."

He was back in half a minute with my drink, serving it without half the disdain the maitre d' had shown. Of course, he was young; he had plenty of time to learn. Then again, he probably figured that if I got in, I must belong in. I wasn't thrilled with that kind of figuring, but there wasn't a whole lot I could do about it. Besides, according to some doctors, we all belong in. So, what the hell, I thought; I decided to just toast the medical profession and not worry about it.

I let a short gulp wash its way down as I looked over the rest of the bar. I hadn't seen any signs of anything that might either be Sterling's office, or at least lead to it, on the way in. I'd decided to see if I could find him without any employee help first. Something was giving me the feeling that the boss left everything he could up to his hired hands. Unfortunately, what I needed him for couldn't be handled by proxy.

The crowd wasn't giving me any ideas, either. They were

heavier in the dining room than in the bar, but there were enough customers footing the rail to let me know something was out of place. The one- to three-hundred-dollar differences between most of their outfits and mine had me pretty well convinced it was me. The looks on their faces told me they were convinced of the same thing. One guy, good-looking in that matinee idol kind of way, maybe ten years my junior, came over to see what I had to say.

"First time here?"

"Yeah," I told him.

"What do you think of it? It's a pretty new place, you know."

"I'd heard. Know anything about the owners?"

"No. Why, is it a good story?"

"I don't know. It may be."

The youngster looked me over again, trying to get the right reading. You could see it in his face. He knew there was something wrong, but he couldn't figure it out. I was inside, I was having a drink. He had come over and expressed an interest—what was wrong with me? he was thinking—couldn't I see how beautiful he was?

This one had me stumped. I didn't necessarily need a "cover." I wasn't bounty hunting; there wasn't nothing wrong with me being where I was—nobody was going to attack me or even ask me to leave if they found out I wasn't gay. But aside from not wanting to attract any more attention to myself than my outfit already was, I really didn't see the need to hurt the guy's feelings if I didn't have to. Looking back at him, I said,

"My name's Jack."

"Hi Jack. Bud. 'Eugene' to my parents and other outsiders, but you can use Bud."

"Thanks. Listen, Bud, can I be honest with you?"

"Well, sure," he told me, meaning it in a sincere kind of way that made me hope I wasn't going to have to be a heel about the whole thing. "What is it?"

"This just isn't my first time here. This is my first time anywhere. If you catch my drift."

"Ohhhhhhhh." It was an exaggerated sound, meant to

convey shared knowledge and a feeling that understanding was there for me. He touched my wrist gently to assure me he understood. It was a firm but brief squeeze, one not looking to suggest anything but contact. He withdrew quickly, sensing my discomfort. Pulling back into his own space, inches from mine, he told me,

"It's all right. Everyone's got to have their first time for everything. I guess you're not in a mood to dance just yet."

I told him "no" as politely as any timid girl has ever turned down her first high-school advance. I didn't have to fake the blush. He smiled at me in an amused but warm way, telling me,

"This must be really new for you. Listen, don't say a word. I understand. I'm at a table over near the stage—few friends—you'd like them all. And they'd all understand. If you feel like breaking the ice a little further, I promise no one will bite you. Not till you want them to. Okay?"

I nodded, jerkily, not really knowing what to say. I was grateful for the chance to start blending in, but I was also as nervous as any other straight thirty-year-old guy surrounded by homosexuals, trying to stop himself from acting as if they were mad dogs and not just people. I started to say something after that, but Bud put a forefinger to my lips and reminded me:

"No, no. Not a word. Not till you're ready. I'll be keeping my eye on you. I'll let you know when you are."

I nodded again, one hand waving with a shake at his receding form, the other tight around my drink, trying not to squeeze the tumbler into shards. My mind shattered in a dozen panic directions for a split second, and then recomposed itself. I felt stupid, angry, nervous, and relieved all at the same time. Pushing away everything except the relief, I raised my glass to take a drink. As it neared my mouth I suddenly noticed the rim of the glass coming upward, almost in slow motion. My mind's eye showed me Bud's finger pressed against my lips, a voice reminding me that maybe I was about to wash something vile down my innards.

The split second passed and I downed my drink, saying the hell with such worries, making it as just another toast to the medical profession.

• • •

Having wasted enough time, I decided to leave the bar and get down to the business of looking for Sterling. Circumstances forced me to slow down, however. Before I could desert my post the lights notched down lower everywhere in the club except on the dining room stage. I threw Moustache a hand signal which he interpreted correctly, practically tossing me a second Gilbey's. Taking a short draw, I moved to the archway to see what was passing for entertainment these days in places like the Ostrich.

"These days" apparently called for torch singers. The piano introduction accompanying the slow-moving figure's approach to the stage would have given it away, even if the costume hadn't. She was tall, almost too tall, too willowy, too perfect. Almost everything about her was too perfect. She was a cross between the most recent scarecrow, lesbian-overtoned fashion ads, and an old black-and-white three-hankie matinee queen. She looked like a young Bette Davis, or maybe Garland, jerked forward out of time and given that certain, today hairstyle, and outfit, and pair of heels, to make her just the kind of vulnerable bitch goddess that would appeal to this great new world in which we live.

Her head down, she held herself until the beat came around, and then whispered sadly into the microphone, stirring all the hot souls around her with a voice as soft as cat's fur and as damning as prints on a bloody knife. She wailed her tune quietly, and the only thing I could think to do while she was on stage was listen.

You didn't have to be so cruel;
You didn't have to eat and run;
When you dined on my heart, you got the best part,
And you sucked on the bones just for fun.

I didn't mean to be a fool;
I didn't mean to lay myself bare;
But when you arrived, common sense took a dive,
And my head took you on for a dare.

Do you get your kicks from wrecking hearts
On the rocky shore of your soul?
Do you savor the error of inflicting terror
On someone who sees you as love's goal?

As she went back into the chorus, I wondered if the management made it their policy to turn up the air conditioning during her act, or if it was just me. I noticed I had stopped sweating, had taken on a chill to match the one in the singer's voice. Maybe it was the gin, or the fact she didn't move while she sang, just stood before the mike as if she were chained to it, using her hands in a defensive way that suggested there was pain in just letting out the words of her song. Maybe I was only remembering how many times a week I felt the same way, or wondering how many times I'd given others reason to—just like anyone else in the audience.

Gasping out the chorus, she beat at us with the rest of it.

You didn't have to work too hard
To prove me undeniably weak—
That up against your style, and your
      snakecharmer's smile,
I'd have to lie down in defeat.

I'll admit I'm fair and easy game,
And half of the blame is my own;
But when you think you're in love,
      you welcome each shove,
As the price of not being along.

I didn't want to ache again,
I guess I should have kept my cool.
My excuses are lame,
And I'm greatly ashamed
Of even playing your game . . .
But you didn't have . . . to be . . . sooooo cruel.

By the time she was done, half the audience was crying, the other half was ordering more drinks. I was in the latter half, but not by much. Moustache had already splashed a clean glass for me. I traded in my empty, tossing another handful of singles on the bar to keep it company. The applause began to die down as I knocked back the top half.

Somewhere in the ceiling the lights changed and the second number started. I decided not to watch. I had come on business. As I waved a last toast toward the stage, though, I finally stopped looking at the image and noticed the singer wasn't as "she" as she appeared. Oh well, I thought, that's show biz. If it didn't matter to the guys in the three-piece suits throwing roses onto the stage, it didn't matter to me.

Deciding it was time to stop drinking up Miller's money and start doing what he'd asked, I opted for the direct approach and just asked Moustache if the boss was in.

"Ralphie . . . ?"

"No. Bill Sterling."

"Mr. Sterling; no, sir. I doubt he'd be in this early."

I wondered at what kind of life style it was that considered eleven-thirty "early." I must have let it show. Moustache told me to wait and then went over to a phone at the back of the bar. He talked to someone for a moment, looked back at me, and then rattled off a little more. Whether he was describing me to Sterling or someone else, I couldn't tell. He was too young; his face hadn't yet developed to where you could read the lies clearly. He asked in a loud whisper,

"Can I ask your name, please, sir?" He was young, all right. I told him,

"Jack Hagee. I called earlier, but I haven't been able to get through to him."

I studiously ignored him as he talked further to the phone, pretending to be engrossed in the singer's rendition of "It Had To Be You." Moustache finally hung up, but was called to mix a few more drinks before he could get back to me. Once he did, though, he said,

"I'm sorry, sir. Ralphie says he's still out. He remembers you calling earlier today, but he's afraid he really doesn't know where Mr. Sterling is."

I smiled my biggest of-course-I-believe-all-of-this-nonsense smile, shrugged my shoulders, and "oh welled" my way off toward the bathrooms. Hoping Moustache thought little enough of me to buy my routine and forget about me in favor of his other customers, I moved through the darkened room slowly, watching the movements of those around me. I figured the archway the couples were disappearing through was not the way I wanted to go. Walking around the fringe of the dining room in the other direction, I let my eyes play in all directions, looking for anything that might tip me off to where Sterling's office might be. Nothing made itself apparent.

From what Ballard had told me, Sterling wasn't a homosexual. Of course, all that meant was that he hadn't been one in Plainton. People have been known to change after moving to New York.

Actually, the city takes a lot of heat for that rap, which it really doesn't deserve. People don't get changed by New York as much as they simply grow comfortable with what they really are after they get here and find out the busybodies behind all the next doors aren't watching that closely anymore.

Thinking about that made me wonder what kinds of things Mara might have started getting comfortable with since her arrival. Somehow I didn't get the picture of her big orchid blues filling with tears over all the trouble she'd been causing. That would make things too easy.

Ignoring such distractions, though, I continued looking for Sterling. I'd given everyone I'd seen so far a casual once-over; no one was looking much like the high-school snapper Hubert'd delivered. Having finally made my way around to the side of the dining room where the restrooms were, I continued watching the singer, using him as a cover to ignore the signs pointing back behind the curtains. I spotted another doorway back toward the corner. Since it was the only thing that had even a chance of keeping my trip from being a total waste, I decided to check it out. Applauding and smiling when everyone else did, I worked my way back to the door. As I got closer, I could see its wood veneer was chipped at the bottom revealing a flat metal surface underneath. Steel reinforcements—a good sign—if it wasn't an office, it would do until one came along. I reached for the knob, but a hand came to rest on the panel in front of me before I could turn it. A rat-faced boy decked out in a silky, raglike affair whined sharply over the noise of the crowd.

"Where you into, flake?"

"Just looking for the bathroom." I smiled to show I meant it.

Half-believing me, he pointed back over my shoulder, brushing my jacket as he did. "That way, white shorts."

I turned to look behind me, "noticed" the sign I'd spent so much time carefully working my way past before, and then thanked him ever so much for his help, wondering which crack he'd crawled out of. He grinned after me like a sick dog, talking to my back.

"That's ace, flake. Don't get raped."

I smiled again, with a bit more difficulty, and headed back in the direction of Ratty's still outstretched finger. Sighing to myself, I walked straight to the men's room and went in. Since Sterling's policies seemed to not make his office any more accessible than himself, I decided to just use the facilities and head back down to my own office. I wanted to run all my bits and pieces past Hubert and see if any of it added up differently for him. I was standing in front of one of the open urinals, debating whether to put Hu on looking for Miller or Sterling, when the door opened behind me.

I didn't think anything of it, and just kept working the excess out of my system. I certainly wasn't looking for any trouble; nothing I'd been up to recently had cued me to looking for any where I was. Big mistake.

I heard a noise like trouble, but before I could do anything about it, something smooth and hard crashed down between my shoulder blades, knocking me forward into the smooth stone of the upper wall. My hands flew up a little too late to catch me. My face hit the glazed granite at an angle—flat on and painfully. The pain struck again—left side below the

ribs—then again—abdominal hit—stunningly hard. Before
I could turn, my left leg was hooked out from under me. I
went down in a tangle, slamming my chin on the top of the
urinal, soaking myself with my own arching spray all the
way to the floor.

I curled around defensively as I hit, trying to angle around
for a look at what was happening. The thug standing over
me loomed up like Godzilla to my Tokyo. I could see Ratty
in the background, shoving a spectator out of the room. I
tried to crane my head to look up but it didn't feel like
moving. My vision blurred from the effort as tears forced
themselves loose. With the side of my dripping face
helplessly plastered to the floor, all I could tell about my pal
was that he kept his shoes well-polished.

The shiny shoes each took a step forward. Something
blurred above them, and suddenly my shoulder screamed at
me as I shut my eyes, biting down, trying to ignore the pain
and the blood squishing through my mouth. I couldn't.
Stabs of torment rolled through me until I couldn't tell just
where each blow was landing. Godzilla stepped back when
I started throwing up on myself, worried about his shine. He
couldn't have been worried about me getting away. I wasn't
going anywhere. Bits of steaming food lay in a puddle on
the floor before my face, pooling further away from me each
time I hacked a little bit more of my guts out. My playmate
whispered,

"Your type is always so fuckin' stupid."

I nodded weakly. The man was right. I lay on the floor
wondering how many of my bones were broken and how
many only felt that way. Spasms began to shake me. I didn't
bother trying to rein any of it in. The worse I looked, the
longer 'Zilla would wait before he started in on me again. I
must have looked pretty bad; nothing else fell out of the sky
for a while except words. While Ratty kept shooing patrons
away from the door, 'Zilla shared some fatherly advice with
me.

"Now—you wise it straight. Leave Mr. Sterling alone—
leave his place alone. Leave Mara alone; leave Carl Miller
alone; leave it all alone. I'll tell you why. If you do, then I'll

be happier; you'll be happier; Mr. Sterling'll be happier—
get it? We'll all be happier.''

He nudged me with his foot, just hard enough to catch
my attention and assure me that he was still in charge.
"Right?"

"Yeah," I sputtered weakly. "I'm just dying of happiness."

"Good." He leaned for a minute on a thick ebony cane,
the one matching the soon-to-be yellow and purple blotches
up and down my body. With my vision clearing slightly, I
found I could turn my head with the sensation of only
grapefruit-sized rocks being dropped on it. I dragged myself
slightly upright, only causing myself to transfer the little bit
of fluid which had stayed in my stomach to the front of my
shirt. A ragged break in my lip opened wider as my
coughing renewed, blood leaking down my chin to drip onto
my chest. I wanted to stand but knew I couldn't.

"So," asked 'Zilla. "Any questions?" I nodded. He
asked, "Like what?"

"What's your name?"

Surprise registered for a full second, after which he told
me, "You don't want to know that." Pulling together what
little strength I had left, I said,

"Yeah. Sure I do."

He smiled at me, and then suddenly he was no longer
leaning on the cane. Before I could react, it slammed into
the side of my face, knocking my head backwards into the
baked enamel metal partition to which I was plastered. My
eyes welled over—tired, stinging—flowing freely. All I
could see was a long, tired gray metal plane covered with
throbbing stars. Through the exploding darkness a voice
asked me,

"Now . . . what did you want to know?"

Answering against the tide of blood and thickening spittle
pooling in my mouth, I told him, "Your name."

Hands reached down. They dragged my head forward by
the hair and then suddenly snapped it back against the
partition. Twice more I was thudded against the coated steel
until a small flurry of paint chips and hidden rust loosened

by my head began swirling in front of my swollen eyes. I was told,

"That's something I don't think you really want to know."

"No. Honest," I croaked, my voice thick with the gurgling choke of semi-fluids trapped in my throat. "It is. You know, maybe I'll . . . a drink, maybe. Call you for a party—something . . ."

And then, suddenly, 'Zilla looked at me in a way I could see even Ratty didn't like. An unspoken understanding passed between them; Ratty started to say something, but 'Zilla cut him off with a hand motion that apparently meant something to them both. Ratty quieted; my playmate asked, "So you want to know my name, huh?"

I nodded again. Every square inch of my skin screamed in anticipation of the pain 'Zilla had taught it came with defiance.

"Could you write it down?"

'Zilla went through his pockets wearing an amused look. Turning several of them inside out, he finally reported, "Not a scrap of paper."

"Damn." I sighed, the noise forcing me to cough more bloody phlegm. "Guess I'll just have to try and remember it."

The cane struck once more. "I guess you will." My face rang off the wall again, and then a fifth time, then a sixth. The cane crashed against my leg, making the pain scream through me, cutting shrilly, the way the phone does at three in the morning when you don't want to wake up. It was a flashing, wrenching, hateful kind of pain, one that came three more times as 'Zilla said:

"My name . . ."—head pain—"my name is Jeff . . ." —leg pain—"Jeff Anthony," the third blast of pain a slash that tore through me from my legs to my eyes, ending as the sick throb of some guy dry-heaving whom I was sure I'd met in a mirror earlier in the day.

"Jeffrey Anthony. Think you can remember that?"

I curled on the white tile hurting and crying and bleeding, sputtering blood bits of drool over the floor and myself, thinking over and over and over, Jeff . . . Jeff Anthony . . . Jeffrey Anthony, knowing that—yeah, sure—I could remember that.

Long after the laughter had stopped, long after the pain of being dragged quickly out of the room and out of the restaurant, I was still remembering. I closed my eyes while I was pulled through the kitchen and stuffed out in the alley with the rest of the trash. That would have been too much to watch; I didn't want to see it.

Luckily, I passed fairly quickly into that state where I didn't have to see anything.

# CHAPTER 13

I WOKE UP in a sewer; I could tell from the smell. My eyes were taped shut—my guts kicked out. I hurt like a run-over dog, not able to see or hear anything except blackness and a dull, echoing throb. I stayed brick-still and quiet after my first attempt to roll over sent a jolt up my spine that told me I'd already found the most comfortable position in the world—no matter how much it hurt.

The sewer caved in on me suddenly. Mud and slime sludged over my body; broken pipes and rushing water battering, magnifying all my pains a dozen times over. I screamed, shouting at the top of my lungs, not caring about the rush of garbage washing into my mouth and down my throat. Not caring who might hear me. I screamed out of animal hurt—as loud as I could. Then, I caught my breath in drowning bubbles and did it again.

Rats bit at me, tearing at my shoulders, biting my eyes out and swallowing them. I couldn't even feel it. Minor sufferings like those had to take a ticket and get in line. I barely noticed them. Then, abruptly, the mud and garbage faded away. The sewer was a hospital; the odor was disinfectant. The rats were Bud's hands on my shoulders, shaking me gently.

"Jack—wake up."

"I'm awake," I told him. "I'm awake. I don't like it much, but I'm awake."

He released my shoulders, stepping back. The smile on his face grew from one ear to the other as he told me, "Glad to see you're alive."

"Yeah," I croaked, my voice a mix of dry cracks and pain, "me, too."

"God, no offense, but you sound terrible."

"How do I look?"

"Huummmmmmmm . . ." I knew if he had to think about it the answer had to be pretty bad. "Let's just say that if you look like this every morning, you're going to have a very tough time finding anyone to share a life with you."

I went to make a snappy response but my throat didn't think it was worth it. Neither did Bud. He told me to be quiet, then said he'd go and find the doctor to see when I could be released. Ten years felt about right.

My brain hurt with questions while I waited. Who'd found me—brought me to the hospital? Bud? How many of my bones were broken? What day was it? And, why in hell had Mr. Jeff Anthony trashed me?

I hadn't asked Bud anything, simply because it hurt too much to talk. I figured someone would fill me in later. In the meantime, I tried to take in my surroundings. It looked as if I was in a hallway off an emergency room. I couldn't have been there too long if they hadn't found me a room yet. Feeling beneath me, I realized I was on a gurney; they hadn't even found me a bed yet. Oh well, I thought, it was better than a chair.

Across the hall from me, a blond girl was sleeping with her head against the wall. Blood was dripping from somewhere under her hair, streaking its way down the porcelain. Next to her sat a cop's wife—had to be. She had a cop's hat in her lap, a pair of glasses folded neatly inside, a stub of green pencil fast in the leather hatband. She had a roll of paper towels under her arm and a look on her face that showed she'd stopped his bleeding on other occasions. She was resigned to whatever was going to happen—afraid of it as well.

I looked away. My own pain was enough to concentrate on. Out in the center of the room, a mixed pair of cops and a young male orderly were fussing over a John Doe. From what I could hear of their conversation I gathered the old

man had passed out in front of a restaurant and fallen
through the front plate-glass window. Now the orderly
wanted to cut his crusted clothing away so they could find
the source of the bleeding soaking through his rags and
trickling down his feet, but Street Boy wasn't about to let
them.

"No, sir; no. No, sir. No. Little white fucka wans mys
money. Little doctor shit hungry for all'da quatas, all'da
pennies. No, sir. No, sir. Mys money. I keeps mys money."

The lady cop tried to bribe the old drunk with a sandwich.

"Come on now, old-timer. Take it easy. No one wants
your money. It's yours. Here; wouldn't you like this
sandwich? Let's get rid of these clothes, and we'll feed you,
and take care of you, and get you a new set of clothes.
Okay?"

"Fuck you, bitch," the old black man snapped. "Whore.
You just wants mys money. I knows. I seed it all inna
dream."

Tired of the uselessness of the situation, the orderly told
the officers to hold Street Boy down and began snipping his
way through the layers of rags he had draped about himself.
Once he did, though, several dozen cockroaches spilled out
of the wino's clothing, zipping off in all directions, several
running across the sandwich and up the lady officer's arm.
She screeched in surprise. The sandwich flew away.

Flinging roaches in all directions, the female officer
stepped on the ones she could while cursing them all.
Disgusted, the orderly and the other cop strapped Street Boy
in his wheelchair and moved him out of the room. Most of
us ignored his screams, turning to watch the body of cops
who'd suddenly entered the room. They were ushering in
several more bleeding people—some of them in tears, some
in handcuffs.

Another John Doe sitting against the far wall ignored the
new show, though, laughing as his comrade was wheeled
away. Stumbling down from his chair, he hit the floor with
a thud but pushed himself back up to his feet, staggering the
few yards to where the various parts of the bribe sandwich

had fallen. Scooping it up with bits of floor soot and a few of Street Boy's roaches, he wolfed it all down, still laughing, spitting bits of white bread about the room. Wads of it landed on a kid holding his bleeding groin. The kid was obviously underage, which meant they were waiting for the proper release forms before working on him. Which meant he got to sit and wait in pain, muttering in agony with his life soaking through his fingers until someone could be found to give legal consent to work on him.

That was all I could look at. Deciding to give up on the passing parade, I stared at the ceiling, counting the little squares and circles which made up its fading pattern. I'd found 483 when Bud returned with a young but friendly looking hospital employee who turned out to be my doctor. While he looked over some papers that'd been stuffed under my pillow, he asked,

"Mr. Jack Hagee—right?" I nodded. "Well, Mr. Hagee, you may be surprised to learn you can get out of here soon." I looked at him as if he'd grown another head. He continued.

"You probably don't remember earlier when your friend brought you in. We've already done a battery of X-rays; no, we don't need your permission to take X-rays. The results were quite good. You have bones as thick around as kitchen plumbing—did you know that?—just as durable, too, apparently. We found a hairline fracture in your left wrist, but nothing else. It seems you passed out from exhaustion and pain responses, but not from a concussion, which is, of course, quite good."

"Yeah," I said. "Why? What's the difference?"

"The difference is that this is not television or some cheap novel. In real life when people get hit over the back of the head and they pass out, they do so because their brain has been denied oxygen. Denying the brain oxygen is just the nice way of saying brain damage. It's why fighters who go down too often talk as if their connections are scrambled. You took some nice punishment along the left jaw line but nothing dangerous."

The doc stepped back, folding his arms over his chest.

"So, I'll make you a deal. I'll set your wrist and write you up as a simple emergency room visit. I'll fox the papers for your insurance company so they take the fall for your tab—if you get yourself out of here in the next hour."

Not liking to needlessly spend money any more than the next guy, I liked the idea. Not trusting doctors any more than the next guy, though, I was a bit suspicious. I asked what was behind his generosity. He told me.

"Three reasons. One, I can use the bed you're slated for for somebody else. Look around you. I could use the gurney you're on for somebody else. Two, you just got beaten by someone who apparently had quite a lesson they wanted to teach you. One lesson that brutal a day is enough. You don't need a crash course in the high costs of modern hospital care as well. And, three, your wallet says you're a private detective. Let me tell you, all I do is listen all day long to people scream and cry and groan and beg poor. I think it would be a novel experience to set a tough guy's fractured wrist while he told me about getting beaten to a pulp in a back alley."

I gave him the second-head look again. He explained.

"Let's just say I'm bored with television. I'd like something good and violent—but at a safe distance—in my life. So, I patch you up, you tell me your story of New York City woe. I bill your insurance company in a way that lets you off the paying end, and you use some of what you save to buy me a Bloody Mary some night when you have more fun stories to tell me.

"That way I have some fun, I get an empty gurney and a free room faster than anyone expected, and I look good in the end-of-the-month reviews for keeping a well-oiled, fast moving, happy, happy ship." Folding up the papers he'd taken from under my pillow, he threw them in a nearby trash basket and then stuck his hand out to me, asking, "Deal?"

I shook his hand, laughing as much as I could at the same time. "Deal," I told him.

Using his hand as a brace, I slipped my legs over the edge

of the gurney—surprised when they almost didn't hold me—surprised that they could. As the doc, with Bud's help, walked me down the hall toward his office, he asked,

"My. My God, but you are big. Any more at home like you who might want to go out dancing with a doctor?"

That got me to chuckle. Groaning in mock horror, I rolled my eyes and answered, "Oh Lord, save me. I'm in the clutches of a big city homo. Oh, me—what shall I do?"

"First thing you can do," he joked back, "is drop the outmoded references. They don't call us 'homos' anymore."

"No?"

"No. Honestly, don't you read the papers? We're Godless, diseased, damned, child-molesting scum who ought to be taken out and stoned."

"Oh yeah," I admitted, recalling the famed impartiality of the modern American press. "I heard that. I just forgot."

"I know. It's part of what makes you so likable."

Bud spoke up in equally mock offense.

"I don't like you, Jack. You were just using me last night, weren't you? Just a big Sam Hammer, toying with my affections."

"Sorry about that."

"Oh, sure, that's all right," he answered, his voice filled with exaggerated pain. "After Bill sets your wrist, he can do my heart."

"Now, Bud . . ." the doctor said.

"You two know each other?" I asked.

"I guess it shows, eh?" replied the doc.

At that point we arrived at his office. By the time I collapsed into a chair, I could feel every bruise and welt and broken piece of skin with which Jeff Anthony had left me. It was wide-eyed pain, the kind of hurting that keeps your mind on only two things—how much you hurt and why. The first was beginning to die down, but the second was getting stronger. I could feel my wind coming back slowly, by the thimbleful. Eventually there would be enough of it to allow me to go out and show Jeff Anthony how much I'd enjoyed our last chat. Right now, though, the best I could do was sit up straight and talk with the little doc and Bud.

The doctor's name was William Norman, but I couldn't help calling him Doc. He looked too young, too carefree to be a full-fledged candidate for malpractice. While I continued to work through my pain, we all swapped stories of what brought us to New York in the first place. Bud's was easy—he was born here. Mine was a need to get away from a townful of memories after a short, messy marriage and a quick, ugly divorce. The doc's was a desire to escape the condemning eyes and tongues of a family of farmers who didn't understand his choice in singles bars.

He'd come to the city at age nineteen and put himself through medical school with little more than odd jobs, coffee, and determination to keep him going. He and Bud were okay guys—I liked them. Hell, they were a lot less depressing than most of my friends.

It wasn't long before he was ready to put the finishing touches to the cast on my wrist.

"All right, now," the doc said. "Hold that wrist nice and straight now."

"After all," minced Bud exaggeratedly for effect. "You wouldn't want to end up looking like one of us."

I laughed in spite of the pain. Wearing an expression of mock hurt, Bud continued,

"Sigh. I just try to help and he laughs at me."

"Bud," said the little doc with a weary tone, "leave the nice man alone."

"Sure, watch a guy get dumped in an alley, drag him to a hospital at great personal risk, miss a fabulous party . . ."

"You got me here?" I asked. Bud just smiled. "Thank you. I was wondering."

"Quite all right—but please, no applause." Standing with a flourish, Bud finished, "And sadly, I must make my farewell. The big city beckons and, weak spirit that I am, I must answer its call. Adieu, adieu."

I laughed. So did the little doc. Hoping I was catching him at a good moment, I asked for a favor.

"Hey, Doc. You got a scalpel in here?" When he answered in the affirmative, but with a question in his voice, I told him, "I just got an idea." Pointing to the cast, I asked, "Do you think you could layer one inside this thing?"

"What?" The little doc was more than a little shocked.

"Just finish whatever you have to do to make this thing work, and then put some extra plaster over the scalpel so I can walk around with an little extra protection until I get rid of the cast."

"Mind if I ask why?"

I told him the story of Jeff Anthony. I told him about the caning I'd taken, and the lack of reason for it. I told him about having to go back to Sterling's to clear the whole mess up once and for all. He did what I asked without hesitation. I thanked him.

"Forget it." Magic Marker in hand, he told me, "Listen; all you have to do is tap this thing against something hard, right here where I've drawn this dot. That'll release the scalpel without breaking the blade. Hopefully."

"What does 'hopefully' mean?"

"It means that I've never done anything this crazy before, and so I don't know if it will work. But, hopefully, if you need it, it will. Understand?"

"Gotcha."

After that I asked if I could make a call. The doc shoved his phone across the desk. Ringing Hubert, I told him where he could find my car and asked him to pick me up. Somewhere in the middle of a string of inane chatter he said "sure," and told me he would be out in front of the hospital in half an hour. I didn't bother to ask what he would use for keys—it would've just insulted him.

While we waited, the doc and I talked about more routine stuff, my job and his. He gave me a few pills to take. I didn't ask what was in them; he didn't tell me. After a while, he walked me down to the front door, half just wanting to talk, half measuring the effect of his painkillers. The conversation was good—the pills were better. If I was walking on my own, I knew they were strong. He slipped half a bottle of them into my jacket pocket with a finger to his lips. I got the message. Thanking him for everything, I promised him a night of drinks whenever I came in to get my cast off.

Then, much as the little doc hated to admit it, he had to get back to work. I shuffled out through the doors toward Hu and my car. I had to get back to work, too.

# CHAPTER 14

THE FIRST PLACE I had Hu take me was Tony's so I could shake the aroma of back alleys and hospitals. My locker had just enough clean clothing left in it to complement a shower and shave. After a hot-water dousing and another pill, I almost felt human again.

While I was showering, Hu made a few calls looking for information about the Ostrich. It turned out the place had picked up quite a reputation as a bop joint recently, with more than one guy finding himself in the same alley I had with the same stars dancing in front of him.

None of them had pressed any charges, which only indicated that they had probably been up to something inside that they didn't want lawyers fighting over in court, let along showing up on the front page of the *Post*.

Storing that information, I called Ray, discovering that his sweep had been successful—they'd brought Miller in a few hours earlier. When he'd returned to his hotel in the early hours of the dawn, he'd been as plastered as a stucco bungalow. The only answers he'd given the cops so far had been snores. I told Ray I would be right over to see my client. He let me know that was just the thing he was waiting for to make his day complete.

On the way over I stopped at the bank to finally deposit Miller's check. The way New York banks are run, with luck it might clear before my fiftieth birthday. While I was there I withdrew enough from my savings to pay Ray what I owed him and give myself a little coasting money as well.

It was ten thirty by the time we got to the station house.

Miller was awake and talking with Ray. Officer Mooney greeted us as we came in with all of his usual charm.

"Hey, Jack," he said, pointing toward my face. "I like this new look. It really suits you. Wish I'd been there to help you select it."

"Keep off my back, you pock-faced mick, or so help me I'll rip off your head and spit down your throat just to hear the splash."

Mooney laughed.

"Charming as ever, aren't you?" He walked us back to the interrogation room where we could find his captain and my client. His hand swept to point first at Miller, and then at Hubert and me. Keeping his voice light and happy, he said,

"I sure don't know what we poor, dumb ratheads around here do to deserve such high-class visitors like your clients and your friends, and of course, you yourself."

I couldn't say much. I looked like hell, but Miller looked like death warmed over twice and burnt once. The life was out of him. I could tell by the way he was clumped in his chair he wasn't going to be trouble for anyone anymore. Ray took me aside.

"Take him home. Take yourself home. Clean up the both of you."

"You clearing him on the George killing?"

"For now." Ray shrugged. "Keep him around but, between you and me and the walls, in my opinion this guy never killed anybody." When I just stared, Ray explained.

"I was there when he got the news about George. His reaction seemed on the money. He didn't look to know anything about the shooting. He admitted right away that he owned a Saur. Claimed it got stolen from him a few months back. I checked it out with his home town blues—they confirmed. He reported the bulk of his collection raked a while back. Their report makes it look pretty clean for Sad Sack there."

The lab hadn't found any prints on the shell recovered the night before from the roof. Ideally that would have made it easier to hold Miller, but Ray didn't feel like bothering. His

instincts were telling him what mine had already suggested—
that the Dumptruck wasn't a killer—that he wasn't much of
anything, really, except a nuisance.

What I did wonder at was Ray's lack of emotion. Usually
losing a prime suspect puts him in a worse mood than the
one I was witnessing. He explained it.

"Who could get mad? This guy is too depressing. Do me
a favor, get him out of here. Get him sober and explain
things to him. Make him give it up and go home."

"Didn't you try?"

Ray just looked at me, a bleak, soulless stare which
would have upset me if I didn't understand where it had
come from. Shifting past belligerence, I told Ray,

"Yeah, I know. I won't make any promises I can't keep,
but I'll try and get him straightened out."

Ray and I went back to where Mooney and Hubert were
taunting each other while Miller waited in hungover silence.
By the time we broke it up, Hubert'd already reached the
point where he was dancing around the office, picking up
paperclips and throwing them at Mooney, dragging his
gimpy leg behind him. The big cop used a lot more restraint
in dealing with Hu than with me—which made sense. The
police department needed him a lot more than they did me.

"Good thing you came back for your monkey, Jack. I
was getting ready to tie a firecracker to his tail."

"F-fat chance," laughed Hu. "Tyin' knots takes an
opposin' thumb. Somethin' you lower species haven't developed yet."

"Shut up, you exhaust fume," growled Ray. Turning to
me, and indicating Miller, he snapped, "Get this mental
case out of here. Either clean up his act, or get him out of
town."

"Good advice," added Mooney. "Take it yourself, Jack.
Either way it would make for a nicer city."

"When I want to do my part toward making New York a
nicer city, I'll suggest they stop pinning badges on sacks of
shit. Granted, that'll raise the Irish unemployment level by
two hundred percent, but . . ."

I let it trail off. Mooney and I were at our usual draw,

already turning our backs on each other to get back to business. A lot of people around the station house keep waiting for the two of us to start swinging at each other. We haven't yet, but a number of guys feel it's only a matter of time. Mooney's one of them. I'm another.

Once Hubert and I got Miller outside, we walked him to my car, hoping he would start responding to some sort of stimuli soon. He seemed vacant, as if nothing else mattered anymore. I wasn't as sure he was innocent as Ray was; I've seen a lot of drunks lie through their teeth with perfect conviction. Until he was sober, there'd be no way to tell anything for sure.

Hubert wanted to tag along, but I told him to flag a taxi. My only plans were to sack Miller out at his hotel and then head off for a nap myself. Hu nodded, saying,

"All right, b-but keep me posted. Okay? I'm sure interested in how this one is going to p-print."

Yeah, I thought, so were a lot of people. Once Hubert caught his cab, I loaded Miller into the back seat of my Skylark. Breezing back downtown to his hotel, I parked in the space reserved in the back for their kitchen deliveries. Slipping the dishwasher a deuce made sure that wouldn't cause any problems. I managed to propel my client inside and upstairs to his room without turning too many heads. Getting his key from him, I aimed him through the door and then toppled him onto his bed, loosening some of his clothes so he could get some air.

He lay where he struck without moving, only his sagging chest and gut moving up and down in time to his deeply liquored breathing. I watched the fat sliding back and forth, wondering just what kind of game was going on around me. Why had George been killed? Was he even the target, and if so—whose? And if he wasn't, then who was? Byler, Cerelli . . . me?

I sat in the room's soft chair, letting myself relax. Getting off my feet relieved the pressure on a number of my aches. I tuned out the bubbling snores coming from Miller along with the stale, dusty odor of old beer and urine that permeated the million-year-old room. I'd flopped in places like it enough times to know how to ignore the weak lighting and the roaches and the death smell of age that runs through all of them. The rat scream of the bed springs next door faded with the rest, leaving me alone with my thoughts and my pain.

My facts were few and non-matching; they held no patterns. Which only meant I didn't have enough of them yet. Looking at the cast on my wrist, I knew where I was going to have to go to gather some more of them. I would have already headed there but for the heat and the aches dragging at my every step and movement. It was getting close to noon; sweat was washing my forehead, streaking my face. Heaving my way up out of the chair with a grunt, I pulled my hat off to use as a fan. Outside it was great protection from the sun; inside it was only an annoying sweat trap.

Taking a last look at the Dumptruck, I gave up the notion of waiting for him to wake up anytime soon. Using the little notepad I keep in my jacket, I scribbled a message for him to call me, tore the sheet free, then wrapped it around his room key and left it on the night stand. Setting the door to lock, I pulled it shut behind me. I tried the knob to make sure it stayed closed—proved it would under any normal conditions—and then headed for the elevator. I had a few things to attend to while Miller slept.

# CHAPTER 15

THE ANSWERING MACHINE was glowing when I got back to the office. The caller turned out to be Jean Ward. She wanted to come and see me. There was fear in the back of her throat, the kind with sharp claws that can't even entertain the thought of letting go of its victim. I called her back at the number she'd left. She answered on the second ring—quickly—as if she had her hand over the phone the whole time but'd waited for the first ring to pass for the sake of appearances. When she found I was back in my office, she begged me to stay, saying she could get to me in fifteen minutes—twenty tops. I told her I'd wait. She cut the connection before I could finish my sentence.

Sick of wiping at my sweat, I opened my non-bullet-shattered windows, turned on my fan, and then sat back in my hardwood chair, feeling the slats burn into my bruises. I thought about having a shot but decided against it. Having squirmed my way into an almost comfortable position I was loath to lose it. Besides, I wanted to think, and the pain running through me was distraction enough.

Sweat continued to bead on my face, arms, chest, everywhere. Every few seconds it would chill over as the fan's breath swept past me, not moving while the air brushed it—waiting for its chance to start dripping again. Running over the facts, I found they hadn't changed much since I'd sat with Miller. Ray wanted me to earn my fee by cleaning up the Dumptruck and slapping him on the next Amtrak to Plainton. A day ago, I would have agreed. But that was before someone had pumped a heavy round through my office and one of my guests. That was before

Jeff Anthony shattered a few of my personal illusions—along with my wrist.

It was obvious that something was going on I couldn't see—something that couldn't be read in the tea leaves available. It wasn't large—the security of nations wasn't involved—but it was dirty and it stank, and the poor slob it had in its clutches had come to me for help. I might not have taken his money for the best of reasons, but I'd taken it. Now that mistake had bounced the poor slob in and out of jail, and killed a man, and taught me that in New York you can't turn your back on people even in the crapper.

The knock came eighteen minutes after the call, bringing Jean Ward back into my life. I'd wondered if I'd be seeing her again. She came in in a rush, less cool than the last time, more loose fear and nerve endings in evidence. Her body showed it as she crossed the room—her eyes confirming—she was scared. Something more had happened—something that had pushed the hardness in her eyes to the side for the time being, replacing it with an honest glance inscribed with the pleading sincerity of children and beggars.

She took the same chair she had the day before, skipping right over the "hellos."

"Oh, Jack. What are we going to do?"

"About what?"

"About Carl. About lunatic Carl. I'm so scared. I don't know what to do. I'm not sure what's safe and what isn't anymore."

"Maybe you could fill me in on what you're talking about."

She stared up at me and then she noticed some of what'd happened to me since the last time we'd been together. The yellowing purple of my face and neck was more than what one might call noticeable. She gasped out loud, sitting back in her chair as if trying to put more distance between us.

"Oh," she cried. "He was here, too."

"Miller? You think he did this to me?"

I was actually a little insulted, but I pretended to be a grownup and let it pass. Truthfully, if it had been Miller who'd snuck up on me, he'd probably have been able to pull

off my lumping as easily as my buddy Jeff. That's why
people attack from behind in the first place. When Ward
nodded that she did indeed think the Dumptruck was my
assailant, I told her,

"Nope. Right case—wrong maniac. But what makes you
think Miller's ready to start getting physical with people?"

She started to speak, but then bit the words back, letting
only a slight sound escape. Whatever she was going to blurt
out got reeled back in and hidden away. Getting hold of
herself, she started again.

"Carl . . . came to my place last night. He'd been—
he'd had—ah . . ."

"He was drunk," I finished for her.

"Yes."

She cut the word off sharply, giving it a bitter sound.

"Yes, he was drunk. Drunk enough to talk about getting
rid of anyone in his way . . . to rant all over again about
'killing his enemies.' Drunk enough to do this."

Reaching up to the open collar of her blouse, she pulled
the neckline to the left, revealing a large bruise on her
shoulder. It was a black, ugly welt, one that didn't go well
against her Dresden skin. She showed it for only a second,
but it was enough. I got the idea. I was tired of people
getting hurt because of Miller, especially since most of them
seemed to be getting hurt by Miller.

Ward's recollection of her conversation with the Dumptruck and the time it took place gave some strength to the
argument that Miller's finger might have been the one on
the trigger that blew George's life out through the back of
one of my chairs. Ray was fairly sure the fat moke was
innocent, but Ray isn't always right about everything.
Neither am I, but I had to start somewhere. While Ward
straightened her blouse she noted my cardboard-covered
window and my broken chair. Desperate to change the
subject, she asked what happened. I told her.

She took the news badly. The tears that'd been looking
for an excuse decided they had one. Even after she collected
herself enough to talk, they still kept rolling.

"Oh, poor Fred. Oh, God—I mean, it isn't that we were

close or anything, but . . . it's just that he was such a . . . well, decent man. He was a thinker, a logical person. It just isn't fair—not Fred.''

I was surprised. If someone had told me about Ward's performance, I might have thought it was a cover-up. I'd begun to think of her as not capable of such emotions. But it was real. Why she felt so badly about George's death I couldn't tell. I knew Byler's wouldn't have upset her nearly that much. When she finally got hold of herself and dried away the last of the water dribbling down her cheeks, she checked her face in a small pocket mirror, grimacing at the ruin the tears had made of her makeup. She didn't bother to fix it, however. Wiping the mess away with some Kleenex out of her purse, she apologized for the crying, her looks, for bothering me, and just about everything except the latest trouble in the Middle East.

Putting up my hand, I slowed her down, telling her not to worry about it. That only started the tears again. I stopped talking; there wasn't anything I could say. When I'd first met Ward I'd been hard-pressed to size her up. She'd been too varied a combination of hard and soft edges for me to pass any quick judgments. It was getting easier, though. I felt sorry for her, caught in the dirty middle of the whole sloppy mess along with Miller—or because of Miller. I still couldn't decide.

She came around the desk and put her arms around me, the tears coming long and hard. She pressed against me, her sobs racking her as she let all the grief and anger and fear out in a long, painful series of wails that might have brought the cops if my office was in a building where anyone cared about such things. I held her to me as long as she needed it, feeling the grimness of her mood coming over me as well.

I welcomed her grief, though, not trying to stop her or even calm her. Her despair was a fuel I could use, a force powerful enough to help me forget the fading pains up and down my sides and back and legs and face and arms as effectively as the little doc's drugs—a force I figured I would need soon enough.

After a while she got out of my lap and stood up shakily,

wiping at herself with the same soggy Kleenex she'd used before. There were no apologies this time. She knew they weren't necessary. I asked,

"Are you going to be all right?"

"I—I think so."

"Fine." As she sat back in the chair she'd first taken, I told her, "Here's what I want you to do. Get out of your apartment for a while. Move in with a girlfriend, or a boyfriend—go to a hotel—any place for a few days. The 'where' is not important. Just someplace where Miller can't find you. Let whoever absolutely has to know where you are know, but make sure they understand they aren't to tell anyone where that is. You're a model—a public figure— give them a number about being pursued by an overeager fan. Then call me with the phone number when you know where that place will be."

She pulled a piece of paper from the pad on my desk, scribbling with my pen.

"I know already. There's only one place I'd go—my girlfriend Barbara's."

I took the number and slipped it into my address book while she snapped her purse shut. Then I stood up, ready to walk her to the door. Looking up at me, she half-smiled.

"This crying in your office is getting to be a bad habit."

"It's okay," I told her. "Come in anytime. I'll keep some rags around."

The smile blossomed; the fascinating eyes lit up and the slightly bent nose wrinkled, and I felt the grimness inside tugging at me, whispering that it didn't like the idea of Jean Ward having to cry anymore.

I took her to the door, and watched her disappear down the stairwell, listening to the click of her heels afterward until they faded away completely into the heat. Then I went back to my desk, digging out my shoulder holster and my .38. Sliding the revolver into place, I checked the draw again unconsciously, making sure it came free as smoothly as always. It did.

That made me smile, because where I was headed I was hoping for a chance to use it. I kept smiling as I locked the door, walked down the hall, the stairs, out to the car, and drove all the way back uptown. It almost felt wrong . . . smiling . . . the feel of it, but I didn't care. The weather was worse than ever, but that didn't matter either. Sometimes even a New York summer day can't ruin your good mood.

# CHAPTER 16

I STALKED THE outside of the Blue Ostrich for close to an hour and forty-five minutes, waiting for a glimpse of Jeff Anthony. Some might call that necessary surveillance work. I called it a waste of time; he never showed. My only hope was that maybe he was already inside. I was leaning against a wall across the street from the nightclub, keeping tabs on it in the carefully studied manner of someone who couldn't possibly be watching a place because they never seem to look directly at it. It's one of the things I'm good at.

A lot of guys don't like surveillance work—especially in cars. First off, you have to own a car, and a license, and an insurance policy. It helps if you know how to drive, too. Trying to tail someone in New York City is always a picnic—one that comes with ticket-happy cops, jangled nerves, and wrecks instead of ants. I don't like tail jobs, or stakeout work much either, but I'm good at both, so like anybody with a reasonable job skill I follow the money.

Being good at standing around wasn't working this time, though, so I decided to try a more direct approach, one that involved going across the street and pushing my way into the Ostrich and seeing what kind of trouble I could cause, and what might surface because of it—something else I'm good at.

The sun had helped dismiss some of my aches. So had moving around. So had just living through the slamming that had given them to me. It wasn't as if my ol' buddy Jeffy'd done a bum job on me; he'd been efficient and thorough—like the professional I reasoned he was. It's just that you can ignore a lot if you think you have a reason. I was pretty sure I had one. Waiting for the traffic to thin, I lit a cigarette and then stepped in between the cars whizzing by, dancing my way to the other side of the street. Everyone jaywalks in New York; they only put up traffic lights for the out-of-towners.

My guess was that Sterling was one of those guys who absolutely never answered their own phone, never got their messages—who were never in no matter what time of any day it was. The kind of guy you didn't get to see without some improvisation. I tried my theory out on the guy at the front door. Putting on my best No. 3 smile, I started past him. His arm came up.

"Where you into, grief?"

"Settle your pipes; I'm here to see Sterling."

"The boss doesn't have any appointments for this afternoon."

"I don't need one—or doesn't Anthony tell the curb help anything anymore?"

My buddy's name was all the ticket I needed. I reached for the door, pushing the geek aside. He protested.

"Hey—I still gotta check."

"Check out my ass, shit-licker. All you want to check out is the air conditioning. Walk your beat and sweat it out. I've got work to do."

And that was that. Suddenly I was inside with the air conditioning and a little more information. If the Ostrich was strictly legitimate, the guy at the door would have hollered bloody murder—New Yorkers are like that. Give them a handle on any kind of self-importance and they'll worry it worse than any dog ever did any bone. But when they're not in the right, or even suspect they might not be in the right, they fold up and quiet down like paint-fingered first-graders standing next to a smear-covered wall.

No one much was in the main rooms of the club. A barman I didn't recognize was washing out some glasses; another was pouring dollar-a-gallon sludge into the Jack Daniel's bottles. If Ray ever turned gay, I could recommend the place to him. My attention, however, had to be directed toward more important things. Namely getting back to

Sterling's office, the place I'd backed down from the night before. So much for the common-sense approach of not causing any trouble in public. Now I was doing things my way.

The Ostrich was dirty; what kind of dirt and where it was piled were yet to be discovered, but it was there—the air was thick with the smell of it—it was what had garnered me the thrashing and alley dumping, ruined suit, wrist cast, and kick-myself-in-the-head-itis that'd been irritating me since I'd woke up on my slab that morning.

All I'd wanted was to find the Dumptruck's girlfriend. I hadn't cared about dope or illegal sex or gun-running to Martians or whatever the hell it was Sterling was involved in. I'm not the sheriff of Dodge City. I don't wear a suit of armor or give a damn about righting the injustices of the world. Not usually. Not until someone drags me into the middle and tells me how important they are. That tends to change things for me. Now I was going to find the Dumptruck's Mara, and I was going to bust Sterling's operation to hell and back, and maybe even Sterling, and most definitely Jeff Anthony. Just because I was mad. Just because I'd been told not to.

I made my way back to what the night before I had assumed was Sterling's office—this time with no interruptions. It was looking as if Godzilla and Ratty only worked the night shift. Well, such were the fortunes of war. Wrapping the fingers of my good hand around the doorknob, I held it lightly for a minute, sending the radar out. I could hear muffled talk coming from the other side, some laughter, possibly a television. None of the noise I could filter seemed tense—always the best time to make an entrance.

Opening the door, I stepped through quickly just in case someone was standing a guard on it—wasted effort. Everyone was over at the boss's desk, a big inlaid affair with a portable TV atop it and a guy behind it who matched the high-school photo Hubert had brought to me. Three of the city's new breed of tough-looking leather boys were watching cartoons with the boss. I recognized the Woodpecker from his laugh. Someone else was present as well, trying to compete with Woody for the big man's attention from under the mahogany, her red high heels aimed at me from underneath the desk.

Sterling took charge.

"Who are you? What's going on here?"

His eyes never left the set. As I came closer I could see he was eating a bowl of Frankenberry cereal. Stopping in front of his desk, I watched the spoon go in again, the eyes remaining glued to the Woodpecker and his antics. Dip, bite, chew, laugh. Makes a guy feel real important.

"I'd like to ask you a few questions."

"Awwww, go away, will you? I don't feel like talking to you."

"Not even about Carl Miller and his Mara?"

Dip, bite, chew, laugh.

"Why ruin a perfectly good afternoon? Go on now, take off."

Woody tricked the buzzard chasing him into running into a brick wall. Sugar-thick milk dribbled over Sterling's lips.

Dip, bite, chew, laugh.

The red heels at my feet were growing more animated. It dawned on me that Mara's black-and-white blue eyes might be at the other end of them, buried in Sterling's lap. Before I could say anything, though, the boss's hand dismissed me again, his voice laughing.

"You still here?"

Tired of the way the game worked played by his rules, I asked,

"You want to pay more attention to me than to Woody?"

"Why should I?" asked Sterling, his eyes still glued to the screen. "Are you funnier?"

"Yeah," I told him, plucking the cereal bowl from in front of him. "I'm a fucking riot."

And then, before he or his leather boys could react, I poured the remaining milk and cereal into the back of the television set. There weren't nearly as many sparks as I'd been hoping for, but there were enough. Sterling screamed and fell backwards, toppling his chair. Falsetto screeches echoed from under the desk. The boss must have kicked his playmate. Leather Number One came for me, reaching out with both hands as if I were some drunk who needed help to the street. Stepping inside his reach was easy; so was sending him over the desk.

Number Two came forth a little warier—fists up. Three was stuck helping untangle the pile of thrashing bodies on the other side of the desk. Fine by me. I waited until Two was a half step out of reach and then faded to back up, but suddenly shifted, stepping forward when he did. He tried to swing, but it was too late. I pinned his arms to his sides and then pushed, sending him back into the desk. He caught himself with both hands, but I hooked my foot behind his left ankle and pulled, sending him crashing roughly to the floor. He turned quick to see what I was up to, but only met my heel. It slammed off his jaw at just the right angle to bounce his head off the desk.

I backed away quickly, though, ducking as Three swung a long leather sucker sap at me. It knocked my hat loose, but luckily not my brains. Coming in under his rush, I jabbed him twice with my right, burying it as deeply as I could in his left kidney. His eyes bugged but, he didn't fold. Even though he was still in pain, he managed to grab my arm. Before I could jerk away, Leather Number One grabbed the other.

One's grip was tighter; I hadn't done any real damage to him yet. Three was groggy. I was feeling every inch of the bruises I'd brought in with me but kept shoving them to the background, ignoring them as best I could. Concentrating on shaking Three off, I waltzed the pair of them around the office, keeping them off balance. One tried to dig in his heels but the rug slid, letting me keep the lead. Reaching the edge of the room's open area, I pushed off with everything I had, throwing all three of us toward a series of filing cabinets against the wall. One and I slammed Three between us and the files; his grip disappeared.

Taking the opportunity, I brought my left up and slapped One as hard as I could with the cast. The plaster scraped his face, peeling skin; blood poured from around his nose and

eyes. He didn't let go, though. I slapped him with the cast
again, and then reversed and damaged the other side of his
face. Blood sprayed my chin and jacket. I could feel it thick
and warm, landing in my hair, instantly thinned by my
sweat.

Taking advantage of the moment I reached forward with
my right arm and grabbed hold of One's shirt front. Leather
and hair bunched under my fingers. I gave him credit, he
didn't let go of my arm, but it didn't matter. I pulled him
forward into the cast, slamming him hard against the
thickest section of the plaster. His hold on my arm, and his
nose, broke at the same time.

A few feet away, Leather Number Two was helping
Sterling to his feet. Seeing me standing over his girlfriends,
he started around the desk. I crossed the area between us in
two large steps, wrapping my fingers around the handle of
the still sizzling television atop the desk. As he came to
meet me, I hefted the portable and then brought it down on
top of him. He raised his arms to protect himself. The
television broke through his elbows to slam against the side
of his head. I brought it down on him twice more, knocking
him to the floor. Another wallop against his right ear left
him flopping and crying like his pals.

Seeing they weren't going to be any more trouble, I
turned my attention back to their boss.

"Hi," I said, my breath coming heavy, Three's blood and
my sweat running pink down my face. "Remember me?"

I closed on the desk, pinning Sterling with my stare. The
red heels had finally untangled themselves from the boss
and his chair, revealing the torch singer from the night
before. She started to make some tearful protest but I cut her
off, saying,

"No one's asking you to stick around, pal. All I want is
your boss. Why don't you head for the powder room and
freshen up a little? This won't take long."

The red heels disappeared out the door without a second
thought. I never turned my eyes from Sterling, keeping him
pinned. "Pick up your chair," I barked. He did it. "Sit

down.'' He jumped. I was finally beginning to warm up to the guy.

"Now, see . . .'' I told him. "Here we are talking nicely, like old pals, or something. Isn't that better?''

He nodded. His head would shift off to the left and then the right, looking for something more hopeful to show up, but in the end it kept coming back to my stare. I'd started sweating because of the exertion. He'd started out of fear. His little eyes rolled in his head, his skin growing pasty as the blood drained from his face. I didn't know if I'd scared him enough to spill the information I needed but, I knew I was going to enjoy finding out. I asked him,

"So tell me . . . where's Mara?''

"Oh, Jesus—oh, God!'' he spat, the little eyes getting bigger. "That cunt?! This is all about her? I knew I should have never seen her. She was always trouble and she still is.''

"I don't care how much trouble she is, I just want to know where she is.''

"I don't know. She—she spent a few days with me when she first got to town, crying about how she had to get away from Carl—about how crazy he was getting—she even got me to give him a call.''

His eyes shut for a second as he remembered something he didn't quite know how to relate.

"Me . . .'' He said it almost like a question. "Me, calling Carl Miller. Me trying to talk him into leaving her alone. From what I can tell, I guess he hit town the next day. Guess that was a phone call I shouldn't have made. Carl hit town, Mara splits with a few grand in my evening receipts, and I've been living behind closed doors ever since.''

His composure was already realigning itself to the changes in the situation. I recognized his type—everyone does. Sterling was a manager—a cold, emotionally retarded accountant, one with minimal pleasures and desires outside of watching his piles of cash grow. I asked for more information. Now that he knew it wasn't going to cost him anything, he spilled what he had.

"Scared? Yeah, sure, I've been scared. Carl's crazy.

Everyone knows that. Then again, I guess we were all crazy back then. Everybody slept with her—Mara, I mean. Everyone, even Karras—even that little jerk slept with her— Fred made special trips back home to hang out with Miller just so he could sneak away and dork her on the side. Twice he did that. Twice!''

George had had a special sort of force. He might have intrigued Mara enough to fit into her plans—whatever those plans were. Maybe he was convenient as something to throw up in the Dumptruck's face, which might explain the bullet that had snuffed him—but Karras? What possible scheme could he have fit into? Why she would sleep with him was a question that needed an answer and not speculation. I asked Sterling for an answer.

"You see, Karras and Carl, they hung out a lot together. Carl trusted Karras more than anyone else, really. That's why Mara used him.''

"Used him for what?''

"She and Karras had a plan to get their hands on all of Carl's dough.''

"How?''

I took a little glance around at the Three Stooges. Since they seemed content to stay where they were, I turned my attention back to their boss.

"Mara said that Carl had a lot of stuff they could grab—his investments . . .''

"What kinds of investments?''

"Physical ones . . . stuff . . .'' he explained. "His gun collection, original artwork, a lot of antiques and all. While Mara worked on getting his bank accounts, Karras set up a way to back up a truck and clean all that stuff out.''

Not being one to trust a guy like Sterling because of his good looks or his nondiscriminatory hiring practices, I prodded him for more.

"And how is it that you know all this?''

"Because they wanted me to help them move the stuff.'' His eyes met mine for an instant, then filled with fright. "Now, now—wait a minute. I didn't do anything. I told them no way; no way at all. Steal from Carl Miller—

hahahaha—like I don't have enough troubles. I meant it, too. I mean, man, there's no way I wanted to get mixed up with that jerk again. I left Plainton a long while back to get away from him and, well, his kind. I said no and I mean no. Honest."

"Then what happened?" I asked. "Why is Karras still home, dirt poor, and considering himself Miller's friend? Where did Mara go after she left you? Where is she now? Why did your goon bounce me off the porcelain last night and warn me to stay away from this case?"

I grabbed his shirt front then, hauling him up off his feet, bending him toward me over the desk. A thin, reedy noise steamed out of him. The Stooges stayed where I'd left them. Shaking Sterling like a child who's pushed you to the limit, I shouted,

"Tell me what's going on! Everything you know—give it. Now!"

I threw him backwards into his chair. He hit hard enough to almost tip it over again, but not quite. Shaken, his voice jumped upward as he answered.

"I don't know; I don't know. Oh, God—please, honest. Honest—honest. Mara must've found someone else to fence the stuff they took—she, she cut Karras out, I guess. You know she would—look at him, look at her. How could he make her do anything?" He was speculating, but he made it sound good. "She used him and threw him away. Would that be a surprise to you? The little bitch. She did it all the time, to everyone she knew. Once she gets her hooks into you, you find yourself doing the stupidest things—things you just couldn't ever imagine that you'd—that you'd really do. That time—that time in . . ."

And suddenly his voice trailed off and he was somewhere else, his eyes letting me know the past had captured him. He rambled on for a minute about some motel on the outskirts of Plainton as if I knew where it was and everything about it. He talked about going there with Mara and a camera, and some vegetables, and a dog, and a box of assorted restraints. Who did what to whom he left a little unclear.

He swam back to the office then, his face streaking with

tears. Looking up at me, his earlier bluster long gone and forgotten, he told me,

"I don't know what's going on. I don't. Please believe me. It isn't me. Honest. I just wanted to get away from everybody. Run this club—be a big shot—you know what I mean? Honest—I don't know anything!"

I eased up, asking a few more questions in a softer voice, knowing I'd just about run out of time. It wasn't what I wanted, of course, but just what had to be. What I wanted was to slap Sterling around—just a little—just once at least. I didn't though. It wasn't worth it. Much as I hated to admit it, mainly because it made my job harder, it was time for me to make my exit.

No matter how satisfying it felt, the law was unlikely to care that I had good personal reasons for both my trespassing and assault-and-batterizing in the Ostrich. Private investigators have no special powers—if a citizen gives you an answer, those times they don't just slam the door in your face, even when you don't believe it—you say "thanks" and then turn around and leave.

I'd thought going into the Ostrich that I was going to find all the answers I needed. Anthony would be there and I'd be able to give him his. Mara would've been there, too, and I could've just dragged her out and back to Miller and sent the two of them packing out of my life. Yeah, whoever'd killed George would've been found out as well, somehow, and that could've been put to rest, too. Surprise, surprise—things hadn't worked out the easy way.

I was sure Sterling wasn't George's killer, or responsible for any of Miller's other problems, either. He'd convinced me of those. I wasn't so sure that he wasn't the one hiding Mara. If he was, though, I was just going to have to find some other way to prove it.

Sterling confirmed that Anthony came in for the late shift. He told me he was sorry about what had happened the night before. Everyone had been waiting for Miller to cause a ruckus. They thought I was it. Sterling could've lost his voice apologizing. I told him "forget it" and headed out of his office. Having laid out three of his employees, it was the

best end to a bad deal. As my hand caught the doorknob, he
called out,

"Are you . . . finished? I mean, are you coming back?"

"Only if I have reason to."

Exiting back into the main body of the club, I was aware
that everyone's eyes were on me. They were sensible
enough to keep their distance, though, so I didn't care. Red
Heels was nursing a drink at a small table near the bar. She
shuddered as she saw me, her Adam's apple bobbing with a
noticeable gulp. I slowed as I passed her table. Looking
down at her, I told the poor guy,

"Caught your act last night—you put me away."

The fear in her eyes vaporized, the white-knuckle grip
around her glass going to pink. She answered,

"Thank you, thank you . . . ah . . ."

"Jack."

"Thank you, Jack," she answered, a smile starting across
her face.

"Any time, baby."

As I crossed to the door, I wondered about where I should
go next. I stood in the doorway debating. Miller, Ward,
Byler, Karras, Cerelli, Ray? Andren, the Phillips family,
Ballard? Who to visit? Maybe an afternoon-time drop-in at
the morgue to see if my bedside manner could get something out of George. I was stiff and sore from tussling with
Sterling's dress-up dolls, all of Anthony's damage reawak-
ened, my wrist screaming at me.

I dry-swallowed one of the little doc's pills, but it was too
little, too late. The seconds wore on like years, each more
tiring than the last. After a couple of decades I knew there
was only one place worth going.

I went home.

# CHAPTER 17

I CAME THROUGH the front door of my apartment to find Elba Santorio combing out my dog, Balto. I'd forgotten it was her day to clean. Actually, I'd forgotten what day it was, period. Balto ran over to try and knock me down in the hallway—not a very hard task for a hundred and ten pounds of half-shepherd, half-husky.

Elba stood up brushing her hands, one against the other. She might be only twelve, but she collects my mail, keeps my apartment straightened out, feeds Balto when I don't come home, puts food in my cupboards, and has probably tucked me in when I wasn't looking, on more than one occasion. As I crawled through the doorway, she asked,

"*O, Dios mio. Qúe pasa?* What have you been doing now?"

I should have thought, I cursed myself, should have remembered she'd be there. Two years back, the Santorios had moved into my building. It didn't take me long to realize that someone was teaching what should have been a smiling, happy little girl her life lessons with a length of leather. I looked into things. Turned out her mother had died, and her father didn't know any better way to handle things than to take off his belt. Especially once he'd started drinking, a habit he didn't bother to save for the weekends.

"Not much, mama chiquita. I went dancing."

"With who—the Cosa Nostra? Jack, you have to start taking care of yourself."

"Yeah, I know," I told her. "That's why I came home to you."

"Don't be a wiseguy. *Quitase esa ropa!* Blood and dirt

and wrinkles. Take everything off and throw it in the hall and get in the shower. And use the hot, hot water. And you stay under it. Do you understand?''

"Yes, mama.''

Her voice came through the bathroom door, ''And use the old towels first—don't go grabbing a new one. Do you understand?''

"Yes, mama.''

I could hear her in the hall, gathering up my clothes, mumbling something most likely fairly accurate about ''men'' under her breath. She was, as they say, wise beyond her years. Unfortunately, like most people in that situation, she'd gotten there the hard way. As I dragged myself under the steaming water, feeling it soak into all my throbbing aches, I couldn't help remembering.

One night, the screams—the sounds we'd all gotten used to, in all the children's different pitches—went on longer than usual . . . too much longer. Why people allow these things to happen is understandable. Interfering in domestic situations is nothing a person does lightly. The law is on the side of the family. Aside from that, there isn't a cop alive who won't tell you that stopping one loved one from beating on another is a good way to make yourself the target of both of them. It doesn't make any surface, logical sense, but that's because people's emotions don't lie on the surface. You've always got to look deeper if you want to know the truth.

That night the screams weren't stopping. They came up through the funnel of the building's side courtyard and echoed through my apartment until I couldn't pretend they weren't there anymore. Not able to sleep, I crawled out of bed and scratched myself and checked out the refrigerator. The screams followed me to the kitchen—waited for me inside the G.E.

Not fully awake, cursed by the pealing wails, I walked out into the hallway, tracing the anguish through the air until I found its source two floors down. Silence struck then, filling the air just as I stopped before the Santorios' door. I did not know who lived on the other side, did not know what the screams were all about. I'd merely been driven to that spot by my inability to tolerate whatever was going on there—sometimes every night.

Truthfully, part of me felt relieved to not have to intervene. As the quiet seconds passed, I began to feel foolish, standing in the hall in my bare feet and pajama bottoms. It dawned on me I'd left my front door unlocked. Go home, that sensible part of my mind said, the section that favors modern civilization and its notions on how things should and should not be handled. I wavered for a second, and then, at the moment of decision, a sob came to me from the other side of the door. Not a scream or a wail, not even crying. Just a deep-in-the-throat choke of despair, a heart-breaking noise that signified a sense of hopelessness that the past was the future and that neither would ever change.

He was still holding his belt free in his hand when I kicked their lock apart. Elba was on the floor, half-naked, covered with lashes that stung just to look at them. Maybe a third of them were bleeding. I walked into their home and dragged him to another room and did him in. I kept hitting him past when he said he'd never do it again, and past where he begged, and past where he threw up on both of us and the rug and the walls. If she hadn't opened the door to watch, all welts and wide brown eyes, I might have kept beating him until he was past breathing. I almost did anyway.

I let him up, though, self-possessed enough to stop short of murder. He scrambled away from me on all fours, chittering viciously like the nasty, greasy little rat he was. He never beat Elba, or her sister or brothers again, though. A few days later when her swelling had gone down, she came to my apartment offering to do the cleaning. No mention was made of the last time we'd seen each other.

In some kids it would have been a dodge, a way to run a scam on *el gringo*. Get his keys and clean him out. Hell, sometimes the whole family will be in on a beating con just to soften up the entire neighborhood for the touch. I knew that wasn't the case then, though. No proof—I just knew it. The feeling for trust was right, so I went with it. I gave her the spare key without a word or a rule and headed into the city. Half my brain was kicking me for being a chump—logically. The other half kept whispering about patience and faith.

When I got home that night, Faith smiled in triumph. I came back to a changed world. Whether Elba had brought in an army or tapped her magic wand, I never found out; maybe I didn't really want to know. It certainly didn't matter. All the dishes had come out of the cupboards to be cleaned. Then the cupboards themselves had been scrubbed, and the walls, and the floor. When I'd left in the morning I'd had some old blankets and towels hung over the windows—I came home to curtains. My furniture sparkled from being polished; my windows were clean; my clothes were clean—the gray I'd never been able to get out of my underwear was gone—if Balto hadn't been there, I'd of thought I was in the wrong apartment.

I found her sleeping on the couch, passed out in a deep sleep as if she'd run in the city marathon. Her hair was thick with sweat and dirt, but the face it surrounded was calm. Somehow the peaceful look on it gave me the feeling that I'd been adopted. It wasn't the worst feeling I'd ever had.

Since then, I've paid her a housekeeping fee—half in hand, half socked away for her in the bank. Sometimes Hu or Tony or one of the other characters I hang with will get a whiff of the ponies and I'll take a little out and place some bets. Sometimes we lose, but usually we win. It all goes back in the bank, except maybe enough for a couple of rounds for all her uncles. So far I have about eight and half grand tucked away for her.

The book was made out in my name, in trust for her, but I've begun wondering recently if I shouldn't put some sort of safeguard on it, like writing instructions about it in my will. If I ever turn up missing, or flat-faced down from lead poisoning, I know I can count on my bank to do its best to swallow Elba's account without so much as a burp of guilt. Of course, that would mean making out a will in the first place.

That was all for later, though. Stepping out of the steam clouds roiling over the tub edge, all I could concern myself with was getting some sleep. I'd only been awake for a few hours but, they'd been real tough ones and I needed a nap. I asked Elba to make sure I got up by four o'clock. She scolded me again for not taking good enough care of myself, but promised I'd be awake on time even if it took a pot of cold water in the face. I asked her to exercise any less radical methods she could think of first, and then shoved her from the room with a smile.

Balto came in and curled up next to the bed, ready to defend me from all invaders—even my own nightmares. His wet tongue's proved a good deterrent to my dark conscience more than once in the past. Taking a look at the clock on my night stand, it registered that I'd only given myself two hours to rest. Accepting that you take what you can get in life, I settled back and closed my eyes. When you don't have much, it seems stupid to waste it.

# CHAPTER 18

BY SIX THIRTY I was back on the road, working my way through the thinning rush-hour traffic swarming around Manhattan. I'd crawled out of the sack at ten after four when I finally tired of Elba and Balto's concerted efforts to wake me. If you've ever had your sleep interrupted by ninety pounds of screaming Spaniard and a hundred and ten pounds of slobbering mutt, you can send your sympathy along. If not—count your blessings—you don't have it as bad as you thought.

In between bites of steamed vegetables—Elba won't cook me any meat, she says my system gets enough poison on its own—I'd made a few calls trying to set things into motion so as to finally get the Dumptruck off my back. Sterling's comment about wanting to be a big shot had started me thinking—Andren and Ballard had both made it clear that none of these guys from Plainton were supposed to be that well off. If that was the case, how had Sterling raised the money to start up the Ostrich?

Of course, there were a score of possibilities as to how he'd done it, but they would take a belief in coincidence. I don't have one. No, to me, the answer to that question seemed likely to have the ability to put me back on track. To get that answer I called Francis Whiting, a law student I use for research work. When it comes to legal papers and a lot of random combing research, Hubert's prices climb pretty high—friend or no friend. Not liking that kind of work any more than I do, Hu priced himself out of that end of the business a long time ago.

I told Francis to check out Sterling and his Ostrich. I

wanted to know how it had been purchased, or rented, or whatever. If there'd been any renovations, I wanted to know how they'd been paid for. I told him to get it all to me yesterday; he told me to call him a week ago for a progress report. Funny guy.

After that, I called Byler and Cerelli to see if they could shed any light on things. Cerelli'd just been annoyed by my call; his roommate was dead and all the bills were his and all the fault was Miller's and mine. He had to arrange for shipping George's body and all of his belongings back to George's family in Plainton. All in all, the strain seemed a little too much for him. He didn't care what anyone connected to the case did anymore, as long as they left him alone while they did it. Our conversation ended abruptly when he gave me a verb and a pronoun as a goodbye and then used his receiver to crush the life out of a bug strolling across his phone.

Byler, on the other hand, seemed concerned—edgy. Miller still had him worried. Or at least, something did. His attitude nagged at me, his mood swinging back and forth from minute to minute, one second happy, the next upset. Granted, he'd acted fairly moody when he'd been in my office, but he was worse on the phone. What it could be, I wasn't sure. He had been threatened by Miller, lost his wife, and seen a friend get his chest blown out. He claimed it was nothing—said that with his life finally straightening out for him he couldn't understand why guys like Miller and I couldn't have the decency to leave him be.

It was a growl, sure, but only a puppy's—tiny fangs bared in the hopes of sending a bored enemy in some other direction. What'd made us enemies all of a sudden I wasn't so certain. Maybe we'd been enemies all along and I just hadn't noticed. Whichever, his strategy had worked. I was too bored to care. And, even if I hadn't been, I didn't have the time to dope it out at that moment. I'd just arrived at Miller's hotel. Not having to drag the Dumptruck's carcass to his room this time, I circled the block, finding almost legal parking nearby. I had to park a few feet closer to a fire hydrant than the big, brave, long arm of the law allows, but feeling that my luck had to get better sooner or later, I decided to chance the ticket and headed inside.

The lobby was no more depressing than it was the first time I passed through it—just hotter. The only noise within the dust-smeared cavern came from the desk clerk's fan, clawing and pushing the humidity in a semicircle back behind the counter. The clerk was in a heat coma, sitting atop a three-legged stool, leaning against the wall, his sweat discoloring the moldering plaster behind his head and shoulders.

Stirring him by slapping the desk with my palm—I had to be sure he was coherent enough to understand me—I asked if Miller had gone out. He hadn't. From the shape the Dumptruck'd been in when I'd parked him in his bed, I wasn't sure he'd be awake yet. Having no intention of traipsing back down to the lobby if I couldn't rouse him, I figured it was just easier to take the key with me in the first place. And, of course, the simple truth was that if he wasn't in at all, then I was even more interested in getting inside and looking around to see if the big moke was holding anything back on me. When I asked for the key to Miller's room, though, the clerk got hesitant. He stalled me with,

"I don't know. Things like that aren't good for business."

"Neither is having the cops roust your customers, which has happened once with this guy. You want flat footprints all over your rugs every couple of hours . . . it can be arranged."

"You're no cop."

"Wow. How astute. I'm no cop. Take your cigar . . . go to the head of the class. That's right, goofus. I'm no cop. And you're nobody . . . period. Now—hand over the key before I prove it to you."

The clerk grumbled a few quiet words but ultimately delivered. He'd only been trying for his daily grease. I'd realized that, but heat plays funny games with people—sometimes you're up for polite rules, sometimes you're not. That day I wasn't. Partly it was my aches and the humidity souring my mood, but partly it was the fact I get tired of paying people extra to do what they're already being paid to do. The guy'd seen me drag Miller in earlier—he knew I belonged with him—there was no reason for him to try and shake me down. "My-hand-in-your-pocket" is a common disease of the New York working-class, which seems to be nearing epidemic proportions. It makes me tired.

I waited for the elevator in a small room off the lobby where the building's two animated rust buckets were hidden. Both were off the floor at that moment. No air circulated in the waiting area. I opened another button on my shirt, peeled the soaking fabric away from my chest, and then fanned myself with the flap, trying to dry up some of the sweat running down into my pants.

When the elevator came, the door opened with a grinding noise. One low-wattage bulb flickered as I stepped in, threatening to die completely throughout the entire trip upward. The heat in the rising box was twice that of everywhere else in the world. Steam followed me into the hall as I stepped out onto the Dumptruck's floor. It seemed to, anyway.

I walked through the hazy dimness of the crumbling hallway, feeling the greasy, threadbare carpeting slide beneath my feet. Stopping at Miller's door, I gave it a knocking and then waited. And kept waiting. Knocking again, I upped the volume and length of the pounding, angry at being stuck in a decaying flophouse, banging away on a sloppily painted door, trying to rouse my stupored client. I was angry at fate, destiny—at my own stupidity in following both of them to Miller's door. Maybe at one time I'd had a chance at a real life—I banged harder—but that was gone. I'd misspent my youth on a series of mistakes—wrong jobs, wrong homes, wrong lovers, wrong choices all along the way—now I was dying from the heat, ready to pass out as I slammed my fist again and again against the Dumptruck's door.

The key in my pocket was forgotten. I pounded away, first mumbling at Miller to open the door, then screaming it. When the noise I was making finally disturbed one of the other tenants to the point where they could overcome their fear of opening their door, I stopped, realizing that I had to calm down—that it was more than the heat getting to me. Pulling myself back into some semblance of order, I stopped and thought for a second. Nothing had happened yet on the other side of the door, despite my display. Miller hadn't grumbled, yelled, or even snored loud enough for me to hear him. Either he'd left earlier and the washout behind the desk downstairs had somehow missed him, or he was still passed out and an even weaker sister than I'd pegged him for. Glad for having been as arrogant as I had, I fished the door's key out of my pocket and let myself in.

Miller hadn't gone anywhere. He was still stretched out in the center of the room on the bed. His snores had subsided. So had his breathing. I didn't have any proof—hadn't stepped into the room yet. There was no blood in sight, no signs of violence. It didn't matter. I knew Carl Miller was dead.

All the pains throbbing within me doubled. The heat shot up to 250 degrees. Everything, including my instinct for self-preservation, told me to just shut the door and leave. But, I reminded my instincts, I'd etched my face into the clerk's memory by being such a smart guy and, sooner or later, even in a flophouse as bad as the one Miller'd chosen for his farewell, someone would come to clean the room and they'd find his fat, bloated remains.

Besides, I also reminded my instincts, he was our client.

He'd paid me for a week on Monday morning, and it was only Wednesday. Hating the dead bastard on the bed more than ever, I slammed the door shut behind me as I went in to try and figure out what the hell had happened now.

# CHAPTER 19

I SAT DOWN on the arm of the chair I'd sat in before and worked on piecing together what had happened. Tired and stiff, I looked around the dim room for some clue that might allow me to do that. The first one I spotted was a doozy. Apparently Miller had called the front desk for a typewriter. The antiquated manual hulk squatting on the dresser hadn't been there earlier in the day.

I got up and walked over to it, trying to disturb the room as little as possible. What the ancient machine'd been used for became apparent as I neared it. The Dumptruck had given up the fight and left the rest of us to carry on without him. I scanned his last words:

"Dear Mara: I'm sorry for all the trouble I've caused. Sorry for hounding you. It was a mistake for me to try and find you. I should have stayed home and let you have your freedom. All I've done is cause trouble and hurt people. I've bullied and murdered and I know now I can't face the fact that this is all going to tumble down around me. Please forgive me, my dearest. You were meant for better things. I'm doing this because there doesn't seem to be another way anymore. Forgive me, darling."

And then it was signed, and that was it. I stared at the note, wondering at the wrongness of it. Something bothered me about the Dumptruck committing suicide. It didn't seem to be in his character, and yet, neither had roughing up Ward, or killing George. Wanting to make sure, though, I decided to try and check his signature. I looked around for his wallet, hoping it was out on the night stand or in a drawer. It wasn't—which meant it was probably in his hip pocket, the out-of-towners' favored place for their wallets. I couldn't get it there. Not unless I wanted to explain to Ray what I was doing disturbing corpses in his jurisdiction. Especially their wallets. Everyone knows the police get first crack at all leftovers.

Turning to his suitcase, I popped it open, hoping to find something with his signature inside. Moving through the packed shirts and socks and underwear, I dug down to the spot where he'd stuffed all his non-clothing items. Razor and toothpaste and cologne were all shoved together in a corner with some folded sheets of yellow paper and dried food packets and the Dumptruck's checkbook. That I pulled free.

A wad of canceled checks were rubber-banded together inside the back of the book's plastic holder—paydirt. I checked a few of their signatures carefully against the one on the suicide note. They matched. Even given the number of points one has to shave when matching handwritings due to all the possible influencing factors—stress, time taken signing, possible state of intoxication, et cetera, there was no doubt the same person had signed all the pieces of paper at which I was looking.

That avenue closed, I went back to his case and pulled free the sheets of paper I'd originally passed over. Taking them and the checkbook back to my chair, I started reading. The canceled checks held no surprises. Dozens of them in the last few months were made out to Mara in ever-increasing amounts. Not all the checks were from the personal checking account book I had in hand—most of the larger ones were drawn on his hardware store's account. That tied in with what Sterling had told me.

Switching to the folded tablet papers, what I found was intriguing, but of little help. The rows of figures and the words attached to them didn't tell me much.

Fractur . . . . . . . . . . . $3,500.00
Wind-up Blackface . . . . $925.00
Mettllach (1) . . . . . . . . $530.00
Mettllach (2) . . . . . . . .$775.00
Mettllach (3) . . . . . . . $1,475.00

The Mettllachs went up to twenty-three, and their price went up over three thousand, but that didn't tell me much about Carl Miller, or why he was dead in his bed. Neither did J&E Norton deer crock, or Joseph Filius Guarneri, even at the price of $93,450.00, or any of the other things in the columns. Refolding the papers, I slipped both them and the checkbook into my pocket and then headed down to the desk clerk. He looked even happier to see me the second time.

I told him to hand over the phone. He asked,

"Why?"

"Because I want to call the police to report a body upstairs."

"What! Oh Christ. What for? I can take care of it. We don't need another load of cops flopping through here. Let me just get it dumped—okay?"

He wheeled some more, but I reached over the counter and pulled the phone to where I could use it, telling him to shut up before I reported his conversation along with the stiff. Calling Ray directly, I let him know where I'd gone and what I'd found.

"This isn't one of your half-assed shenanigans, is it?"

"Ray," I exclaimed, sounding as hurt as I could. "Come, come now, ol' buddy. I told you before . . . this is the beginning of a whole new Jack Hagee."

"Yeah, right. And we should all love the fucking homeless, just like the Democrats and the goddamned *New York Times* keep telling us to. You shit-stuffed bastard. Don't you move. I'm sending the boys over there right now. Before now! You be there or you start thinking up some new way to make a living."

"Why, I'd be happy to wait here and assist your officers in their various duties, Captain."

"Stuff it up your ass and choke on it." Ray was not happy. It's his habit during those periods to make sure no one else within range is happy, either. "Say what you like, do what you want, but . . . leave that hotel, fuck with that room, pull any shit at all, and you can use your license for toilet paper."

"I'll tie a string around my finger so I won't forget."

"Tie it around your throat. Save Mooney the trouble."

I didn't get to say anything in return. Ray slammed off the connection, most likely switching to another line to order an investigation team to the hotel. Figuring I might have only a handful of minutes, I handed the phone back over to the desk clerk, telling him,

"You're lucky it was me and not you found Sleeping Beauty. If you'd dump that stiff, you'd be sucking trouble long past forever." I made my lie more elaborate. "The big boys in the department have been looking for this guy to off himself for some time now. A team'll be here any minute to check him over. I'm going to get some air and catch a smoke outside until they get here. Don't let anyone into that room until I get back."

I was out the door before he could get his mouth working again. Racing around the corner to my car, I popped the trunk and then stashed Miller's checkbook and the yellow sheets under a loose flap in the carpeting. Sliding the car's emergency kit over the spot, I looked it all over to make sure it appeared natural and then slammed the trunk. Firing a cigarette, I walked back around the corner, smoking and waiting outside the hotel for the first of the departmental boys to show up. Edgar Collins was in the first car.

"Jack," he called. "Hear you dug up another bundle for us."

"Didn't have to, Ed. This one's still above ground."

"Good. Good. The wife's getting sick of cleaning the dirt out from under my fingernails. Says the graveyard moss is ruining her nail file."

"What're you going to do about it?"

"Ahhh—for now, I got her a new nail file. That don't quiet her down"—he laughed—"I guess I'll have to get a new wife."

We shook hands and headed into the hotel with the others in Ed's forensics team. I gave him the gist of what had happened so far, telling him anything I thought might give him some insight as to what'd led the Dumptruck into taking the last shortcut. He went into Miller's room with his

usual look of anticipation, the same keen grin he's worn to
every unnatural death I've ever shared with him. Ed likes
the cases with a little mystery to them.

I'd told him I didn't think Miller was the kind of guy to
take his own life, but also that I really didn't know him well
enough to bet the rent money on it. Ed told me to give him
a while to get intimate with Miller, and then once he had
some facts, he'd be sure to make some time to debate my
theories with me. I told him, "Swell," and then let the door
shut between us.

There was no reason for me to go in—I'd already been
there. All I could do would be to get my prints or shoe dirt
or bellybutton lint in the wrong place, which would only
upset some official type. Cooling my heels in the hallway,
I lit up another cigarette, waiting for Ray and Mooney to
show. It didn't take long. The pair of them came at me,
double-timing it over the greasy carpeting, Ray starting to
shout as soon as he saw me.

"What are you doing out in the hall?"

"Trying to stay out of everyone's way. It's no Madison
Square Garden in there."

"I don't buy it—you're so full of shit your eyes have
gone brown. Give it straight, snoop."

I blew up.

"What the hell do you want from me, Ray? You and the
Ape here send Miller to me just to bust my nuts, and then do
nothing but carp at me after. I've given you everything on
this one—everything! All the way up and down. I deliver
the drunk fatbag back to his room, go home, come back,
find him with a suicide note on his night stand and a definite
impediment in his breathing, and what happens? I play by
the rules and report it A.S.A.P., and you come down here
with an attitude the size and shape of a red-hot poker just
itching to massage me with it. Give it a break, Ray. I've
been through too much lately to want to waltz around about
this now."

The speech left me panting in the heat. I took a hungry
drag on my cigarette, spewing words and smoke at the pair
of cops before either could edge in.

"You wanted Miller out of town? Well, he's about as out of town as he's going to get. If you want to choose to believe his farewell to arms in there, then your fucking casebook is closed. You've got what you want, so get off my goddamned back!"

Ray held it for a second, realizing the heat had gotten the best of him, and that he had nothing to gain by not at least listening to the facts before he said too many of the wrong things. Seeing that we were all calm again, I filled him in on my day from where I'd left his office until when we'd met again in the hall, making only a few tactical omissions here and there for the sake of brevity. Ray mulled my story over, then asked,

"So you don't know how Miller did himself in?"

"I don't even know why he did himself in. I can't see the angle in it. Maybe he did, maybe he didn't. In all honesty, I don't know. Maybe I'm just too tired and stiff to care anymore."

"Yeah, maybe."

The Ray who could be dealt with began to seep out of the shadows, coming to meet me halfway. "All right, listen. You hang around a little longer and we'll see if we can't piece this whole mess together. You're out a client, but—ah, hell—that jerk, you're probably better off for it."

Ray worried the knot in his tie, pulling it loose to the point where he might as well have taken it off. Mopping at his neck with his handkerchief, he growled,

"God, it's too fucking hot. Anyway, you hang out. If we can get this all wrapped up neat enough, we'll just get your statement here and get this thing over with. Okay?"

It was as nice as he was going to get—as nice as any cop ever gets. I told him, "Sure" and went back to nursing my cigarette. He and Mooney squeezed into Miller's room. I closed my eyes and leaned back against the wall—waiting. I waited a long time.

By eight o'clock, though, Ray and Edgar and I were walking away from the hotel, the sounds of the ambulance boys wheeling the Dumptruck down to their wagon off behind us. Ray felt the case was closed, which was making him almost human. As far as he was concerned, the letter was Miller's and it neatly sewed up all of our loose ends. Miller killed George. Miller killed himself. Ray believed it. Edgar said the facts backed it.

"Makes sense, Jack," he offered. "The signature on the letter is the same as the one on his driver's license. Shakier, true, but with the liquor he had in him, it was a wonder he could write at all. That's why he called for the typewriter. There were a lot of crumpled attempts to write the letter in the wastebasket—a few typed ones, too, along with an empty bottle of rodent killer. Lots of 'forgive me' crapola—barely legible, but his handwriting. It's all there—finally he gave up, got the front desk to send up a typewriter, ground out his all-important message, and then did his dose of poison. It looks pretty clean."

And it did. Miller's prints were all over the paper and the typewriter and the bottle of rat juice that'd puckered his stomach lining and closed his eyes forever. All the facts were staring me in the face—the bad guy was dead. The case was closed. Ray was giving me all the facts so I could play along with the party line and take my profit and drop my investigation with a clean conscience. Although I kept my face still and my comments to myself, my thoughts weren't agreeing. He was satisfied and, if he was satisfied, the rest of the world was supposed to be satisfied, too. He and the rest of the world could go to hell.

He wanted too easy a ride—if he didn't, he would've had Mooney frisk me in the hall. The fact that I'd been prepared for him to check me out while he hadn't bothered to do so told me I was a lot more interested in this case than he was. Part of my brain understood—Ray's a public servant of the city of New York. Miller was from out of town. George was just another nobody. Ray, like all cops, was hired to keep the peace, not wield an avenging sword. He'd done all the job anyone expected of him. I, on the other hand, don't have anyone to answer to except myself. Somehow I never thought I'd end up being such a tough boss.

I split off from Ray and Edgar at the corner, claiming my car was down a different block. Heading away from them,

I circled the block back to the hotel entrance. None of the cops were still around. They and their cars and trucks and equipment had come and gone, taking away the Dumptruck's body and their disruptive presence quietly, disappearing into the humidity much to everyone's relief, including mine. If they were going to write Miller off to keep their books tidy, then the quicker they were off the case, the better.

Stepping back into the lobby, I smiled to see the same desk clerk still flopped out behind his counter. His little fan continued to sputter, grinding the stale air in the lobby through its blades. Trying to catch part of its meager breeze, I leaned over the counter as I told him,

"Okay, everyone's gone. Except me. And, since I have a real problem about being the last one to leave, don't make this take any longer than it has to."

"So leave," he said, his head not coming away from the wall. "Who's stoppin' you?"

"Don't push it."

His face took on the look of someone who'd wrecked an expensive apartment trying to kill a fly, only to find it squatting unharmed on the wreckage of the most expensive thing that got trashed. He squawked about already having told his story. I explained,

"So now you tell it again."

"You make me sick," he snapped. He thought about trying to blow me off—you could see it in his eyes—but then decided it might not be smart. Wiping the sweat away from his forehead, he rubbed his hand dry on his shirt, saying, "Okay, okay, okay. Shit. So what now? What else do you want?"

"Play me back the statement you gave the badges. Then I'll ask you a few questions, and your duties as a citizen will be complete for another day."

What he gave me was enough. He'd bought a couple of bottles for Miller; later on he'd taken up the typewriter. That was it. He gave me Miller's check-in time, telling me he'd paid cash each day. I wasn't surprised Ray and his boys had accepted the story and taken off. People sweeping dirt under a rug rarely take the time to see how much is already there.

"An' that's it. That's all that's gone on. Total."

"Total?" I asked. "No meals? He didn't go in or out? Ever? You didn't bring him anything but two bottles and a typewriter? No one else brought him anything? He didn't have any visitors, or phone calls . . ."

He stopped me.

"The only visitor he had didn't bring him nothin' but comfort an' joy."

"Speak plain, geek."

The clerk warmed up his favorite leer and put it on. It went well with the plaster mold stuck in his hair.

"Our boy there had a visitor, all right—nudge, nudge. Bayyy-be. Nicest piece of ass this neighborhood ever saw."

My interest woke up. I told him to give me the complete rundown—who she was, where I could find her—all of it. In one way he was less than helpful, in another he seemed to fit the last piece of the puzzle together for me.

"I wouldn't know where to find her—shit, my left nut for her phone number—Christ, God, yes." His eyes glazed over with Christmas-morning joy. "She was no regular nigger-hustled street skank—uh-uh-uh. He called her down from uptown. That's for sure. Double sure. What a sideshow. Tits like baseballs—round, firm, perfect—shape like a center-fold. She was a blonde, that kinda dewy, honey blonde. Jeeeezzzus. She was one hot cunt, all right. She cost him the limit, let me tell you."

She'd cost him—I had to agree with that. She'd cost Miller the limit—the limit and then some. She'd come in with a smile and a plan, one that had worked. The Dumptruck was dead, poisoned by the one person who could get him to do anything—even, as Karras had put it, "cut his own throat for her"—if she said to.

It looked as if Carl Miller had found his Mara after all. Doing so'd gotten him even more grief that I'd told him it would. All of which made me think, if a joke like Miller could find his Mara . . . then I could, too.

With that thought in mind, I thanked the desk clerk for all his help, flipping him one of Miller's twenties because it seemed like the right thing to do at the time, and then left the hotel. I walked back to my car pondering my new information, looking to see what kind of sense it made during the ride back uptown. If Mara'd emptied the Dumptruck's accounts and pawned off all his guns and antiques and the rest, it fit that she would take off. Maybe she never figured Miller to come after her. She knew her parents wouldn't make much of a search, and if you think your own mother doesn't want you, why should you figure anyone else would, either?

But she'd figured Miller wrong. He'd wanted her—not his money back or his junk or anything else—just her. He'd pinned all his hopes on her, made her his dream woman, his sweet, virginal love to be adored, and she'd sensed what that had meant and hung him out to dry by his ankles until every last nickel'd hit the sidewalk. Then she'd blown town and left him with his check stubs and his cryptic papers and his broken, bleeding heart, thinking he'd mope around for a while but would keep quiet, too embarrassed to make a stink for fear of looking the fool.

But since looking the fool was no big deal to Miller, he'd come to New York and lived in a flophouse. He done that to be able to pay me the outrageous amount of money I'd asked for because I'd pissed too much of my own money away—and because he wanted his Mara. And now it looked like he'd become a big enough annoyance to her to cause her to come out of hiding and give him a transfer off the one-way street.

A cop named Spenser I'd been friends with a long time ago once told me that you get what you pay for. He told me that the day he tried to kill me. I'd ended up with a bullet in my shoulder and he'd ended up dead. The image of that day came back to me there in the car as sharp as it always does. I could see Spenser clearly, not wanting to kill a fellow officer, but not wanting to go to jail, either. It had been him or me, and we'd both gone down. The only difference was I eventually got up again.

Sometimes I've had the feeling Spenser stood his ground and took his bullet because it was the only clean way he could see out of his situation. I've always said that every second of every day, everybody does exactly what they want. No gods pull our strings—the decisions we make are nobody's fault but our own. And that's why I didn't believe Miller committed suicide.

He had wanted his Mara. Period. A guy willing to go through what he did just to find a woman who had done what she had done, ready to forgive her, didn't take the easy way out. There were enough holes in Ray's case for me to force it open if I wanted to—but I didn't want to. Having a bored and resentful police force grazing in the same field I was, was not my idea of how to break a case in a hurry.

Besides, I was fairly sure circumstances were going to drag Ray and his boys back into things soon enough.

# CHAPTER 20

I PULLED UP to Freddie's newsstand, docking the Skylark as close to our police sign as I could. She headed out to drag it back but I waved her off, sliding out the passenger side to do it myself. As I brought it in the side door of her stand, she reminded me that her charm was a twenty-four-hour affair.

"What're you doin' here this late, you unctuous prick?"

"Just wanted to know what time to pick you up for the junior prom."

"Be here in just forty fuckin' years ago and you'll be right on time."

I snorted a laugh, digging some change out of my pocket for the paper and a Three Musketeers bar. As she herded the coins across the counter, she asked,

"How you been, Stud?"

"I've been better."

"Yeah, ain't we all." Then she studied my face, catching some of the bruises despite the surrounding darkness. "Although I must admit you do look as if you've been playin' on the big kids' side of the recess yard."

"How bad's it look, Freddie?"

"Ahhhh, don't sweat the small stuff. Yer still hung together well enough to sweet-look a lady inta buyin' ya a drink."

She handed a bottle of Wild Turkey over the counter to me. I eyed the street quickly for cops, not in the mood to be hassled for being a big bad criminal, then tilted the bottle back three fingers worth, letting the warmth of it chase back a little of my mood.

"There. Now how d'ya feel?"

160

"Well, I'm not up for singing in the rain, but it ought to keep me from drawing a razor across my throat."

She grinned approvingly. "Big improvement."

"Thanks," I told her.

Freddie snorted at her own humor, then took back the bottle to knock back a few knuckles worth of her own. She asked what'd happened to me and I told her. I gave her everything on Miller and Mara and Sterling and, of course, my ol' pal Jeff Anthony, and all the rest of the cast. Sometimes Freddie's extra thirty years gives her an insight that I might miss, but not this time. If there was an angle hidden in what was going on, it was hidden well enough to escape both of us.

After a few more snorts I told Freddie I had to call it a night, and headed across the street. Once upstairs I went into my office, crawling out of my shoulder holster as I stiff-walked to my desk. My bruises were calling to me, reminding me of just how much I really did hurt. I'd put on a great act for a day, but the curtain was down, and between the heat and the Wild Turkey I didn't have the energy left for any curtain calls. After opening the windows that could still be opened and hitting the fan, I planted myself behind my desk and then flipped on the message machine to see who had called.

I listened while I stashed my shoulder holster and .38 in their drawer. The first two calls and the last one were unimportant, but the third intrigued me enough to call back even though it was already past eleven thirty. Ted Karras had called and left his number, asking me to phone him back. I didn't have the faintest idea what he could want, but I was curious enough to find out.

He picked up on the third ring. His voice had an edge to it, as if he was hoping it would be me on the other end of the phone. He'd already heard about Miller. The news'd apparently run a wildfire path through his little burg. He wanted to get my opinion of what'd happened. I told him.

"I don't think he did it."

"Why not?"

"That's my business. What's it to you?"

He explained. Mara's father had called him, asking him what he had thought. It seemed Mrs. Phillips' pride hadn't run out to the point where she didn't care if the town knew men were killing themselves in flea-bait hotels over her daughter. The old man'd been hoping Karras might've had some different news. His call had gotten Miller's ol' pal thinking. Now he was worried about what was going on.

"I, I tried to call you the other morning but, I didn't get no answer, and I, like I didn't call back. But, this got me, sorta . . ." He paused for a sharp moment, then said, "Aww, look. I don't think he done any of it, either. Not killing Fred, or like himself, either—you know?"

"Yeah. So what?"

"Listen. I'm coming up to the city tomorrow. I want to, ah, well like talk to you. You know? I don't know. I think maybe I can, well, you know, maybe tell you some stuff you don't know about."

I was surprised. I hadn't pegged Karras as the kind of guy to help anyone but himself. But then, maybe my first impression had been right. Maybe the loss of a friend, even one as pathetic as Miller, had left too big a hole in Karras' life to allow him to just let it pass. And then again, if I was right and the Dumptruck hadn't killed himself, then maybe giving me some put-away-the-bad-guy facts might just be in Karras's vested self-interest after all.

I asked him if he wanted to talk about it right then and there, but he said, "No." He didn't trust the phone—it had to be in person. I told him I'd be happy to talk to him, gave him the address of a hotel to check into where he wouldn't get robbed blind and where they had parking to boot. He said he'd call when he was settled. I told him that was fine.

After hanging up I called Hu, telling him about Miller's list. I asked him to put a little brainpower to the job of deciphering it all. He told me to read the list over the phone while he taped it. I told him there were easier ways to get him a copy. He admitted that there indeed were, but that they were all easier on me than on him. Then he told me to start reading the list. I did.

After I finally hung up I pulled my Gilbey's bottle free

from its resting place and took a slug just to chase away the stiffness in my back and the dryness in my throat. I shoved the windows full open then, letting in every scrap of the trickling breeze that had found its way up to my level. After that I turned out the lights and fell back into my chair, eyes closed, taking a sip now and then from my bottle, mostly just trying to dry up the sweat. My wrist was itching under its cast, the kind of itching that spreads up and down your body like a runaway flood wall because you can't get your nails at its source.

Ignoring the irritation, I took another slug and checked my watch in the glare flashing in through the window behind me. It was already well past midnight. Sighing, I stood up and stripped off my shirt. Hanging it over my desk chair to dry, I followed up by emptying my pockets into my top drawer. Kicking off my shoes, I made sure the door to the hall was locked and then finished peeling my sweat-sticking clothing away from my body.

I lay on the floor, feeling the dust and grit sticking instantly to my back as I made contact. The wood was dry and hot, like the rest of the world, but my sweat soaked into it, cooling it and making it seem softer. The fan whirred quietly, stirring the sluggish humidity. I closed my eyes and lay in the darkness, thinking about the Dumptruck, and his Mara, and my best friend Jeff Anthony, and all the rest of them, feeling the steam rise off of me, getting madder every second.

That wasn't smart. Calming down, I dropped them all in the porcelain bowl and pulled down the lever, listening to them all whirl away down through the pipes. I'd have to think about them all again in the morning, and that was soon enough. Instead, I thought about being out of town the day they nuke Times Square and vaporize this reeking dump of a city.

Pleasant dreams always help me get to sleep quicker.

# CHAPTER 21

I WOKE UP early. The sun stabbed at me, moving through my office, coming at me from all sides. I surrendered immediately, groaning like the walking dead out of one of those old George Romero films. Dragging myself into a sitting position, I shook my head until my vision cleared and then worked on getting myself up onto the couch. Eventually, despite drifting off for a few minutes here and there and just plain laziness, I got both dressed to the waist and my office back in a workable order.

Stumbling out to the utility sink in the hall, I splashed my face and arms and chest with cold water out of the only working faucet. Then I borrowed some of the cleaning crew's soap powder and rubbed myself raw whipping up enough froth to chase away some of the smell of the day and night just passed. A handful of paper towels later I was feeling good enough to set up for my morning coffee. Waiting for the perking to start, I went back to the hall where I washed my T-shirt, wrung it out, and put it on damp. Its cool wetness felt good as a shield against the heat brewing both inside and out.

Later, after I'd knocked back my first cup of brew and was working on my second, I checked out my other calls from the night before. One was from a bunch of my old Army pals. Every year the group gets together and hits some place like Miami, or the Grand Canyon, or Hollywood, whatever, for a week-long party. It's not always the exact same crew, but it's always the same party.

I've made it a few times, but never in a plaster cast, or in the middle of an unsolved case. The guy in charge of details that year was Mike Bowen. It was good to talk to him again, even if I had to disappoint him by turning the group down a third year in a row. He understood and accepted the facts, good-naturedly letting me know that he and the rest of the guys were getting together to come over and set fire to my car. I told him I'd bring the hot dogs.

The other two calls were for work—an investigation gig from a law firm that'd thrown me a few bones in the past, and a run from a rich woman who wanted someone to babysit her mansion while she went to South America for a month. I nixed the law firm, telling them I was too busy. The work they had in mind called for the worker to do a lot of traveling in the Midwest, and I wasn't in the mood to agree to a thousand miles of driving with a fractured wrist.

I called the rich lady and told her that guarding expensive mansions was one of my specialties. We set up an appointment for a week later to sniff each other over. After that I called my pal Peter Wei. Guarding mansions is more his specialty than it is mine, which gave him some experience I could draw upon. He gave me a handful of tips I was sure would never have occurred to me. I promised to split the detail with him if I managed to actually snag the job.

I thought about giving Hubert or Francis a ring, to see if they had come up with anything for me, but decided not to. Neither one of them had ever sat on anything important in the past. I didn't have any reason to think they were going to start now.

The reason was that I was edgy. I wanted to solve Miller's case for him, even if he was dead. But as I'd told him the day he'd walked into my office, finding missing people in a city the size of New York—especially if they wanted to stay missing—is not the easiest thing in the world. On top of finding Mara so I could nail her for the Dumptruck's fall, I also wanted to find the gumball who had taken out George. That one looked even harder.

The only thing that made George's death look even vaguely connected to the case in the first place was the fact he was killed by a not-so-common type of rifle that Miller had once owned. He'd reported the rifle stolen, and I had the information from Sterling that it probably had been stolen. Could that be one of the things Karras'd decided to come to New York to talk about? There was no way of knowing until he arrived.

Until then, I didn't have anything to do except drink coffee and read the paper I'd bought from Freddie the night before—or so I thought. I froze as the door to my outer office opened. I'm not usually such a jumpy guy, but I'm not usually involved in a case with as many unknowns as Miller's, either. Holding the newspaper quietly with one hand, I slid my other into the drawer where I'd stashed my .38 and pulled it free. Two seconds more proved there'd been no need.

"Hi," said Jean Ward, coming into my office.

"'Hi' back," I told her.

"You look cool enough."

I lifted my arms to show off my T-shirt, sliding the .38 back into its hole first.

"Like my new summer look, huh?"

"Love it. Let's try and interest Bloomie's in a whole line."

"Think they'll go for it?"

"The wet T-shirt as high fashion? Sure; those pretentious yups will sell anything they think their even more pretentious customers will buy."

She was hesitant, not nearly as happy as she sounded, and yet clearly relieved. She kept moving around the office as we talked, not taking a seat. Finally, I said, "You heard."

She nodded, quietly asking for details. I gave them to her. I told her everything—from Andren to Jeff Anthony to Karras to Ballard to Miller's note. She was glad the whole thing was over as far as the police were concerned—I could hardly blame her for that. She must have caught something in my voice, though.

"They're satisfied, but you're not. Are you?"

I admitted I still had my doubts. When she quizzed me, I laid the blame at Karras' feet, not wanting to tell her I suspected her onetime best friend of murder. I try not to spread my theories around too much. Facts upset people enough as it is. I told her he'd hinted he might have some news for me, and that I was going to meet with him later in the day.

She was as amazed as I'd been that Karras might actually go to some trouble for Miller, especially if it meant sticking his own neck out. She insisted on hearing the whole story, what little there was of it. I gave it all to her, down to where I'd told him to stay, but it still seemed too unbelievable to hear.

"You just don't understand," she said. "Ted Karras is a creep. A major creep. It just isn't like him to do this. If he really did help Mara rob Carl, I simply can't imagine him admitting it later. I mean, who would? It just isn't like him."

I had to admit the same thoughts had crossed my mind. The main impression Karras left one with was that of an upright weasel, one who maintained the position only through skeletal arrangement. The idea that his call might be some sort of setup had been growing since the sun had first burned me awake. Ward voiced the same idea.

"Don't go. Look at what's happened to you already. You can't trust that little snake. He was always the worst, filthy little scum—his eyes—the way he would look at you, and the way he would talk to you—auuggghhh, that slimy . . . that—oh, oh, oh, I know I sound silly, but I'm serious. Jack—God, please . . ."

And suddenly she was around the desk and holding me, trying to talk and cry at the same time. Her words told me that what might happen to me would make a difference to her, and that she knew it was crazy, and then suddenly her lips were still moving but she wasn't talking anymore. Her teeth tore at my ear and neck, her tongue smoothing over any damage they did. Her breath was hot and wet and I breathed it in like a tonic.

I crushed her to me and felt the pain in my back and neck and side and wrist but shoved it aside, running my hands over the woman in my arms as if she were my last ten girlfriends and my ex-wife and all the other ruined relationships I'd ever had come back to give me one last chance to make it all up. My eyes fogged over and I moved out of the chair. We stood for a moment but soon found ourselves on the floor, tearing at each other like a couple out of the 42nd Street twenty-five-cent loop films.

She pushed at me with one hand, but held on with the other, whispering from far back in her throat, "Let's go to my place. We're only a few minutes away." She looked at me with her hard eyes, begging for a chance to soften them. "Please. Let's make this good."

There was a promise and a hint in her voice that let me know the sweat-stained floor of my office would not mean nearly as much to her as her bedroom would. Somehow the little voice inside got through to me as well, reminding me that after the passion, her memory would see a guy who just had to have it when he wanted it, no ifs, ands, or buts. I wanted her, but I wanted her for more than an hour. It had been a long time since anyone had shown any concern for me—real concern, worried, connected concern—I'd almost forgotten that sometimes people can still do that.

I grimaced, but nodded, consoling the raging voice of need that kept pumping blood through my brain with the fact that our throbbing back and side and wrist might like a bed better than a hardwood floor as well. Jean and I got up off the floor, smiling those teenage smiles of regret, holding ourselves in check from grabbing each other and just having to untangle all over again. Catching up my shirt and a pair of sunglasses, I herded her to the door like a sheepdog barking the last lamb back into the flock. We took the stairs two, three at a time, racing each other to the street, laughing like lunatics by the time we got out into Union Square.

Practically dancing to my car, we were in it, uptown, parked, and dancing down her sidewalk in under fifteen minutes. We were in front of her door in less than another two. As she slipped her locks and opened her door, though,

we were hit by an unrelenting wave of hot stale air. She
gasped.

"Oh, God. I forgot; when I moved in with Barbara I
locked up all the windows."

We stepped further back into the hallway, catching our
breaths. Waving a hand in front of her face, Jean said,

"Look. The bathroom is to the left, back around the
kitchen. You go and get the shower going"—her fingers
played with my chest— "and get in"—twining hair around
their nails— "and wait for me."

"Yeah." I grinned. I actually grinned. "And what are
you going to do?"

"I'm going to get the air conditioners going."

"Trying to put out the fire?"

"Trying to keep it concentrated."

I laughed as she pushed me off toward the bathroom,
taking in her apartment as I went. It was a bit more classy
than I'm used to, a mostly white-and-pink Art Deco affair
with colored stripes and patterns in all the right places.
There were a lot of posters from museum art shows—some
from Manhattan, some from Paris. The soft whirr of the air
conditioners came up in the background. They were a signal
to keep moving, which I did, all the way to the bathroom
hall, where I got stopped in my tracks. It was another poster
which stopped me, one of Jean Ward the model at work.

Byler's nasty little speech about his ex posing for "faggot
underwear ads," came back to me. The central figure was
one of those thin-lipped, disinterested pouting boys who
seemed to be selling us everything from cars to mutual
bonds a year or two back. He was well-muscled but
soft-looking. His sneer was a pose with no strength to back
it up—just contempt.

Jean was kneeling at his feet dressed only in a torn teddy,
gartered stockings, and one high-heeled shoe. Her arms were
wrapped around his legs, the fingernails of one hand half
under the elastic of his cotton briefs, clawing toward his
crotch. There was a hint of lipstick halfway between the
claws and his groin, one that matched the way Jean's was
smeared. He didn't seem up to noticing, though.

Music came up behind me suddenly then, the Tchaikovsky they used in some Disney cartoon. Taking my cue, I stopped staring and headed into the bathroom. I flipped on the hot water and stripped out of my too-warm clothes, dropping them in a heap on my shoes. Reaching in through the mounting steam, I cooled the flow enough to make it tolerable and then stepped inside. I let the water scald me, burning away the pains I was still lugging around, softening their effect. Keeping my cast from getting wet was a problem, but I managed fairly well.

I soaked for a long time, feeling my pores open and my pains fade away. It felt good—so good I barely noticed how long Jean was taking until she arrived. She knocked on the glass door almost shyly.

"Room for anyone else?"

I slid the door open a crack, telling her, "I think so."

She slid the door over the rest of the way and my heart skipped. She'd made herself over in soft pink and black—blushing makeup surrounded by dark lace and soft ribbons. Her hair was all swept to one side, little wisping curls of it playing across her face. She was more beautiful than her ads, more beautiful than my imagination. I reached out and pulled her inside, sliding the door closed behind her.

Then, I spotted her eyes staring at one of the bruises on my shoulder. I hadn't stopped to think about what I looked like, all welts and bruises and crusts of blood where the broken skin had scabbed over. And then I remembered the ugly black patch on her shoulder and suddenly realized why she'd worn a negligee into the shower.

"Oh, Jack. You've got so many bruises."

"Why don't you kiss them all and make them better?"

She kissed my lips instead, running her tongue over and between them, dueling with mine. Pulling back, she kissed her way down the front of my neck, and then my chest, pulling at the hair there with her teeth. Hot water splashed over us, turning our skin red.

"I wouldn't know where to begin," she whispered, her knees sinking beneath the water level in the stall, she finished, "so I think maybe I'll kiss something without any bruises at all."

Like I said before, I try not to argue with beautiful women; it makes them cranky. Happy to accept her logic, I breathed in the steam in gasps, my hands on her shoulders, moving back and forth to the rhythm she set. The misting clouds all around us narrowed the world in sharply but, it was all the world we needed.

# CHAPTER 22

IT SEEMED LIKE years later when I returned to the office. Actually it was only two thirty. The shower turned into a long romping session that ended in a lunch filled with joking and teasing, which led to another session. The carrying-on put us in almost every room in Jean's apartment and loosened every muscle in my body to the point where picking up a pencil seemed like too much bother.

I made it back to my office, however, as cheerful as a man could be in my circumstances. I felt good, was stuffed with a great meal (although why women seem intent on loading me with salad and tofu is beyond my comprehension), and had started something with a beautiful woman that for once might stay alive longer than the first flowers I sent her. Throwing my sunglasses back in their corner of my top drawer, I shoved the windows open first thing, getting the fan going second. My message machine told me Ted Karras had arrived and was checked into his hotel.

I sat back, listening to his taped voice, trying to decide from what I was hearing just what his game might be. Then I rewound it and played it twice more. He sounded sincere; I had to grant him that. Search as I might, I couldn't find any sense of danger in his call and, after my run-in with Jeff Anthony and my warning from Jean, you can trust that I was listening with care. My instincts told me he was clean, though, and I decided I could stop worrying about the little weasel.

Also deciding he could wait a little longer, I headed back outside, walking down to 12th Street to a florist I knew. I blew more cash than was reasonable but less than I had, sending Jean a large mixed bouquet of everything in the shop that looked good. It'd been a long time since anything besides the sun had made me feel warm, and I wanted to do something about it before I let it all slide and whatever was beginning to happen between us piled up on the same rocks as all the other whatevers I've begun.

I hadn't forgotten about Miller, or Mara, or my good pal Jeff Anthony, either, but somehow they weren't as drivingly important as they had been a few hours earlier. People murder and get killed and dish out beatings and steal from each other every second of the day in New York. Miller and his crew were nothing new or special. In fact, in a world where airplanes fall from the sky on a routine basis, where people kill grandmothers and children with bombs just to emphasize a point, and cops get shotgunned to death by people trying to avoid speeding tickets, murderers with a reason that makes sense were almost refreshing.

With Jean's flowers on their way uptown I walked back to the office, gearing up for getting back to work. Having basically committed myself to my rich lady and her guardless mansion, I couldn't afford to waste a lot of time on a closed case. Of course, that wasn't much different from my regular attitude. I'm not a patient man; I don't like waiting. Whenever a case bogs down, the itch starts to get me. I was already restless—having Jean come into my life wasn't helping me concentrate.

By the time I was back in my office, though, I was ready to get back down to work. Resigning myself to not throwing in the towel until I'd gotten to the bottom of the problems the Dumptruck'd left behind, I picked up the receiver and called Karras' hotel. The switchboard put me through. The phone rang; I waited. Nobody picked up the other end.

I let it ring ten times, and then ten more. Finally the switchboard girl came back on, informing me that no one was picking up in the room. I thanked her for letting me in on the secret, then asked her to connect me with the desk clerk. She did. An older woman's voice came on the line.

"And how may I help you, sir?"

"You should have a Mr. Ted Karras registered . . ."

"Yes, sir. Room 403."

"Right. Do you know if he happened to step out? We were supposed to meet as soon as he got into town but, I was, ah, delayed. Now I can't seem to reach him."

"Mr. Karras . . ." she said, trying to remember. "Slight build, dark hair, not a handsome gentleman—yes, yes, he's in. Shall I have the switchboard ring his room for you?"

"No. We just tried that."

I was a little confused, but then suddenly, the Sick Feeling grabbed me and squeezed—hard. Everyone knows its touch—it's that stabbing feeling that springs into the brain and then drops to the guts like lightning—when you see a person you know you'll never have a chance with, or a house you know life is never going to let you enter, let alone buy and enjoy. It's that quick flash of pain that invades your system every time Fate doesn't play fair with you. I had no facts, just a feeling—but it was enough. I asked the woman,

"Humm. Well, could you tell me if Mr. Karras has had any visitors?"

I asked because I knew the place I'd sent Karras required its visitors to sign in. The desk clerk begged off for a second to check her records, and then got back on the line with me.

"Yes, yes he did. A Mr. Jack Hagee came to see him at ten o'clock."

She was so good with names and descriptions I tried her out again.

"Is that the Jack Hagee who used a cane?"

"Yes. A big gentleman. Heavy shoulders. One wouldn't think a man that large would need a cane."

No, I thought, not for Karras. I thanked the clerk and depressed the receiver button with my finger, letting it up and calling Ray when the line went clear. Television detectives might get away with hiding out and making fools of the police when dead men are piling up with the P.I.'s name checked off in the suspects' box, but since no one'd offered me my own show that week, I thought perhaps I'd handle things differently.

"Jack," he started, "I'm in no mood for bad news."

"Then hang up, 'cause that's the only type I got."

"Tell me this is connected with that Miller shit and I'll kill you."

"Better men have tried."

I told him the what and the where, the how and the who. I didn't tell him the why because I didn't know it—yet. He told me he didn't have time to run around town chasing down my hunches. I told him,

"Fine. I don't care. I'm going to Karras' room and have the house dick open it for me. You've got better things to do . . ."

Ray sighed, telling me not to go in until he got there, promising to meet me in under half an hour. I said "Swell" and hung up. I sat looking through the phone for nearly five minutes, my vision boring out through the walls to the street beyond. Whatever good mood I'd gathered to myself over maybe having established something with Jean had gone down in black-clouded flames crashing against the rocks of Karras' death. A small voice, pleading for the life of my newfound cheerfulness, tried reminding me that I really didn't know the Dumptruck's bony little friend was dead.

After all, it told me, all I had was a hunch. Just a couple of unrelated facts cobbled together to tell me Karras was smashed up and broken in his hotel room. Maybe his visitor only went there to frighten him out of town. Maybe there was no answer in his room because he'd snuck out and run away from New York and the murderous lunatics who went mad within its boundaries.

But I knew that wasn't the case—deep inside—I knew it. He'd been beaten once before, most likely for the same reason he'd been killed this time, for trying to stick by the only person ever to stick by him. I knew it as surely as I knew Ted Karras was dead, beaten to death slowly and cruelly with a cane with which I was extremely familiar. And I knew that if it was the last thing I ever did I was going to make sure that cane never beat anyone else—ever.

Once I got my wind, I threw myself up out of my chair, mopping at the sweat on my face and forearms with my al-ready soaking handkerchief. I checked my .38 over, loading it and making sure it was ready for work. Slipping on my shoulder holster I secured the small revolver inside and then checked the draw as I always do, making sure everything felt comfortable and ready. Then I shut down my fan and closed all the windows, again. I knew it was going to take me a long time to disentangle myself from the cops.

I also knew it was going to take me a long time to track down Jeff Anthony, but that this time I was going to do it. I'd allowed my own good fortune and Jean's tearful smile to distract me. I wasn't about to blame myself for Karras' death; anyone who thinks they'd have done differently has never lost at love and thought they'd never have another chance at it, which makes them one lucky son of a bitch. If taking the first bit of happiness that's come my way in years was a crime, then book me and let it be.

It bothered my conscience that a man might have died because I wasn't near my telephone, but not enough to make me wish what took me away from it had never happened. I wasn't there—someone died. Okay, I'm not God. I can't predict the future—I can only clean up the messes the present drops off on my doorstep.

Checking the draw on my own brand of cleanser again, I slid it back into my shoulder holster and then left the office, locking the door behind me. The time had come to end things.

Great, I thought. I'm ready.

# CHAPTER 23

WE STOOD IN front of Ted Karras' hotel room, Mooney knocking on the door over and over, waiting for an answer I knew wasn't coming. Ray warned me three times between the lobby and the hallway we were in that he was going to run me through the wringer if we didn't find anything. I was beginning to get the idea he was going to run me through it whether we found anything or not.

Finally tiring of listening to Mooney's ham-sized fists bounce off the metal door, Ray ordered the house detective to open it. He did. As it swung open, nothing showed itself to be out of place. The room was a bit sloppy, newspapers and clothing strewn about, but nothing to indicate a murder. Nothing at first, anyway.

Something in the air kept everyone from yelling about their wasted time. Maybe it was the way the broken lamp on the dresser jagged its way upward from under Karras' shorts that kept everyone from jumping down my throat. And things only got quieter from there. We walked around the corner to the bathroom. That was where the real mess started.

Karras was smeared from one corner to the other. Apparently, the beating that spread his brains across three of the four walls had started near the door and then continued inward until he'd been forced down into the bottom of the bathtub. Possibly he'd tried to lock himself in the bathroom—whatever'd been happening, however, the end result was that Karras was dead, dead in a harsh and lonely way.

He'd been subdued quickly—bound and gagged with his own clothing. Then, once there would be no noise except the muffled thuds of a heavy object against flesh, and the occasional cracking of bones, the poor little weasel'd been systematically thrashed until he'd become no more than a sack of jellied meat and goo. His blood was all around us; it coated the floor like wall-to-wall carpeting—an arc of it had even made it to the ceiling. One of his eyes had been dislodged. It lay clogging the drain, backing up a puddle of hardening, blackening blood. The other had been completely ruined, splattered like a sideshow balloon at the dart toss.

Bones stuck out of his skin at odd angles, cracked bits and pieces littering the floor, stuck to the tub and walls by dried blood and other fluids. The gagged head was propped in an impossible pose, screaming up at us out of the porcelain grave even though he was chest down over the rim of the tub. One of his legs was broken up underneath him, the other hanging half over the edge. When Ray made to nudge it more into the tub, skin blooded fast to the edge tore away, leaving a small patch behind for someone to scrape off later. Maybe it would be buried with him. Maybe it wouldn't.

"Christ," muttered Mooney. "I hope this guy never wasted time taking out an organ donor's card."

My hands started for Mooney's collar. I wanted to take his laughing, beefy face and bounce it off the wall—a lot more than once. It didn't matter to me that he'd seen enough scenes like the one before us over the years to grow insensitive to them. I didn't care that the heat had made us all irritable and more prone to relieving the pressure without thinking.

The body of a human being lay before us, broken and splattered. A man had been murdered, viciously, insanely. It could've been done a lot more easily, quickly, but the man swinging the cane had wanted to have some fun. His enjoyment showed in the extra time he had taken—fingers crushed, toes smashed to miserable pulp, one ear ripped off and hanging sickly by threads of flesh. It was nauseating . . . period. It was an abomination, not something to make jokes about. I was sick of the excuses people use to justify their behavior. More than that, I was sick of Mooney and just wanted to bounce his head off the back wall.

I let it pass, though. Doing something as crazy as the handiwork in front of me wasn't going to help Karras, or Miller, or me for that matter. Swallowing my anger I turned from the scene in the bathroom and went out into the hall. Leaning back against the wall, I slid down it suddenly, my knees weakening under me. I'd taken too much punishment over the past few days, pushed myself too hard. I fumbled the little doc's pills out of my pocket, swallowing two more of them dry. It was too late for them to help, though. The toxins were building up in my system, breaking the balance of my emotions up like driftwood in a storm. I felt tears I couldn't find a reason for cooling my stinging eyes. Wiping the trickle away, I sat on my heels, exhausted. Waiting. I didn't have to wait long.

"Okay," came Ray's voice from above me. "How did you know?"

"A hunch," I told him.

"My ass."

I looked up, all the weariness of the world crushing me toward the carpeting. "Fuck yourself, Ray," I told him. "It was a hunch. That's it. I called him back and was told I'd already visited him. The last time I tried to rouse someone waiting for me in a hotel room, they were dead—remember? When the desk clerk told me the 'Mr. Hagee' who visited Karras used a cane, then it just hit me that he was dead." The breath came out of me in a ragged sigh. "I just knew."

I looked back down again, resting, not caring what was going on in Ray's head. Until he made up his mind on what was going to be, there was no use in doing anything but getting some rest. I settled for it, waiting for God to make up his mind over what the future held for us all. God finally told me we had to talk. I told him, "Swell."

"Come on; get up off the floor. We can't talk here."

"Why not?" I indicated with my hand. "There's nobody around."

"Because bodies bring crowds and if we're going to talk about this one, we're going to do it in private."

Mooney was told to call headquarters and get Ed Collins and his crew down to the scene. The house dick was told to lock the room and make certain no one but the police team entered. I was told to get up off the floor again.

I always get the hard jobs.

# CHAPTER 24

A FEW MINUTES later found Ray and me in my Skylark parked a few blocks from the hotel. While we watched the splendor of the city pass by the windows, my best friend on the force outlined my options.

"Okay. Ready to hear how this one plays?"

"Yeah. I can hardly wait."

"Fine. I love having people's undivided attention. Now, Mr.-Hagee-who-checked-in-as-a-visitor-at-ten-o'clock-this-morning, how would you like to go down to the station and go through the routine?"

"About as much as I'd like to take a bubble bath with your mother in Room 403. Skip the threats. I know what a tough guy you are and I'm not up for a day or two of rotting in your iron-bar resort spa. What's rattling?"

The Trenkel smile lit up—the one that means trouble—the only one I've ever seen.

"I figure you for a real public-spirited citizen, Jackie-boy. I really do. This new image of yours you've been bragging about is paying off. I believe in this whole new Jack Hagee. In fact, I believe in him so much, I'm going to let him do the NYPD a favor."

"Let me guess. Karras couldn't make me throw up, so you're trying."

"Funny boy. Laugh all the way to the Gates of Hell. Abandon hope. Do not collect two hundred dollars. Shut yer yap."

"Yass'suh, massa, suh."

"You'll learn your place yet."

Yeah, I thought, going upside your miserable dustbucket

of a head. Like with Mooney, though, I left it at an impulse. Going with the feeling that I might get what I wanted if I played my cards right, I decided to keep quiet and let my host do the talking.

"You're pretty sure this Anthony character did in Karras, aren't you?"

I nodded.

"Much as I hate to admit it, I think you're right. I looked into this guy after you got your lumps. Bad news, this clown. He hasn't been in town long, but he's got a sheet. A lot more suspicion than facts, but he's down as a very bad boy."

"So what?"

"So, I want you to take him down. I'll cover the action. At best this punk has friends in low places—no one goes out of their way to help hired psychos. Not even the ACLU'll rattle our cage if you powder his brains. The only bad news is, you're going to have to break the case before you break his back."

"In English?"

"You give me all the answers on this one and you can skag Citizen Anthony. I want more circumstances. If you can pin Miller's murder on someone, go for it. Nail them to the barn door with Jesus-sized spikes. Same for Karras. Find some proof that'll stand up and you have carte blanche for a day. Anthony'll be all yours."

Normally Ray is as cooperative as any other part of City Hall. For him to stay out of the way is one thing, offering presents was another. His sudden about-face had me wondering. I asked the necessary question.

"Why?"

"Because I'm a great guy."

"Yeah, and there's a dime under my pillow from the tooth fairy. Don't send me into this blind, Ray. Give it."

The cop face stared at me sharply. Ray was used to giving orders, not explanations. Maybe he realized it was a fair request; maybe after looking at the mindless ruin upstairs he was too shook to play his normal tough-guy self. Whatever it was, he gave me his answer.

"Ever since Miller went down, and I know that isn't so long ago, there's been some pressure to find a different answer to his 'unfortunate demise.' Someone up high is apparently friendly with someone from Miller's home town."

It made sense. I could even name the someone—Joseph Phillips. It was his call that'd propelled Karras to come to New York in the first place. Perhaps the weasel's motives might not have been so noble after all. I could see another check being written, one to help spur Karras on toward the truth—one that wouldn't have been reclaimed at the door-way. Having a future son-in-law murdered is one thing—having him make a grand suicide exit, citing your daughter as the cause of grief, is another. Mrs. Phillips was having a hard enough time staying a part of the social register without the Dumptruck's swan song adding to her prob-lems.

"We could have quieted things down," Ray went on, "but this is getting to be too much to keep wrapped up. You know that son of a bitch Violano from the *Post*'ll be upstairs before we're done talking. I got no doubts he'll make the connection between Miller and Karras—two guys from the same home town die in Manhattan hotel rooms in two days—he'll catch it. I can see the two-hundred-point type already. That prick's been kicking for a Pulitzer ever since Breslin got his."

And now I knew the source of all Ray's cooperation. Rich Violano was one of the toughest crime reporters the city had ever known. He'd lit a number of fires under the city's smug rump in his time, zeroing in on Ray's precinct more than once.

The grudge between Ray and Rich was well known in Manhattan. Neither had gone to extremes—the police hadn't started tailing Rich's car, watching for busted taillights, or one-mile-over-the-limit speeding, and Rich hadn't started doing columns dogging every cop for every apple ever taken from a fruit stand—they were both too professional for that—but they watched each other closely, looking for moments to pounce. So far, the non-drinking, non-drugging, heterosexual, and basically honest Violano was pretty far ahead of the game.

Not knowing how to handle an honest man, the city had started with placation and ended with cover-ups and running away. If Ray was worried about Rich before we'd even seen him, that meant he'd already been nosing around. Maybe old man Phillips'd called him as well as Karras. Maybe Rich was the super-reporter the *Post* keeps claiming he is.

Whatever the case, it meant I had a free hand—if I could deliver the case in a box with a pink ribbon, and if I could catch up to my ol' pal Jeff Anthony, and if I could keep my name off the credit for both of the previous "ifs," which might not be as simple as it seemed on the surface. Turning to stare at Ray straight on, I told him,

"Don't worry. I already have some ideas on what's been going on. I have a couple of feelers out right now, which, if we're lucky, will pull Anthony and Miller and Karras into one stew pot. If I can paint them all into the same black corner, trust me—I'll do it. And I'll turn it all over to you and do the quietest fade you ever saw."

"You bet your ass you will, or I'll bring you low and lay your deranged client and your working past the time he was dead and you were off the case at the media's feet and let them gobble you down. You'll have no credibility after that. Trust me." Ray stepped out of my car, leaning back in through the open window. Pointing his finger at me, he shaped up his warning.

"Get it through your head—I could just as easily take George being murdered in your office, and your name on the register back there, and the fact that through your own admission you were supposed to meet with . . . with—what the hell was his name . . . ?"

"Karras."

". . . with Karras, and all the other money-assed bull-shit in this case and clear it all out of my lap. Those TV boys love something new. How about a private eye who gets some citizen killed by pushing a closed investigation? By the time the Fourth Estate gets done with their electronic tar-and-feathering, your rep will be so much dog food. And, by the time it all gets straightened out, if it ever does, it'll be old news and not worth anyone's time. Even Violano only beats a dead horse for a day or two.

"But, you made it clear to me earlier this week that I still owe you one. Okay—here's your payoff. I'm going to talk misdirection about 'special investigators.' You have some facts for me quick, before they start turning up the heat on me. You bring me George's murderer, and Karras'. You clean up this Miller suicide/murder, you find this Mara bitch, and I will cover any quiet disposal you make of Jeff Anthony.

"You keep your fee from Miller, and anything else that comes your way, and my department keeps the credit for busting the case. Agreeable to you?"

I wanted my money to stay in my pocket, and I wanted whoever'd killed a man in my office, and I wanted the killer who did in my client, and I wanted the bastard who'd beaten me silly and another man to pulp. And since if I didn't want those things badly enough to go after them, the police would feed me to the press one black-tarred slur at a time. I saw little choice in saying anything but,

"Yeah, beautiful. It's a great plan—it sings. I love it."

"Funny man. Just deliver on time."

"Sure, sure. Stop drooling on my upholstery."

Ray stood away from the car, circling it warily as if he expected me to try and run him over. It didn't sound like a bad idea to the mood he'd left me in but, I had a sneaking suspicion I wouldn't get away with it, so I let it pass. Besides, anything that put Mooney closer to the Captain's office was not something in my best interests.

I pulled away from the curb carefully, avoiding both Ray and the car waiting to back into the parking spot I was creating. Due to the shortage of spaces available, New Yorkers are always circling blocks like vultures, waiting for openings. Maybe four percent of the city's residents who drive have a place to lock up their cars. The rest of us get to fight it out in the streets. Just another one of the marvelous devices the city maintains to keep tempers high and the

citizens hating each other instead of their thieving admin-
istration.

I put thoughts other than those about the case I was on out
of my head. I had to concentrate. Between the heat I was
getting from the sun and that which I was getting from the
police, I didn't need anything else to set me off. I was still
a little surprised. Ray Trenkel was supposed to be my pal. If
anything, I thought, it was his fault I was in the mess I was
in. Of course, that was only half true. Just because Mooney
and he thought it would be humorous to send the Dumptruck to me didn't make it their fault I took the case. Much
as I hated to admit it, being mired where I was was my fault,
and the only way I was going to get out was by clawing my
own way clear.

Karras' hotel was fairly close to my office. By the time I
got inside my own eight walls it was past eight thirty. First
duty was opening the windows and getting the fan going.
Second was to check the message machine. It had a call
from Francis. He was ready to report. I called him back, but
found it was his turn not to be in. Leaving him a message to
get back to me pronto, I dialed up Hubert. He was in.

"Y-your dime, start yakkin'."

"It's gone up, Hu."

"Hey, hey, Dick Tracy. Movin' in to c-consumer report-
ing now, eh? What's the word?"

I laid out Ray's current method for paying back favors.
Hubert laughed his duck screech, letting me know what he
thought of me for believing a cop could be anyone's pal.
After taking what I deserved, I said,

"Okay, okay, calm down. Don't get a hernia. What about
your end of this? Get anywhere with that list?"

"Yeah, sure. What'd you expect?"

He actually sounded a bit hurt. I hadn't expected him to
come up dry—even on the short notice he'd had—I never
do. Normally I wouldn't have phrased things to sound as if I
had, but I wasn't in the mood to think of anyone's feelings
but my own . . . which is always a bad move. I placated
Hubert.

"Sorry, Hu. I'm not riding the right tracks today. Do you want to give it over the phone or meet somewhere?"

"Did you have dinner, yet?"

"No. Not really."

"Great. You c-can treat me to a steak."

Why not? I thought. I told Hu to meet me in an hour at Louie's, a steak and seafood place on the border of the Village. It was close enough to walk to and worth the trouble. Their steaks were tender, big, and reasonable. Louie served them covered in melting slices of onions and black-burned mushrooms, with baby carrots all around the edges, soft but not soggy, dripping in butter. He also had the cheapest per-pound price in town on two clawed lobsters, an attraction that had drawn me there even during the times I was making my gas money up out of returnable beer bottle refunds.

My coffee pot was still out where I'd left it, a third filled with tepid brown/black fluid. Pulling open the deep drawer, I dragged out my Gilbey's and poured a little into the pot as sweetener. Capping the bottle, I hoisted the coffee, drinking straight from the pot. A trickle ran down my chin. I caught it with my wrist and then drained the glass bowl with two long pulls. Taking the Gilbey's again, I poured several fingers worth into the pot and then swirled it around, collecting up the last dregs of caffeine clinging to the bottom.

Once I was satisfied I had all I was going to get, I knocked back the now tan-colored gin, setting the pot and its hot plate back in their file cabinet drawer when I was finished. Some people might not approve, but I've always found it the easiest way to clean the bowl before I put it away. Besides, like my mom always used to say, find some fun in your work and even the most disagreeable task will suddenly become tolerable.

After that I did a bit of cleaning, trying to straighten up the mess I'd been making of the place for the last week. I didn't put much effort into it. The cast on my wrist was a bit hampering, as was the heat, and the fact I don't really much care what the place looks like. I made the attempt mostly to have something to do until it was time to leave for Louie's other than drinking up all my gin.

The phone rang before I could finish, though. It was Francis. He had the information I wanted. I asked him if he had eaten yet. He hadn't. I told him,

"Hu and I are meeting at Louie's in about a half an hour."

"Room for one more on the check?"

"Sure, but it'll come out of your fee."

"Nix that," he told me. "Pay the check—take it off your taxes."

"You pay it and take it off your taxes."

"If I pay, we eat at Burger King."

Giving up, I offered, "I'll treat a third—the rest bites your fee."

"Only if you cruise the tip."

"Fine—Christ. Whatever; just be there."

I hung up. Leave it to a law student to plea-bargain a dinner check. Glancing at my watch, I found I had just enough time to take the long way around through Tompkins Square Park if I left right away. The park was always relaxing— watching the old men play chess, drug dealers weaseling the passersby, muggers sizing up just who was carrying around their dinner money. Well, maybe not relaxing, but better than cleaning the office. Grabbing my hat, I hit the lights and locked the door behind me.

A little dust never hurt anyone.

# CHAPTER 25

I WAS THE second to show. Hubert was the first. No big surprise. He'd come early to make sure we got his favorite table, the one underneath Charlie. Charlie is Hu's name for the stuffed sailfish hanging from the dining room ceiling in Louie's. For a while the management refused to seat us there. That all started after the time we'd had a few too many rounds and decided we'd determine who'd pay the bill by seeing who could flip an onion ring over Charlie's nose. Louie was not amused—neither were the people we hit with the onion rings.

It'd been one of those bad nights. We'd gone to an apartment in Queens to see Manfield Mills, a cocaine dealer we knew, to get some information. All we got was an eyeful. Manny'd been playing both ends against the middle for some time, shorting his customers on their blow and his suppliers on their cut. As they always do when you're up to no good, the wrong people found out. They'd gagged Manny and his family and done their work slowly—slicing away fingers, toes, ears, breasts, taking their time to leave a clear message. Crucifying the baby to the ceiling most likely got the message across to everybody. Hu and I stood dazed for we'll never know how long—staring at the small drips of blood falling from above.

The killers'd left more than that scene as a warning. To show what they valued the most, they left two, maybe three, kilos of coke out on the dining room table. In one bedroom they left Manny's guns, all neatly arrayed on the dresser. In another they left his money—four boxes of it—one box each for tens, twenties, fifties, and hundreds. We also found manny's ten-year-old son tied facedown and spread-eagled to the bed, his life run out of him from the rear, saturating the sheets and the mattress, covering the ugly slivers of glass they'd left in him. That was it for Hu.

Seeing he was going to lose his lunch, I shoved his head in the box of hundreds. The heaving splatter broke out of him in wave after wave, seeping down through the crumpled bills in the cardboard box. When he finished, we finally came to our senses and cleared out of the apartment as quickly as possible. We took the box of vomit and hundreds with us, not wanting to leave any trace of our visit behind for the police to discover. They've tracked people down before that with less to go on. Besides, money is printed on high-quality paper. It's washable.

Anyway, after we'd locked the box in my trunk we'd gone bar-hopping, trying to drink the scattered limbs and blood and the staring, pleading frozen eyes out of our memories. By the time we'd hit Louie's, tossing onion rings at a sailfish's nose hadn't seemed so crazy to us.

I walked up to the table, narrowing my eyes at Hubert's humor.

"Hey, hey, Dick Tracy—Charlie says we should order the onion rings."

"Tell him Louie took them off the menu."

I sat down, making small talk with Hu until Francis arrived. The law student pulled his chair under him, whistling as he saw the condition of my face.

"Whhhheeeewwww. What happened to you, Jack? Try punching out a bus?"

"Nope. Just took a whiz in the wrong bathroom."

A waiter came up out of nowhere then, dropping off menus, taking our drink orders, reminding us not to bother ordering the onion rings. They never let you forget. Ignoring the hired help's wit, we got down to business. I told Hu to go first. He had plenty.

"I'll give it t-to you short, first. One-word answer. Antiques."

"Okay, fine. Now give it to me long."

"Miller's list is a bunch of antiques. H-here. Starting

at the top of the list. This 'Fractur.' They're a type of Pennsylvania D-Dutch folk art. They're a watercolor thingus. They use them as birth or wedding announcements. Most of them are pretty crudely done, not worth more than a hundred bucks. B-but a good one now, one with the kind of attention to detail a real artist might give it, one like that can fetch four or five grand.''

"Keep going.''

"Okay. The wind-up blackface? That's a t-toy. Little black guy, one-man-band kinda thing. If you got one that ain't rusted—that still works—easy grand plus profit.

"The Mettlachs're beer steins. King o'beer steins. Mettlach is a town in Germany—they been makin' the things there since about a hundred and fifty years back. Price depends on style, age, the n-number of that type in existence, et cetera. Can be worth two, three grand apiece.''

Hubert kept working his way down the list and I began seeing the pattern. Almost all of the antiques were German or Pennsylvania Dutch in origin. A natural interest for a man of German descent living near the Amish areas. Especially for one with a shrewd business sense. Hubert spelled out the fact that a lot of the things on the list looked fairly worthless to the untrained eye—they weren't the kind of antiques that got any clown on the street thinking they could be worth big money.

So Miller had spent his weekends going from backwater farm to backwater farm, searching out treasures to build a nest egg for his and Mara's future. Sterling'd said Miller had heavy physical investments that Mara and Karras had planned to rip off. The list from Miller's bag was the list of his missing antiques. Why he'd brought it with him was unclear. If he'd wanted the stuff tracked down, he'd have told me about them in the beginning. His reasons didn't matter now, though. Not to him, anyway.

Our drinks arrived then, along with our chance to order dinner. After we did, I told Francis to give me what he had. He had plenty, too.

"How the Ostrich was purchased and by whom. Not small tasks, not easy ones, but as always, you came to the

right source. Listen and learn. The Blue Ostrich was at one
time known under another name. A few too many things of
an undesirable nature happened in the club under that name,
however, and it was closed through the power of the grand
American judicial system. You may remember the former
name—The Silver Mirror?''

I remembered. The place were Joey Sal Pirelliano gunned
down Sammy Bago'Donuts—where the cops found the
money from the Duchler killing. The place was eventually
half-gutted by fire, a blaze started as naturally as the
groundswell that elected our last mayor.

''Nice,'' I told him. ''Who bought it?''

''Nobody.''

''Keep going.''

''It was never sold. Same owners.''

Francis sat back waiting for me to guess. I was in no
mood to play Jeopardy. I told him so. ''Don't play games
with me. I don't have the time.''

''There's no sense of drama left in the world.'' Francis
sighed theatrically to gain his required moment of suspense
and then got on with things. ''The owners, medium-height
members of a certain family of olive growers who for all
IRS-ical intents and purposes don't exist in modern America, after their initial newsmaking days with the club in
question, decided that if the place reopened, their names
weren't going to be on the bar checks.''

''So how did Sterling get into it then?''

''They put the club up on the board as an investment.
They couldn't sell it for beans—all the bad press had
lowered its market potential.''

''They couldn't sell a midtown location?''

''Not for the kind of profit they wanted. So they offered
a pretty sweet deal. They wanted a single investor or
investment group with a lot of liquid capital to take the
place on a lease arrangement. If the investor was willing to
sink his own money into the needed repairs, he could pick
up the place with a ten-year lease on a yearly rate guaranteed to net a large return for the investor, provided the guy
had at least some slight business sense. After the ten years

is up, the lease clears for renegotiation, prorated upward in accord with the success of the establishment.''

"A sweet deal, indeed," I agreed.

"B-but how did the Family take to the notion of being in the b-buggering business?''

"Wouldn't know," answered Francis, sipping at his beer. "Sterling is still alive so, I guess they don't find it any more reprehensible than any of their main capital-generating ventures.''

"Well," I said, "it's swell to know the Mafia's getting so open-minded in its old age, but let's stay on the track. I'm still waiting to hear how Sterling got into the picture.''

"Through an investment firm run by the gentlemen from old Napoli. They were most likely looking for some moron with a pocketful of hot cash who wanted to hide it somewhere legitimate. Not a situation with which they have no experience, eh? Anyway, Hoffman, Howard & Price handled the match-up. They've been sudsing down hot green since the first incorporation days of the mob back in the late thirties.''

Francis drained his beer another inch, coming back up with a foam-flecked smile. "And," he added, "there's no way our Mr. Sterling did not know with whom he was dealing. The record shows his business manager, from the very beginning of the match-up, as esteemed New York financial counselor Raphael 'Bug-Bug' Fanone.''

So, I thought, the squeaking little clown lied to me. That wasn't so bad—people lie to me all the time. What was bad was that I fell for it. I'd bought his story because I wasn't listening, wasn't paying quite enough attention—because I'd torn up his office and his protection like a tough guy, and I was sure, just sure, he wouldn't have the nerve to lie to such a big man like me. I'd let my desire to get my hands on Jeff Anthony blind me to the fact that a guy who had a son of a bitch like Anthony on his payroll already had all the tough guys to be scared of that he needed.

Sterling had misdirected me about everything—the whole way. Karras hadn't had a change of conscience, just a summoning of courage. Perhaps he had called me once before, and when he looked in the mirror long enough, perhaps he called me again—just because he'd decided to do the right thing. He hadn't robbed Miller with Mara. Maybe he'd only been the first one she asked to do it. But just because Karras turned her down, didn't mean little Mara couldn't snap her fingers and find some other greedy home town rat to help her and Sterling do their dirty work. And then it clicked.

I stood up, saying,

"I have to make a phone call. Hu, don't start any trouble."

"W-who, me?"

"No, Bonnie Prince Charlie. And don't you encourage him, Francis, or I'll break your fingers."

Getting an available pay phone, I dialed information twice, first getting the Plainton area code, then Sergeant Andren's home number. Then I called Andren. God bless the small-town life style, I thought. I caught him home with the family, watching a rental tape on the VCR.

He asked me what was so important he had to miss Fay Wray and Robert Armstrong meeting at the fruit stand. I told him.

"Just one little question, Dennis. You remember all the fellows I asked about?"

"Yeah. What about them?"

"I'd like to know something about one more guy."

"Shoot."

"Does the name Jeff Anthony ring any bells?"

"You sure like to mess with the mean ones, don't you, Jack?"

Bingo. I had it all.

# CHAPTER 26

DENNIS' QUICK DESCRIPTION convinced me we were talking about the same Jeff Anthony. I'd known we would be, but I had to be positive. Ray'd made that quite clear. Dennis asked me what was up with Anthony. I told him. His voice shrugged, letting me know my ol' pal Jeff had turned out just as everyone back home had expected. I let Dennis know I'd fill him in on how everything turned out after it was all over and done with. He said "okay" and went back to his movie. I went back to the table.

Our orders arrived a few minutes after I sat back down. My steak looked extra big, as if Louie was finished punishing us for the onion rings. I took my knife and fork and sliced off a good mouthful; the blade slid through the T-bone without effort, almost as if the meat were a mirage. Spearing some onion slices with that first chunk, I swirled the whole affair around in the burning hot, greasy black juice puddled on my plate. My knees went weak from the flavor.

I ate slowly, making each bite last. The baked potato was just as perfect—swimming in melting butter and sour cream, with Louie's specialty, fresh-cooked bacon sliced small and spilling over the sides, thick with fresh chopped chives, scallions, and melted cheese.

Our conversation died down considerably at that point, all three of us far more interested in our plates than in each other. It was doubtful there were fifty words between the three of us after our plates arrived that didn't involve the passing of salt and pepper, or the securing of more rolls, butter, and drinks. Hubert tore through his first lobster as if

195

the things turn poisonous if they sit on your plate for more than five minutes. He slowed up during his order of half-shell oysters and cherrystone clams, but not by so much. It still seemed he was gorging on his second lobster before Francis was halfway through his first pork chop.

Eventually, though, even Hubert started to fill up, allowing us to get back to the business at hand. I was feeling a bit calmer. The process of digestion was spreading the warm, healthy glow throughout my system that it reserves exclusively for red meat. Hubert asked what was next on the agenda. I told him that depended on how well Francis had done his homework.

"Looking for the rest of it, are we?"

"Earn your money, Junior. Tell it—where did Sterling's capital come from?"

I knew the answer. I'd known it since Hubert'd first started giving his report. Watching my law student's face while Hu told me about Miller's list, I was certain everything was going to tie together. Most defense lawyers, whether they know it or not, are frustrated, albeit profit-conscious, actors. A chance to perform is like a Christmas present to them. I could tell the holidays were at hand when I saw the light playing in Francis' eyes as he heard the details of the antique list. That certainty was why I could sit back and enjoy my meal rather than pressing the questions I had right away. Besides, I knew Francis was dying to spill what he had. Having to wait an extra half hour to get on stage was a middling form of torture for him, which admittedly increased my enjoyment of the evening all the more. Someone's got to keep the smart asses in line.

"You mean, where did a low-level paste-up artist from an advertising firm suddenly come up with the requisite, oh dear, what was that figure now—oh, yes—nine point eight million American dollars? Well, he did it in several steps.

"The second of these steps was to default on a dummy corporation. Using a healthy stack of the coins he's pulled to himself, he was able to set another individual up as the head of said dummy corp, one Space Pirate Cookies. It was supposed to be a tie-in with a new Steven Spielberg project—very hush-hush, very do-it-while-it's-hot, don't-ask-questions, get-there-first-and-screw-all-your-friends kind of deal. Thirty-two high-rolling New York, New Jersey, and Connecticut investors bit this one hard and went down for the count. Sterling was supposedly only one of the investors. Thus, he was able to spread the glad-hand talk and back up the man looking for the investments, and then appear clean later on to start a new business.

"Typical of these kinds of scams, the rich suckers who'd had to pry their dentures out of the fool's bait let the rascals run rather than make big headlines. Money is sometimes not worth as much as pride, and Sterling only picked targets with their noses somewhere in the outer stratosphere. He and his partner cleaned up, hid their dirty money in the Blue Ostrich, and the rest, as they say, is history.

"Care to know the identity of the partner and where they got their original investment capital to pay for offices, Italian suits, proposal documents, and all the other riggings of their scam?"

Not having the heart to let him know I'd put it together long ago, I answered,

"I've got a passing interest."

"The partner was a door frame the size of which they used to build small towers out of—out-of-town talent who called himself Steve Ditko. . . ."

When I laughed and Francis looked for a reason, I told him,

"Steve Ditko's a comic-book artist. Here it's an a.k.a. for Jeff Anthony. Go on."

"Anyway, the police don't know about him because, as I said, nothing was reported. After all, would you run to the press with the word you'd invested a quarter to a half mil in a fake company called Space Pirate Cookies? No one wanted to look that silly. It's the kind of thing that does not take you up any notches in the social-gear work.

"The investment pudding was boiled up out of town as well, I think. I have a list of bulk assets that were distilled down into liquid form to finance this questionable sojourn into the world of high finance—all of which can be traced back to Sterling and Dit . . . ah, Anthony. More or less, anyway. I suspect my list here matches the dwarf's.''

I stepped in before Hubert could take offense.

"Yeah; they sold hot antiques to fuel the sting. Do you have documentation for it, though?''

Francis nodded. He had the names of the antique dealers and private collectors who'd helped divide up Miller's collection. His being sure of the final resting places for most of the Dumptruck's pilfered property was a plus. He had records for most of what he'd said, plus one last tidbit.

"I've talked to a few of the stingees. It's amazing how easily everything traced back, all the way to the antique auction Sterling and Anthony had the Hefty-bag-sized balls to run, once I caught onto the Space Cookie thing. Checking out Sterling rather than his partner was the key—after that, the lines were easy to draw . . . but, anyway, as for talking to the poor misfortunates . . .

"They didn't want to make a fuss because the media would have had a field day with their egg-covered faces. But the ones I talked to said, if the tricky Mr. A could be brought low, they'd nail him for the police—happily. In fact, for a fifteen percent finder's fee, I'll be happy to negotiate with the Westchester dental syndicate who wanted to hire you to do that very thing after they got wind of what was afoot.''

"Seven and a half percent.''

"Seven and a half . . . ?''

"That's right. Seven and a half for you. Seven and a half for Hu.''

Hu's deepest head-turning duck laugh erupted. I figured I knew why.

"Hahahaahahaahaaaa. You little d-dick. I told you Jack would catch on.''

"This isn't fair,'' sniffed Francis.

"World's like that,'' I told him. "You thought you were going to fix me, and you might have if you'd used less theatrics. You made a big deal out of saving Anthony and the antiques for the last. But you didn't know I'd already met, 'the tricky Mr. A,' and you didn't know anything about the antiques. You weren't supposed to, anyway. The point is, you wouldn't have bothered to be so thorough about them if you hadn't had prior knowledge they were stolen, and you couldn't have known about that if you and Hu hadn't been swapping information. So it's only fair he get half the finder's fee, because if it wasn't for him, there wouldn't be any fee in the first place.''

"But the little bastard bet me his initial work-for-hire fee against mine that you'd never catch on.''

Hu starting laughing harder than ever.

"Greed, Francis,'' I told him. "Never bet with a man who understands it.''

"But if I lose my fee, and half the finder's, I end up with less than if I'd just done my job.''

"A lesson f-for all beginning lawyers.''

Hubert kept laughing, drawing the eyes of startled patrons from tables all around. I smiled myself, pretty sure I knew how it had all happened. Hu set Francis up, making him think the bet was all his idea. It wouldn't be nearly as funny as if it weren't the third time Hu has pulled the same kind of stunt on Francis. In consolation, I offered,

"Look, since we both know you've already negotiated a fee with these dentists . . .''

"How do we both know that?''

"Because, if you hadn't already wrung top dollar out of them—without my consent, I might add—'' I pointed out to him with only a bit of consternation, "you wouldn't know that seven and a half percent is less than you would have pulled just for doing your work. So, as I was saying, since you've already been so kind as to deal with these gentlemen, you can call them in the morning and tell them to send their check along, and that Mr. Jeff Anthony will be delivered to the police shortly.''

"I thought I might save them that kind of trouble,'' said Francis a bit sheepishly, "and so I brought it with me.''

Francis handed me the check. Noting the number of zeroes had me joining Hubert in his laugh.

"These guys don't learn from experience, do they?''

''Guess you j-just have to be white and w-wear a tie, and
these boys'll give you some money.''

Francis shrugged. Feeling magnanimous, I covered the
bill, tip and all. Then I gave both the boys the checks I'd
brought for them, with Francis signing his over to Hu. I
promised I'd get each of them their seven and a half in the
mail as soon as the dentists' check cleared. Finishing the last
of our coffee, we headed for the door, Hubert still chuckling
over Francis' hung head.

Once we got outside, Hu and I walked Francis over to
where he'd chained his bike to a street-sign pole. Waving
our goodbyes, Hu warned Francis about the perils of
wooden nickels, laughing until the bike and its rider were
out of sight. Then turning to me, he asked,

''Okay. What's next, Dick Tracy?''

''What do you mean?''

''I mean, are we g-goin' to the Ostrich now, or what?''

''And what would we be going to the Ostrich for?''

''Who knows? Maybe this is the p-perfect night to f-fill
our dance cards. Or somethin'. I mean, awwwww, come on,
Jack. You know what I mean.''

I looked down, meeting the little spaniel eyes straight on.
He was in the game for the full count. He knew going to the
Ostrich with me might possibly be dangerous, but that was
the main reason he wanted to go. Well, I thought, no one
knows the odds like Hu. If he wanted to play Sam Ketchum,
it was fine by me.

''Yeah,'' I admitted, ''I know what you mean.''

''S-so? Are we . . . am I . . . goin'?''

I stared him straight in the eye, doing as much to hold
back a grin as I could, telling him,

''What do you think?''

A smile spread across his face from ear to ear. I'd just let
him know he could come with me to the homosexual den
where men were beaten and left for dead. He was tagging
along into a place leased by a thief and a psychopath, from
the mob, a mob in no hurry to pick up any more bad
publicity from the place, possibly to the extent of having
their own people in there watching for trouble. It was a

place where going in looking for something other than booze and a dark room could get a guy iced—fast and quiet—and neither of us could wait to get there.

It's no wonder Elba worries about me.

# CHAPTER 27

SOMEONE DIFFERENT WAS greeting the loving couples in through the front door of the Blue Ostrich when we arrived. Fine by me, I thought. The fewer hassles the better. The greeter eyed Hu as if he'd just crawled out of the sewer. Maybe he didn't like men who limped. Maybe he didn't like men in green-and-orange-checked jackets. Since a lack of manners is the first qualification for a door opener's job anywhere in Manhattan anyway, it's always hard to tell. He didn't say anything obvious, but his contempt was plain enough. He asked,

"Do you have a reservation?"

"Yeah, one about you sp-spittin' in my drink."

The help at the Ostrich just aren't used to people who don't fall over themselves in apology every time someone in a tuxedo gives them the hairy eyeball. I interrupted as he reached for his phone.

"Save yourself some trouble and some teeth. We're here to put the word to your Mr. Anthony."

The greeter's hand jerked back from the phone. He wasn't quite sure what to say, but he knew he didn't want any trouble. Obviously I wasn't the first bruised plug-ugly to come into the Ostrich with business for good ol' Jeffy. He managed to get a few words out.

"But, but, Mr. Anthony isn't here yet."

"Then we'll just go back and talk with Bill."

The man wiped at his neck, glad we didn't seem to have taken any further offense at his manner. Hubert snapped his fingers, pointing behind us.

"Better jump to it, D-Daisy. You got customers."

202

While the greeting smile returned for the tingling pair of soccer players behind us, Hu and I walked through the dividing archway, bearing down in the direction of Sterling's office. The crowd was thick and the lights were down. Red heels wasn't on stage, though. It was a young comic, going on about how silly and awful the straight community was. Oh well, I thought, fair is fair.

When we got to the office, I figured the direct approach was best. Snapping open the door, I stepped in quickly, Hubert wandering in behind me slowly, looking for the best place from which to watch the fun. Sterling was behind his desk, flanked on one side by one of my playmates from the day before and on the other by Ratty.

Before Sterling could react, Ratty pointed at me, yelling, "Oh, Christ. Get him!"

Having tangled with me once before the leather boy started reaching under his vest, deciding he'd rather use something other than his fists this time. Not caring to find out what he had in mind I tore across the room, running into him with my full weight. He bounced toward the back wall, the gun he'd been clawing for coming loose and bouncing across the room.

Pain tore through me. My bruises turned on like a set of electric lights. Ignoring the illumination, however, I spun around to face off with Ratty. He'd pulled a knife with plans to bury it in the general vicinity of my shoulder line. My turn not only threw off his aim, but also delivered him into my range. I swung upward with my right, throwing all of my two hundred and twenty pounds behind the punch. Ratty snapped across the room like a Frisbee.

Turning back to my first playmate, I caught him as he was standing, not yet quite erect. Grabbing the slave collar he wore I jerked his head forward into my waiting fist, once, twice, then a third time until I felt the consciousness leaving his body. He flopped backwards out of my hands, hitting the floor in slamming stages—ass, elbow, head, palm—four hard thuds had let me know he was out of the game for a while.

Soft footsteps behind me let me know the game wasn't

over, though. Hubert sputtered a warning, but he didn't have
to bother. I turned in plenty of time, catching the advancing
Ratty as he tried to move up behind me once more. Shaking
my finger at him, I asked,

Tsk, tsk, tsk. Attacking an unarmed man from behind
with a knife. What would Captain Fair-Play say?''

"Fuck you, old man. You're history."

As he came at me, all I could think of was how could he
call someone only five years older than him at best "old"?
Maybe it was the bags under my eyes. Yeah, I thought, as
the knife tore the air inches from my face, that was it. I reached
out as his knife hand started to pass my face, catching the
wrist just as the point cleared my head area. Yanking down
savagely, I pulled Ratty into my waiting fist, popping his
head back with a crusher that tore open his lips and nose.
Blood sprinkled the rug as I slugged him again, knocking
him to the floor. A strong kick to the side of the head gave
off a sound which made me sure he'd be staying put for a
while.

Then, I turned back to Sterling.

"Bill, old fella. Soooo very good to see you again."

"Don't hurt me," he screamed. "That wasn't my idea.
You saw that. I didn't tell them to do anything. No. No.
I—I—I don't want any trouble. Please!''

I walked over, sitting on the edge of Sterling's desk.
Hubert had already jumped to the task of collecting up the
scattered weapons. While he patted down our two playmates, looking for more, I told Sterling,

"Chill out, man. Nobody wants to hurt you."

He was terrified. He'd gotten mixed up with the mob
thinking he was the hottest thing on wheels. He'd set up a
deal to rob one of his friends, then used the dough to finance
a sting of all the millionaires he could find. The sting money
had bought him the Ostrich, but it had also put him under
the mob's thumb, and apparently it'd only just recently
become apparent to him exactly what that meant. Now he
was just waiting for the hammer to fall from any of a dozen
directions.

"I want to make a deal with you, Bill. Let me make

something clear. I'm not after you. I want Anthony and Mara. Period. You tell me where I can find them and help me get them sewn up, and I could care less what you do. I'm taking Mara down for the murder of Carl Miller, and for setting up the theft on his personal fortune. As far as I'm concerned, she and Anthony can get painted for the whole thing. Your involvement in it will depend on how well you can keep yourself out of it."

I could hear the wheels turning. Sterling was scared, but not enough to lose his only chance. With the warning I'd just given him, he knew there was a possibility of getting clear while retaining some of what he'd set up. He also knew that if he didn't cooperate with me I'd feed him to the cops—piece by piece. Finding his tongue, he said,

"Okay—okay. I can do it. I can. Jeff—he's supposed to be here later. All, all you have to do is wait. Mara . . ."

"Yes?"

"Mara's here."

"She's here now?"

"Yes. Yes."

"Was she here the last time I came here?" I reached across the desk, grabbing his shirt front. "Did you know where to find her then?"

"Yes, yes. Please! Don't hurt me—I, I couldn't help it. She's, she's everything to us. She, she rules us. I, I couldn't . . ."

A rush of disgust mixed with curiosity washed over me. Hubert chuckled in the background. I asked,

"What do you mean, 'us'?"

"Mara. She's our—our queen." Hubert's chuckle turned into a knee-slapping laugh. "She, she tells us what to do and, and we do it. We love . . . her."

Tears were welling. Sterling closed his eyes to fight back the embarrassment the color in his cheeks'd already revealed. His hands shaking, he reached into the upper left-hand drawer of his desk and pulled out a slave collar similar to the one I'd used to drag his pal's face forward into my fist. Snapping it on himself, he rose from the desk saying,

"You're going to take Mara away, aren't you?"

"Yeah. That's pretty much the game plan."

Sterling sniffed, indicating a certain resignation to whatever was going to happen next. While he straightened his collar in the mirror, I thought out our next move. I realized if Anthony returned and found the Sleeping Beauty brothers, he'd know something was up. But there was little sense leaving Hubert behind to wait for him. Even armed, I was afraid the little guy might not be able to handle him.

We checked the bully boys quickly, making sure they were out for the count. Telling Sterling to hold on, Hu and I dragged Ratty and his pal behind the boss's desk. We tried to be careful. I didn't want to leave them out in the open, but after the little doc's warning, I didn't want to ensure them any serious levels of brain damage, either.

Making sure that was taken care of, I gave Sterling the high sign to lead on. The three of us left the office, heading back toward the doorway I'd ignored on my previous visits, the one toward which the couples'd seemed headed. Behind the drapes was a hallway leading to what Sterling explained was a bathhouse area with showers, hot tubs, steam rooms, and the expected et ceteras. An attendant added any back-area service charges to the participating patron's bill.

We turned left, however, going through a door marked Members Only, which Sterling unlocked for us, relocking it on the other side. An unenclosed stairway waited behind it, leading down in darkness further than one could see from the top. As we headed down, Hubert asked,

"What do you faggots got goin' down here?"

"Most of the members," corrected Sterling, "who—who use the underworld, aren't gay."

"Oh, yeah? W-what are they, then?"

"Like me," said Sterling sadly.

We walked the rest of the way down in silence, making our way slowly due to the lack of any handholds. At the bottom we came into a massive cement-block subbasement, dimly lit and broken up into "rooms" by heavily draped dark cloth. The different areas broken up by the black curtains all seemed like bits of cheap movie sets—one contained a small throne room, another a silk-and-lace-covered four-poster bed, another a mock-up kitchen that looked something like the one in the later episodes of *Leave It to Beaver*. The only difference was the number of chains. I gave Sterling a look. Hubert asked the question.

"W-what the hell goes on down here, Billy?"

"It's all part of our—service. It—this—this all, it was Mara's idea. A way to make extra money. One she liked. She, she runs things down here."

We walked forward more slowly, making our way through the labyrinth of drapes and sets, listening to Sterling's explanation. Mara's little underworld was a special club. Men paid a weekly fee ranging from five hundred to several thousand dollars apiece. For that they were given a key, and the freedom to come downstairs on the nights they'd purchased, Tuesday thru Saturday, excepting major holidays, and be abused in the manner of Mara's choice.

At first they'd played things cautiously, worried about the possible bad press and, of course, the police. Then came the night when Mara's games had broken a judge's ribs. Word got out on that one. Business doubled in three days.

It was something for which I hadn't been ready. We opened a number of drapes that had been pulled shut. In the first seven we found men by themselves—gagged, stripped, chained. Some were blindfolded—some had been whipped. Most had painful-looking plugs strapped into their anal cavities. One lucky fellow was glistening with urine, a large puddle of it teasingly out of the reach of his desperate tongue. His eyes met ours when we pulled the curtain aside. There was no remorse or shame to be found in them—he'd only looked up to see if Mara had returned. When he saw that we weren't her, he turned back to the floor, straining to reach the cooling yellow spread out on the cement beneath him. The collar holding him back was tearing into his neck as he redoubled his efforts, threatening to choke him to death. Sterling shut the drapes and we kept moving forward.

We found Mara in a kennel. A pack of seven men straining at the ends of chain leashes were there as well, naked except for the leather restraints and plugs which ran around and into them. We were in their line of vision but they paid us no mind. In front of them with her back toward us, standing with a riding crop in her hand, was the woman who had started it all. Mara. Carl Miller's sweet little innocent, taunting the happily smiling curs chained before her.

Her hair was just the shade of blond I'd pictured it. Isn't it wonderful to always be right? She was dressed in impossibly high-heeled ankle boots, swaying slightly, but in complete control of her movements. She had on the requisite stockings and garter belt needed for the picture, wrapped around with studded leather, black strips that buckled to her boots and then curled upward around her, crossing several times at the waist and then finally buckling to each other around her neck. This was topped by a leather vest that hinted at what was beneath, but which also refused to open far enough to let anyone verify their suspicions.

She was dancing in front of the pack, teasing them with what they knew wasn't coming—what they'd paid her to withhold. Staying on their hands and knees, they followed her movements as best their leashes would allow. Small fights broke out as the naked pack bumped into and fell over each other. One man jumped atop another, biting at him, taking a small chunk out of the guy's ear. Blood dripped down to a floor which looked used to it.

Mara chastised her yapping rich men.

"Now, now. How many times have I told you to be good dogs? How many times?"

She moved through the pack, delivering a blow or two to each of the men as they rubbed against her legs.

"How many times? You're bad dogs. All of you. Just the baddest dogs there are. I think I'll have to leave you now. Leave you to dwell on what bad dogs you are. But—maybe—maybe if you howl for me I'll come back soon. Howl for me, boys."

And, on her command, the seven obeyed, creating a dreadful wailing din that was embarrassing and humiliating just to watch. The howls came from somewhere deep within

the pathetic grovelers chained to the wall—it filled the
sub-basement with a damning echo that brought a smile to
Mara's lips, one which faded when she turned and saw us.

"William! What are you doing down here now?"

"I had to . . . come down, Mara . . . dearest. I had to.
These men . . ."

"They can wait. You vile little toad. You've upset my
doggies. You're going to have to be punished."

"But, but . . ."

Her crop slashed out, drawing blood from Sterling's
cheek. "Shut up!" she ordered. "No one told you to speak.
Now drop your pants."

"But, please . . ."

Her hand rose again.

"Drop them!"

Sterling undid his belt and then quickly slid his slacks and
underwear down past his knees. Sinking to the floor, he
stuck his rear end up in Mara's direction to make things
easy for her. As she began cropping Sterling, Hubert began
laughing. Mara stopped instantly, commanding,

"Stop it!"

Hu slapped his sides, unable to control himself. Mara
snapped at him again, twice as loud.

"I said stop it!"

"Hahahahaaaaa—hoo. God, lady. You talkin' to me?"

"Yes, you filthy little toad. You get out of here—right
now! You don't belong here. William—get up and throw
this little thing out!"

Sterling started to rise up off the cement, apologizing,

"Mara, you don't understand. They know. About Carl,
and Jeff, and, and everything. It's over."

Mara stared at Hubert and me in disbelief. The veneer
she'd worn into her draped catacombs began to peel away,
leaving the queen of the underworld behind, exposing the
thieving whore who'd started the whole ugly mess in which
everyone in sight was mired. Catching hold of herself,
though, she tried to buy her way out of what she could see
coming.

"I'll trust that William knows what he's talking about.

He never puts on this miserable a cringe unless the trouble is real. So, what's the problem? You going to spank me?''

"I'll leave that to someone who wants the job," I told her. "I'm taking you to the cops. Between what you and Jeffy did to Carl Miller and his friends, and what you've been doing here, I think it'll be a long time before anyone's going to have to worry about you again."

She rested one of her palms on my chest, her black-and-white-striped nails twirling the hair where my shirt was open. Pulling the hand to her mouth, she made a show of licking my sweat off her nails, asking,

"Yeah, sure—big tough cop. You just can't wait to throw me in the can in the name of justice. Come on—I've got work to do. Whatever you want, I can supply it. Money, drugs, sex? Just tell me which ones, what kind, how much, how often—whatever the answer is, and let's get this over with."

She pulled the leather vest she was wearing away from her breasts, making sure I could see exactly how perfect they were. Beautifully molded, needing no support, they would have been bribe enough for more men than I cared to number. I had other things to consider, however, and I told her so. She reached for my zipper, letting me know I had no idea what I was missing. I sidestepped her motion, telling her I'd take my chances. She pulled the expected then.

"You faggot—you cock-sucking, cum-mouthed queer bastard. You get out of here. Go chase up a dick for your fucking asshole. Take that troll and fuck each others' brains out. Get out of here!''

"Don't make this any tougher than it already is, lady. Either you get your clothes on and let this happen the easy way or I'll drag your ass out into the street just the way it is."

She swung then, trying for my eyes with the riding crop. Damn tired of people swinging at me, tired of the whole rotten, dirty game, I caught her wrist and jerked the crop from her hand. Then, spinning her around, I slapped her across the face as hard as I could, sending her tripping backwards step after step until she fell in a tangle across her pack.

Righting herself, propped up on one elbow, she ordered, "Kill him. Kill both of them! Get up and do it, all of you, and you'll never believe what I'll do for you! Lucky, Spot, Rover—all of you—get up and get them!"

The chained men began reaching for their collars, freeing themselves from their leashes. They moved forward slowly, not exactly sure what they should do. The desire to commit as simple a thing as a double homicide to ensure the safety of their whore was one thing, but figuring out exactly who was going to do what was another. I pulled my .38, leveling it on the closest one, giving them all pause to think about what they were doing. Mara lashed at them as they hesitated.

"Don't let that stop you—there are nine of us. He only has six bullets. Rush him!"

The bunch began moving again. I cocked the hammer on my revolver, keeping my aim on the lead man. But then, before either he or I could make our decision, three shots rang out, tearing up the cement between us. I spun around toward the source, bringing my gun around, ready to take out whatever the new threat was. I had maybe a full second to fill before the unknown shootist changed his target. My eye caught the gun, but luckily I managed not to squeeze the trigger; the shootist was Hubert.

"Okay, puppies. It's magic time." He was standing squared off with the pack, an Uzi submachine gun in his hands. With everyone's attention on him, he sputtered, "Okay, b-boys. I don't think you'll be wantin' to l-listen to Slut-ella, here. I think you want to be sittin' back down on yer cute little bare asses."

I stared at Hu, wondering at the thought of the little moke carrying around such heavy-duty firepower. Catching my look, he grinned, saying, "Hey, hey, Dick Tracy. With a sense of humor like mine, a g-guy's gotta be able to protect himself. I'm an irritant, not an idiot."

"Sorry, Hu," I said, "I've just never thought of you as armed, before."

"Sure," he laughed. "And legged, too."

Duck-laughing as always at his own joke, he used the compact but menacing weapon as a prod, pushing the pack back toward their chains. With a grin, he ordered them to put their leashes back on and sit down facing the wall.

"Th-that's it, boys. Come on, Lucky. Get movin', Spot." Pointing the gun at one straggler, he added, "You, too, Rover."

"I'm Blackie," said the man weakly.

"Yeah," answered Hu, "I'll just bet you are."

While all of Mara's tricks were being rechained and reseated, I grabbed down a pair of handcuffs from a convenient peg. Pulling the Dumptruck's darling to her feet, I twisted the arm I'd grabbed back behind her roughly, locking the first braclet in place. Giving her the choice again of the hard way or the easy got her to yield the other arm without further struggle, letting me lock it in place behind her.

Sterling had stayed on the sidelines during the proceedings, never really taking either side in the exchange. Once we were ready to leave I grabbed down an extra set of cuffs for my ol' buddy Jeff, stuffed them into a jacket pocket, and then told the boss,

"Okay; let's go look for Anthony."

While Sterling fell into step, Hubert told the pack,

"Boys, after we're gone, my suggestion is that you bad d-doggies get your fur on and get back home to your wives and kiddies, or whatever p-passes for 'em. Things might get ugly around here, so I'll warn you right now—come after us and try to get this b-bitch b-back, and I'll gun you down without a second thought. This city has all the sick fucks it needs. Don't think it'll miss any of you."

I pushed Mara out in front of me with Sterling, heading us all back toward the stairs. Although she had the sense not to try and run for it, she wasn't through attempting to find a way out of her situation. With every other step, she took a slight half-step backwards, trying to rub up against me. Her voice took on a little-girl quality begging to be understood—one promising that no matter what things looked like, what I was thinking had to be a mistake. It was the voice that'd turned Miller's brains to buttermilk and convinced him that every rotten little lie it could come up with was worth believing.

I knew I was right, because after everything I'd seen and heard—despite everything that'd gone on in the last few days—I found myself wanting to believe her. The demon voices that ride side by side with the Sick Feeling were gnawing at my brain, trying to convince me that maybe stepping behind one of the black curtains with a girl like Mara might not be a bad thing. She'd made contact with me often enough during our walk to the stairs that her moistness had soaked through the side of my pants leg. The wetness ran from hair to hair on my thigh, mixing with the tiny beads of sweat trapped there, running faster and faster as it inched its way downward.

I wanted to throw her up against the nearest wall and take her, pinning her to the cement until she screamed. I wanted to wrap us in the black drapes and use her just as she was begging me to, pleading with me to. Such a simple thing to believe the lies and pull down my pants and know that every squeal of pleasure she would make would be sincere, because this time she'd found a real man. Someone she could cherish and do everything for—someone she could finally submit to because this time she'd found love.

Yeah, sure, I thought. That's me all right.

We kept walking. She kept begging. I kept my mouth shut. In all honesty, I didn't have the nerve to say anything. I was afraid that arguing with her might give her some insight into me that she could use to strengthen her position. One look at her firm buttocks swaying in front of me was all it took to remind me that her position didn't need to be any stronger than it already was.

By the time we reached the stairs, she was growing frantic. It seemed obvious she'd expected me to relent somewhere along the line. Mara was a woman used to getting her own way. She couldn't understand my determination to see things through to the end. Halfway back to the upstairs she started getting hysterical.

"Come on, you bastard. Enough is enough. What's the game, for Christ's sake? Just tell me what you want. Tell me! I'll do it—I'll do it! Whatever you want. Anything. Money. We have money. Lots of it. All you could want."

"Shut up."

"A million. A million dollars. One million fucking dollars! I can get it. I can get it tonight. One phone call. I can—I can. We could fuck in it; spread it on the bed and fuck until you couldn't move—until your balls were bloody. Let me have your dick in me—up my ass, in my mouth. I'll suck you off better than you've ever had, better than you ever thought it could be. Every night. Anytime. Always. Alwaysalwaysalways. I can be whatever you want, Daddy. Anything."

I pushed her up against the wall, slapping her twice. Hard. The noise of it echoed as I screamed in her face.

"Shut up! Shut up!! Give it up or so help me I'll twist your head off your shoulders and throw it to your dogs as a last meal. Kiss this cellar of yours goodbye, bitch, because this is it. Dinner's done and the check needs paying. You're finished. It's over."

She crumpled to the stairs then, crying large tears, sobbing over and over that it wasn't fair, that nothing was fair. I was more than willing to agree with her—I feel that way sooner or later most days myself. But that didn't change the facts, and it didn't change my mind. Unfortunately, someone else was around with better arguments than Mara's. High-caliber arguments.

"Well, well," came their voice. "What have we here?"

I smiled without looking up. One way or another, it was all going to be over soon.

# CHAPTER 28

"WHAT WE HAVE here is a slut taking a hard fall. She's going down—so are you. Right behind her."

"Do tell," responded my old pal. His name—Jeff . . . Jeff Anthony . . . Jeffrey Anthony—burned in my memory. "Amusing theory, but I've got the gun and it's pointed at your head. I'd say I have all the cards."

"Having all the cards and knowing how to play them are two very different things. Give it up. This is your one chance to live through this."

We were both angling, trying to work an advantage. Hu had reholstered his Uzi downstairs, putting him out of the first round of whatever was going to happen. Anthony had his weapon, an older, but still deadly, efficient service .45, drawn and pointed straight at me, but he also had Sterling and Mara between us. My .38 was still out in my hand, but my aim suffered from the same blockade. Everyone was quiet for a moment; then Hubert upped the ante.

"So . . . who ya gonna shoot, tough guy?"

"What's it to you, freak?"

"Why," drawled Hu, his hand inching inside his jacket, "it's just that I was gonna get out m-my gun so I could play, too."

Hu's jacket went back. The Uzi started to appear. Anthony panicked. Instead of shooting me first and then going for Hubert, he shifted his aim, trying for Hu first. That pushed everyone else's panic buttons. Mara screamed, throwing herself backwards into me. I tried to plug Anthony, but my shot went a yard over his head. Sterling bumped into Hubert, then leaped away, directly into the

215

path of Anthony's gunfire. Three rounds cut the club owner's strings. He spun and jerked with each shot, flipping over the side of the stairs and disappearing into the drapes below.

Hubert's earlier gunfire had been soaked up by the thick curtaining all through the sub-basement. This time, however, the shots rang repeatedly like a small war, forcing everyone to cover their ears to escape the painful drumming of the sound waves. Hubert fell to his knees, his face going white from the shock. Still handcuffed, Mara's ears had no protection from the brutal echoes. Her skidding heels collapsed underneath her, toppling her into me once more, this time the collision knocking my gun from my hand, following Sterling into the dark recesses below. I caught up Mara before she followed them both, half to keep her from going over the edge, half to use as a shield against Anthony. I needn't have bothered. The only thing on his mind was escape.

He'd torn up the stairs, running in a blind panic as soon as he'd gotten his footing, knowing there was no way he could beat the rap for shooting Sterling. I figured he didn't even know I'd lost my gun. I took off after him, moving up the stairs as fast as I could manage, racing to close the gap between us. I knew stalling even long enough to get Hubert's Uzi would give Anthony the chance to lock us in the basement—and then I'd never get him. Part of my mind knew there was a chance he might turn and fire, but it didn't matter. I wanted him. He was going down. Period.

I could see him thirty steps above me, just reaching the door to the outside. I tried to dig more speed out of my aching muscles, but it wasn't coming. I was too tired—overtaking him didn't seem possible. And then, suddenly, I realized that just like Sterling, Anthony had locked the door to the subbasement behind him.

He dug for the key frantically, getting the ring it was on out of his pocket. Twenty steps left. His fingers searched for the right key, finding it three goes around the ring. Ten steps left. I poured on all the steam I could, biting down against the strain in my screaming arms and legs and lungs. He slid the key home and turned it. I made the landing. He spun the knob. I ran into him with everything I had.

We both crashed through the door at the same time, wild to catch our footing as we burst in off-balance. Anthony clutched his. 45 as he fell, accidentally putting a round into the floor. I dove for his gun hand, catching it in both of mine. Wrenching the muzzle away from me, I watched the flame leap from it twice more. The roar of the shots came like a distant echo, lost in the back recesses of my muffled hearing. We'd fired too many times within the closed confines of the club to be able to hear anything now. Around us, men were bolting in all directions, their mouths working as if they were screaming. I had no way of knowing for sure.

Our rolling around on the floor came to an end when we slammed up against a wall. His back hit first. I dug my boots into the thick carpeting, trying to keep him wedged into place. His legs and free arm lashed out, trying to break my hold. Gripping his wrist with all my strength, I slammed his hand again and again on the floor, trying to knock the possibly still-loaded weapon free. It was no good. His skin split at the knuckle from the constant tearing against the trigger guard, but he wouldn't let go. I changed my tactics.

Easing up on the pinning pressure I'd been trying to maintain, I let him push us away from the wall. We rolled over each other back toward the door to the basement. It was a dangerous gamble, but I had to do something before the crowd or the cops or the mob decided to interfere—perhaps in favor of the wrong guy. Anthony kept hammering at me, punching my back and head—ringing, thudding blows that almost made such possible interference unnecessary. Shaking off the pain, I pulled everything I had together, took a deep breath, and then shoved out from the center. Pulling Anthony's arm forward, I lifted it high and then smashed it sideways against the edge of the open door. One of his fingers cracked, bending back the wrong way. While the pain of that struck and kept him busy, I slammed his uncurled fingers against the metal door edge again—harder.

Blood washed his hand—another finger bent sideways—the gun fell.

I released his hand and rolled away from him then, scrambling across the floor. The gun had bounced out of both our reaches. We watched each other, slowly rising from our hands and knees positions. Neither of us knew what the other was going to do next. We both caught each other sneaking peeks at the .45, wondering at our chances to get at it before the other. I gave up wondering before he did and took a sideways step as if I was going to try for it. Anthony leaped at me, figuring I was off guard. He'd figured wrong. *sp. feinted*

I'd fainted for the .45, hoping for that reaction. Turning and planting myself firm with one motion, I received Anthony's weight on the point of my swinging fist. He bounced off it hard, returning to his knees. I followed that blow with more, first to one side of the head, then the other, finally putting everything into a wide roundhouse left, which spun him around a turn and sent him crashing into the far wall.

He shook off the effects and started pulling himself out of the plaster. I should have jumped him again and kept after my advantage, but I couldn't breathe. I had to take just three crummy seconds to catch my wind. Pain was slowing me down—my wrist was on fire, aching as if its cast hadn't protected it at all. My lungs were red agony, my stomach a churn-mill threatening to spill over. Flaming rags of pain sliced along my nerves, filling my head with a clanking, bone-rattling sound, jangling somewhere back behind the muffled static our gunfire had made of my hearing.

We stood across the hallway from each other, panting large gasps. I mumbled something to Anthony about giving up. Not able to breathe, I don't know why I didn't save my breath. He couldn't hear me. I couldn't hear myself. Straightening himself somewhat, his only answer was to send his hand behind his back. It appeared again with one of those black-bladed Japanese razor combat knives, the kind any maniac with thirty bucks can pick up in Times Square. I wondered at why he hadn't pulled it earlier, for another several wasted seconds, then stopped. *Who cares?* I screamed at that part of my brain, trying to remind it that we had more important things to worry about—like what he was going to do with it now that he had it. I didn't have to wait long for an answer.

He pushed off suddenly, trying to pin me with a wild thrust. I moved—quick but painful—clearing his rush by inches. He turned his blade in time to keep from shattering it against the wall. I backed up toward the interior of the club, looking for something to pick up. There was no one to stop me—the main room had cleared fast.

Anthony came in after me. I hurled the cooling half of someone's dinner at him, following it with a handful of silverware. He dodged and kept closing, a smile coming back to him. He must have found my desperation amusing. Grin on, I thought, suppressing my own smile. I knew I was ready for him—all I needed was a breathing space. Bringing my foot up under the nearest table, I kicked it upward for that needed moment's grace. My ol' pal stepped back, not wanting to risk advancing with his vision blocked by the moving table. Stepping back to the bar, I whacked my cast against it, closing my eyes to the pain and stars that shot through the blackness of my vision, collecting the little doc's scalpel as it fell out of the neatly cracking plaster.

Taking it in the shaking fingers of my right hand, I tried to clear my eyes and bring all the dancing images in front of me back into focus. Anthony came around the upended table, closing for the kill. I backed my way down the bar, hoping to sucker him into another fast rush. He hadn't noticed the scalpel yet. I flipped someone's drink at him, almost getting his head, but not quite. The Japanese blade had nearly eight inches on mine. My only chance was surprise. He kept feigning at me in opposite directions, working me toward the corner. Fine, I thought. I let him work his master plan, worried only about keeping my blade palmed.

Anthony mouthed something I supposed was rather sinister and final. I wouldn't know—still not able to hear him. With a laugh, he closed the box he'd "tricked" me into, slashing the air inches from my chest. Waiting for the blade to go by, I stepped out into his passing arc, putting my back to his returning hand, then drove my right toward his side, pushing the scalpel straight into him. The razor tip was still caked with plaster, but it didn't matter. The blade went through his jacket, shirt, skin, and muscle with little trouble.

Pushing him away with the left side of my body, I pulled the scalpel free and then buried it in him again, ducking down as his knife tried to find me at the same time. Surprised he could react that quickly, I pushed him again from my squatting position—mostly a stumble with weight behind it—sending him reeling backwards over a table. Leaning on the wall for support, I used it as a crutch to work my way back to standing. Anthony crawled over the edge of the table, dragging himself to his feet, not looking that much the worse. Either I hadn't managed to do very much damage with my two hits, or he was as tough as he looked. Stupidly, I hadn't counted on that.

One hand pressed down on the table next to him for support, he started forward again. The sight of his weapon coming toward me again forced my eyes to dart to my own. Then I saw it—my blade had snapped off—probably still buried inside Anthony. I threw the bloody hilt at my ol' pal's face, but he sidestepped it.

While he did, I picked up a chair. The chairs in the Ostrich were neither extremely light nor deadweight. The heft felt just right. I could see the question form in Anthony's eyes—charge the chair or back off in the hopes of a clear shot. He chose the intelligent tactic. I was getting tired of that quality in him. Most guys get wilder, sloppier as a fight progresses. Not my buddy. He was growing cooler—more rational. I pushed at him with the chair legs, lion-tamer-style. He avoided the poking without much difficulty.

I pushed again, and once more, backing him up another two steps. He moved warily, watching for his opening. Afraid he might find one, I pulled the chair back behind me suddenly, faked left, and then hurled it right. Finally, something connected. The chair hit him in the shoulder as he tried to dodge. I picked up another quickly. He shrugged off whatever damage the first might have done with a look that said he was ready for a lot more.

Crouching more than before, favoring the side I'd scored my scalpel hits on, he kept circling tables as I poked at him, trying to get one in between us. Tired and aching and not really watching what he was doing, I let him put the space between us that he wanted there. He'd been moving slowly, as if I'd done some serious damage to him. That was a trick. When he had me close enough, he lifted the end of the table in question fast, flipping it forward at me. I managed to step out of its way, but caught my foot in the rungs of an overturned chair. I went down badly, slamming my head against the table behind me on the way. Anthony came forward again.

Dazed, I scrambled backwards crab-style, ducking under table after table, knocking chairs in all directions. Anthony plowed his way through the debris, trying to catch me in the open. Suddenly, though, I reached the edge of the tables, out of cover, back to the point where we had first entered the room. A glance showed my ol' pal closing fast. With no other options, I braced myself and then stood quick and fast, lifting the table I was under into the air above me, then flipping it backwards into Anthony's path. It hit him.

He staggered a few feet while I limped back into the hallway where our fight had begun. He came after me. I was headed for the fallen .45, the one we'd abandoned when the blades had come out, ready to plaster the ceiling with Anthony's brains. There was only one problem—the gun was gone.

It was impossible—there'd been a lot of people running around, but the room had . . . Cutting the panic off, I pushed the thought aside and tried to find some new option. I couldn't get out through the dining room—Anthony had me cut off. The door to the sub-basement was closed. I tried the knob, but it held firm—Anthony's keys probably still hanging in the lock on the other side. With no other choice, I turned and staggered to the bathhouse area behind me. My ol' pal Jeff followed. I knew he would. We'd reached that

point where we knew it had to end—that it would end
sooner or later, with one of us catching up to the other. He
was the type that preferred to get things over and done
with—especially when it looked like he was the one who
was going to walk away when it was all over.

As I approached the baths I recognized the door structure
and the make of the paneling ahead of me—soundproof—
no one inside knew what was happening yet. They would
soon enough. I grabbed a towel as I passed the check-in
point, ignoring the muscleman in a little booth near the
entrance. Wrapping it a couple of turns around my left hand,
I glanced about me frantically for anything that might serve
as a weapon. By this time the muscleman was out of his
booth, barking orders I couldn't hear as Anthony came
through the door. The attendant put up his hand to stop him.
Anthony gutted him with one vicious circular motion,
jerking his blade free and coming on after me without a
second thought.

I went to the right, away from the lockers and back
toward the baths. Anthony followed. Heads turned as I came
in panting loud and gasping. The heads protested as they
saw me; they screamed as the bleeding madman with the
knife came into view. I could actually hear a bit of it. Going
back toward a large whirlpool, I headed for a broom I'd
suddenly spotted. Men ran away from us on both sides,
sliding along the walls to escape our presence as we passed.
As I neared the broom, Anthony rushed me, stabbing down
with the knife.

I grabbed it by the blade in my towel-wrapped hand,
feeling the sharpness of it eat through several layers of the
cloth without effort. I brought the broom around clumsily,
trying to clip Anthony in the head. He managed to get his
arm up in time, swatting it back. I swung again—bearing
down with everything I had. The force of the blow cracked
the broomstick in half, but also jarred Anthony's weapon
out of his hand. The knife dropped free, skidding across the
moist tiles. Anthony made a grab for it but slipped, kicking
my pins out from under me accidentally on the way down.
I lost what was left of the broom trying to catch my balance.

I fell anyway, landing sloppily on my side. As I tried to stand, Anthony grabbed me from behind, the combined motions throwing us both into the whirlpool.

Hot water flooded my clothes, burning me all over. We went under the foam line together, grappling with each other, both of us trying to simultaneously find the surface while keeping the other under it. We turned body over body, floundering in the bubbling water, slapping each other with water-slowed punches, ripping at each other with our nails, trying to find exposed areas at which to tear. Then, suddenly, my feet scraped the bottom for an instant. I planted them automatically, pushing up with all my remaining strength. My head broke the water—Anthony's a second later.

I grabbed the back of his collar and pulled, dragging him back beneath the scented froth churning in the pool. He bucked frantically but I held him under, using my hands and knees to keep him pinned down. I dug into his skin, trying to force the last of his breath from him, trying to keep my nose above the water line. Wet hair plastered down over my eyes, blinding me. Anthony's thrashing kept the water churning violently, constantly splashing my head, making it almost as hard for me to breathe as I was making it for him. I was also getting weaker, unable to maintain my hold. Finally, one of his hands broke through to the surface, catching my shirt front. Before I knew it, both our heads were submerged, our hands around each other's throats.

Digging my fingers deeper into his neck, I did my best to kill the man who was trying to do the same to me. Then I redoubled my efforts, and then again, fighting wildly with every ounce of strength I had left. His grip tightened as well, unhampered by a towel as was mine. We wrestled underwater for long, panicking seconds, feeling the precious bubbles slipping out between our lips. And then, Anthony's head broke the surface. He sucked in what air my grip would allow, oxygen giving his hands new pressure, which filled my brain with heavy gray shadows.

Struggling for any advantage, I suddenly felt my foot behind his. Pulling desperately, I brought him back down under the water. His hands automatically released me as he grabbed for a handhold. Mine released him as the weight of his fall pulled him from my grasp. Bobbing to the surface, I dragged myself up the side of the tub, pulling in the scalding air around us my only concern. I hacked out a great gush of warm phlegm, stringing wads of it exploding from my nose and mouth. Anthony surfaced again as well, his face red and twisted, hacking chokes shaking his frame for a moment—but only for a moment. While I was still gagging, I watched him flexing away his pain, unsteady, but ready for another attack. Frantic, I looked around to see if I could find any advantages at all. The only thing was the shattered broom handle, just two feet from my grasp.

Anthony charged across the whirlpool, sloshing forward through the water, only a second away. My fingers wrapped around the broom handle, pulling it to me. As we closed together I brought the sharp end of the wooden length up with all my might, driving it against the force of Anthony's charge. The stake went straight through his chest, the grip he was reaching for never materializing. His head locked against mine, he screamed his last breath into my ear—mouth wide open, eyes bulging—only a whisper of his hate reaching me. Blood splashed out of him all around the broom handle, sluicing out to splatter me and the wall behind, tinting the roiling water around me crimson in seconds.

His dying body stepped back from me and stared, not able to comprehend that I'd finally managed to stagger him with anything. More blood heaved up out of his mouth, his stomach emptying red-soaked globs of food into the air, most of it splattering against my face and chest. Then, his knees buckled and he slumped forward under the churning water. I crawled up out of the tub, heading for the door, still spitting up water and hacking for air.

It was finally over, I thought. I went looking for Hubert and my gun and Miller's Mara, knowing that the whole damned, foul nightmare was finally over. Sure, I knew I was lying but, I didn't have the energy to struggle with the truth at that moment. That I left for later.

# EPILOGUE

HUBERT HAD GONE after my gun when I'd lost it, knowing I wouldn't want to leave it behind, even if I hadn't put any bullets in anyone. Just discharging a licensed weapon into the air to scare away a mugger can run you ten thousand dollars in court costs in New York. Just another reason I don't go out armed any more than I have to.

He'd dragged it and Mara up to the restaurant by the time I'd crawled out of the baths area. Together we hobbled out to my car, clearing the building a few moments before the police finally arrived. The sight of me soaking wet and covered in Anthony's gore gave little Mara something to reflect upon during our trip to the car and then downtown.

She didn't fight us anymore. The energy for that seemed to have run out of her. She wasn't trying to trick anyone with a good-girl song and dance; she just didn't have anything left to say. We took her straight to Ray's precinct and turned her in. Ray wasn't on duty that late, of course, but they were able to find him. He was with us twenty minutes after he found out what was up.

Hu and I gave him the full report on Sterling and Anthony and how they'd made their rise to fame and fortune. We turned over all of Francis' documentation and what notes Hu had made. Ray was understandably pleased. Getting out of bed and driving downtown in the middle of the night didn't seem to be bothering him nearly as much as sitting around in my blood-soaked suit was bothering me.

I laid out for him how Mara and Anthony had robbed Miller, where the money had gone, and everything else that had happened since the theft. Mara backed it all up, waiving

225

her right to counsel. When it got to the murders, though, she claimed she didn't know anything about them. Ray looked to me for the answers. This time I backed her up.

We all agreed Anthony had killed Karras. I went along with Ray's official notion—Miller killed George and then did himself in out of regret for the whole mess. The people putting pressure on Ray for another answer wouldn't like it, but with Mara turning out the way she had, they didn't have a great deal of choice other than to accept the facts the way we were painting them. You can only cover up so much. Besides, Ray likes rubbing people's noses in whatever they find distasteful. If it was all airtight, it was good enough for him. The deal broke down that I was never in the Blue Ostrich. He and his men had compiled all the pertinent information in the case and moved when the time was right.

Ratty and the leather boys I'd been dancing with had all turned out to be Mafia street soldiers. Information linking me to knocking around Mafioso employees is the kind I don't mind having suppressed. The .45 with Anthony's prints on it turned up before the night was out, closing the books on the Sterling murder case. And as to who had actually done in Anthony, when men get killed in the back rooms of sex clubs in New York City, it isn't hard to keep it out of the papers. Not if the right people wanted it kept out—and plenty of them did.

The last detail was what to do with the Dumptruck's sweetie. Having gotten everything he wanted out of the case, Ray's answer there was simple—he bent to the pressures over him, perfectly willing to not notice Mara slipping out the back door, as long as she returned to Pennsylvania—and stayed there—released into her parents' custody for five years. I wondered if he knew just how severe a punishment that was going to turn out for all the Phillipses? My guess was that he did. Ray's got a good sense of karma that way.

When I finally escaped the station house I came out into a darkness more complete than I'd ever seen—no moon, stars—even the traffic lights seemed somehow muted. The humidity was near one hundred. People sprawled all around me on the sidewalks, fanning themselves with bits of cardboard, or magazines, or whatever, drowning in their own sweat. The slate-black clouds filling the sky looked packed with rain, but even the first hint of just a tiny shower didn't seem available. Somehow, it no longer mattered. The heat and mugginess had been with us all so long now they just felt natural.

When Hu and I got to my car, I took a bedsheet out of the trunk I use to keep the seats clean whenever I have something filthy to haul. This time it was me. I draped it over the passenger side and got in. Hubert drove. As we pulled away from the station house, the thought occurred to me that at least one good thing had come out of the whole case—the next time somebody tells me to go to hell, I can tell them I've already been there.

• • •

I arrived at Jean's apartment at around two in the morning. I'd been home, showered, shaved, changed, and dropped Hu in front of an all-night club near the Bowery where everyone in sight seemed to know his name. He strolled past the bouncers holding back the crowd, waving to me over his shoulder, and then went in through the loud neon-splashed doors and into the even louder music, throwing back his head, rolling his eyes in time to his own mad laughter. I figured he'd be okay.

The doorman called Jean, woke her, and then let me in without hesitation. She was waiting for me when I got to her floor, looking as if she'd missed me and that waking her at two in the morning didn't matter. She was a wide smile and a taut body and a set of eyes that let it know it was really all for me. My throat went dry from the unfairness of the situation.

She kissed me as I came through the door, a long, hard pressing to which I responded with everything I had. It was an honest, deep warm kiss that tore through me and littered the floor with the pieces. She shut the door with one hand, holding on to me with the other, giggling like a schoolgirl. The air conditioning was on. We made our way to the couch. I pushed her away, gently, letting her know I had something I had to ask her. She waited. I gave it to her.

"So tell me—do I get it before or after Joey?"

"What do you mean?"

She looked at me, startled. It was plain she didn't understand what I was talking about. It wasn't that I was on the wrong track—she just hadn't realized I was ever going to figure things out. I explained her mistake to her.

"What I mean is, who gets croaked next? And how are you going to do it? Jeff Anthony is dead. You won't be able to call him up and send him after anyone else—like you did Karras when I so stupidly told you where he was and then waited in the shower like a good boy while you sent your murderer out.

"You were the only person besides me who even knew he was in town, let alone where he was. Just like you were the only person from Plainton who knew Anthony had given me a beating. You could have told me who he was, if you were on my side in this, but you didn't mention it—didn't find that little fact important enough to reveal. Like you didn't bother to tell me why you were so upset at George's murder. I wondered why you were a lot more emotional over his death than Miller's. Maybe that was because you'd planned to kill Carl when you made yourself up as close to Mara as you could, and then went down and got the poor dumb slob drunk out of his mind, got him to pen up all the letters we found in the wastebasket, then typed up the one he finally signed."

I rose from the couch, putting distance between myself and Jean.

"How did it play? What did you tell him? 'Write a love letter, Carl? I'll help you. Oh, these are no good—you can't even read them. Call the front desk and get a typewriter. We'll get your Mara back for you.'"

"Jack—oh, God . . ."

I ran over her words.

"Dressed in her style—the makeup she'd use, her hairdo—easy enough for a model, I guess—easy enough to tell him what to do all the way to the grave."

"Jack, please . . ."

"But George—you didn't mean to kill him. You wanted it all neat and simple. Kill your ex-husband with one of Miller's guns—Jeffy was probably happy to supply that for a favor or two—I'm sure—then who was going to take the fall? My guess is Miller, since Sterling and Anthony were probably going to have to get rid of him eventually anyway. That would have tied everything up nicely and you'd be in the clear. But you'd never handled a rifle that powerful. Television always makes things look so easy. The recoil threw off your aim—killing George instead of Byler. But you used that to your advantage, too. You got me to distrust Miller by showing me the bruise you'd given yourself with the Saur. Then you went ahead and got rid of Miller. Maybe you were even forced into that by Anthony—I could believe it. But the end result was you caused the death of three innocent men, not even getting the one you wanted, letting Miller take the fall."

I took a breath to calm my straining voice, then asked, "Am I close?"

"Jack, you don't understand. Joey, he slept with Mara—while we were dating, while we were engaged, after we were married—when he was supposed to be mine. Everyone knew—everyone. They all laughed at me. That was why we got divorced, why I had a nervous breakdown . . . why, why I hate him.

"I hated him for the way he used me. I wasn't anything to him, Jack. He married me because he wanted to accomplish the feat . . . not because he loved me. Just because it was the thing to do . . . he, he . . ."

She started sobbing then. She tried to contain it, but it shook her too violently. The weight of everything caved in on her. She explained it all. Fred George had just been a nice guy who had liked her for herself. When she accidentally killed him, everything had slipped. Karras had simply been an annoyance who could've told the truth about who'd stolen what, a truth which could've led back to her and George's death. She'd panicked and told Anthony to lean on him, but Anthony'd already done that once, back in

Plainton. The second time he got carried away. By that time, the panic pushed her over the edge. By that point Miller hadn't mattered to her at all—his death became just a means to an end.

After she got hold of herself, she asked calmly if I was going to take her to the police. I told her "No." When she asked me why, I told her that, too.

"Because it wouldn't serve any purpose. You're not going to kill Byler now, are you?"

She shook her head. I'd known she would. Self-pity and fear and depression had driven her crazy—crazy enough to go climbing around on a roof shooting at people—crazy enough to help Miller kill himself because he'd been trying to save the woman who'd ruined her marriage. But that was passed. The shock of all she'd done had made her sane again. And sanity is the worst prison of all.

"Jail wouldn't do anything to you or for you. If you go to any prison, it's going to have to be one of your own making. If you don't suffer for any of this, then you weren't meant to. There," I said, taking another step away from her. "Isn't that simple?"

She looked up at me, her eyes red with the strain of real tears. She half reached for me, pleading with all the intensity she could muster for me to stay. There were no words, no pitch—it was more. She sent back every good feeling I'd had about her at me, rocking me with the joy I'd felt in finding her—in knowing she could love me. She'd been everything I'd ever hoped for, the dream package I'd fallen for like a bird that's been shot out of the sky, tumbling head over heels in free fall, not knowing what's happened, headed for the ground and oblivion with the speed of a falling rock and the certain guidance of gravity.

But the moment had come. I'd hit bottom and was finally awake, which meant it was time to leave. With all that I knew, with all that had happened, there was no way I could stay. And we both knew it. Rain thundered against her window suddenly, a wild, flying sheet of it striking the glass with the sound of gravel on tin. I stood and turned, seeing the flowers I'd sent her. She'd put the whole affair in one vase, a massive one at the end of the hall to the bathroom. They'd taken the place of the large poster of her first photo layout, the only sign of it being its outline traced in the wall's faded paint. The last strings inside me tore apart and I felt everything toppling inward. It was a lot, but it was too little, too late. Some things just aren't meant to be.

I left the apartment in silence, not saying anything to her, not hearing anything from her. I waited a year for the elevator and spent two more getting back to the first floor. When I hit the lobby I looked across the marble flooring out into the torrent. It smashed against the building's ground-level bay windows in fierce barking waves.

I stood with my back to the elevator, watching the rain fall. All I wanted was to go home and go to bed—maybe just curl up in the back seat of my car and try to forget. I thought once more about turning around and going back upstairs. I wanted to go to Jean and tell her all was for-given—take another chance on the cat in the box and the big happily-ever-after—closing my eyes to everything that'd been done. I wanted to with almost everything inside of me. The strong, pure voice within us that believes in happiness above everything justified it all for me in an instant, telling me to step back into the elevator before the doors slid shut behind me.

It begged in a voice that filled my ears—keeping me from walking away. I wavered for a moment, wondering if just maybe . . . Then I listened to the soft metallic click at my back. Crossing the long miles of the lobby to the front doors off in the distance, I pulled my collar up against the rain to come as the doorman said,

"Hell of a night, huh?"

The rain outside was a flood. It wasn't falling; it was slamming the ground, beating the sidewalks in icy ripples as if it intended to clean all the filth away once and for all. I told him,

"You don't know the half of it, pal."

Then I stepped through the doors, stopping under the building's canopy. Looking through the darkness, down the street to where I knew my car was, blocks away, I pulled my collar down suddenly and smoothed it back into place. Finally, I walked into the rain, letting the building disappear into the torrent behind me.

My old man was right. There's no such thing as a free lunch.